YOURS FOR THE SUMMER

H. S. Luna

Copyright © 2024 Haley Luna

All rights reserved

The characters and events portrayed in this book are fictitious. Any similarity to real persons, living or dead, is coincidental and not intended by the author.

No part of this book may be reproduced, or stored in a retrieval system, or transmitted in any form or by any means, electronic, mechanical, photocopying, recording, or otherwise, without express written permission of the publisher.

ISBN-13: 9798323340842

Cover design by: Joshua Cintron-Alvarez
Library of Congress Control Number: 2018675309
Printed in the United States of America

To Danny,
My favorite pieces of you are in this book.

AUTHOR'S NOTE

This story is, at its core, a romance. The characters are meant to reflect real people with real problems and some of the scenes might not be appropriate for a young audience. The recommended reading age is 18 and older for this new adult story.

Trigger warnings include: anxiety, panic attacks, underage drinking, descriptions of consenual sex, flashbacks of sexual assault, and discussions involving nonconsensual sex.

Your mental health matters.

1

My whole family was in the car on the way to drop me off for my summer long counselor job at Camp Odyssey. My sister and myself were in the middle row, with my brothers in the back, all lost in whatever activity they had brought to keep them occupied during the hour long car ride. My dad was driving and mom was upfront making sure he followed the right directions. I've been coming to Camp Odyssey every summer for the last 10 years so he should know the way. But every year he misses the exit onto route 24. Every year we have to flip around at the sketchy gas station. Every year my mom nags him about it. Every. Year.

This time my mom wasn't distracted by one of my younger siblings and reminded him far enough in advance to avoid the sketchy gas station turn around. I usually don't pay attention to where we are going during long car rides, but I know this route. The billboards have faded or changed over the years, but when I see the faded bright orange sign for 'Aunt Judy's Nut Store,' I know it's only 20 more minutes until we turn onto Odyssey Lane.

As the car turned off the highway and onto a smaller two lane road, I felt my phone vibrate, notifying me I had a text. I looked down expecting to see my best friend Sarah's name on the screen. Instead I saw a phone number that I knew by heart even though I had deleted the name attached to it.

My ex, Keith, was texting me.

"Who is that, Hadley?" My mom looked back in the rearview mirror to check on me. I was only allowed a certain number of texts a month and if I went over that limit my mom lost it.

"It's Sarah just wishing me good luck at camp!" It was a quick excuse to get her off my back.

"Okay, hon." She seemed satisfied with that and turned her attention back to the road.

I looked back to my phone, trying to seem unfazed. Why was he texting me now?

We broke up over six months ago and hadn't really talked since, because I demanded it be that way. It was hard enough having to see him when we worked together, but I didn't have to talk to him outside of that. After what happened between us, a no contact strategy was best.

The text simply read: **i no wut rly happened. sry. ily.**

My first thought was *finally*! He was finally willing to accept what had happened. Then that relief morphed into tingling excitement that he said he still loved me. There was still hope we could be together. But then why would I want to be with someone who said what he said to me? Why would I want to be with someone who had done the things he had done to me? I never wanted to go through that.

So I just texted back: **ty. t2u l8r <3**

It was simple. I couldn't worry or focus on him when I was about to start this new summer adventure. Besides, my phone would be off and in my duffle bag most of the time and I would only really be able to check it at night. My dad wanted me to check in with him at least once a week by sending him a picture of me to let him know I was okay. That's why they got me a new phone with a camera last week. I knew he only did it because he's paranoid but I still counted it as a win.

Last summer I was a counselor-in-training for a week, but that's because I hadn't graduated from high school yet. This summer instead of being away for a single week, I'll be gone for nine weeks as a counselor. It was hard losing the summer right before I went to college, and I was almost as sad about it as my parents were, but I've been looking forward to this moment for so long.

Nothing was going to ruin this for me.

I put my phone away then settled back into my seat and watched the swirl of green leaves roll past me as the car made its way closer and closer to camp. I started to twirl the light brown curls that had escaped from the low bun my hair was in.

Suddenly, my phone buzzed intensely because Keith was calling me. There was no way I could answer with my parents around so I ignored his call. My mom shot me another look in the rearview mirror.

He called again, so I ignored it again. I expected another call and I was ready to text him to leave me alone because I was in the car, but nothing more happened. He must've finally got the hint because my phone was silent. A sigh of relief left my lips as I settled back into my seat.

As we drove down Odyssey Lane, the car began to gently rock as it rolled over the slightly uneven dirt road. The trees began to thin as the dirt turned into gravel causing the car to shake as it crawled into the parking lot.

My stomach was somersaulting from the car rumbles and anticipation. This summer is a culmination of all the years I have been coming here as a camper. I remember the first year I came to Camp Odyssey, I told myself one day I would be that counselor that all the kids love. This was it. This was going to be that summer.

The wooden sign posted up at the front of the camp had seen over 50 years of rain, snow, wind, and sun. The letters spelling out Camp Odyssey had been freshly painted black for the start of summer. Soon the sun would fade it into a dark charcoal gray color, but for now it was fresh and vibrant against the aged wood.

My dad parked the car, giving a cheery, "Alright, we're here!"

We all got out of the car to walk me into camp. My dad and I split from the rest of the family and headed towards the giant white banner that said 'CHECK IN' in bright green letters. We pulled up to the table where Mrs. Hamilton, the camp director, was sitting.

"Welcome back Miss Sullivan," Mrs. Hamilton beamed as she highlighted my name off a list. "We were so excited that you signed up to be a counselor this year." She took out a small folder that had Hadley Sullivan written on the label and began pulling out papers.

"Hadley!" Kelly, who has been my counselor on and off the last few years and was also the camp director's daughter, got up from the table to wrap me in a hug. She gave me a tight squeeze before letting me go. "So good to see you! Gosh, you look almost like an adult now! Is that eye liner?"

"Yeah, figured it would help me look less like an actual camper."

"I told her," My dad interrupted, "that she won't look like a camper because she'll look like a raccoon, but she didn't listen."

"Dad, stop." I grumbled. The eyeliner and mascara helped make my gray-blue eyes pop, and while I probably wouldn't wear makeup everyday, I wanted to look good on the first day.

"Mr. Sullivan," Mrs. Hamilton stuck out a manicured hand with bright red nail polish. "So good to see you again."

"You as well!" My dad eagerly shook her hand. "Take good care of this one. I need her back in one piece for tax season."

"Well, you have three other ones, just in case!" The two shared a laugh that made Kelly and I roll our eyes.

"What size shirt do you want?" Kelly asked, her hand above a box containing a pile of burgundy fabric.

"Large, please. I want some wiggle room."

"Good call." Kelly nodded and fished a large sized t-shirt out of the box before passing it to me. I opened it up to look at the Camp Odyssey logo on the front with 2004 underneath it. When I flipped the shirt over, the back had the word 'counselor' written across the shoulders. My own counselor shirt. I beamed a smile at Kelly.

"Mom, let's hurry this along." Kelly motioned to the other counselors who were in line behind me trying to check in. Some had their families with them and some were alone or with friends. I recognized a lot of the faces from my years coming to camp, but there were also a lot of new people in the crowd.

"Yes," Mrs. Hamilton pulled out a small stack of papers. "Now, Hadley, for the first time in 10 years, you need to sign!"

"With great power..." My dad started as Mrs. Hamilton handed me the pen.

"Yeah, yeah, responsibility." I didn't even read the paper as I signed my name above the counselor line.

"Just one more that you have to sign. This covers the camp just in case anything happens for the duration of your stay here."

I signed as my mom returned with the other kids separated by her arms. "Apparently, finding sticks can turn violent." My siblings were still trying to whack each other with the skinny sticks they had found on the ground.

"Alright," Mrs. Hamilton shuffled the papers back into a stack and put them in a folder. "You are squared away."

"Perfect!" My dad shook Mrs. Hamilton's hand again then grabbed my duffle bag. We walked off to the side for official goodbyes.

My brother, John, went first, barely looking up as he hugged me and grumbled, "Bye." At 13 and he was in his moody teenager phase, so getting a hug from him was a big deal.

The twins, Emmy and Joey, hugged me at the same time, whimpering that they would miss me. They turned eight months ago but my mom didn't want to try to send them to camp this year. John had such a bad time when he went, that he ruined it for the twins. So I gave them an extra tight simultaneous squeeze.

My dad gave me a big hug, "Miss you, kiddo. Stay safe. Don't hesitate to call."

"Will do." I mumbled as I hugged him back.

My mom gave me a tight hug. "Love you, sweetie. We're all gonna miss you."

"Love you too, mom."

"Alright," My dad clapped. "Time to get the monkeys back to the zoo. See you in nine weeks!"

Watching my parents corral my siblings back to their silver SUV, I meekly waved as they backed out of the gravel parking spot and faded into the trees.

Regret instantly flared in my stomach. Despite how at home I felt here, it was weird to be left there feeling all alone. I shuffled my feet, unsure where to go next.

Thankfully, I wasn't alone for long. Aly, who has been my camp bestie for the last four years, showed up and we quickly found our friend, Sam. We met her last year when we all did CIT week together.

Aly and Sam are complete opposites but we all get along really well. Aly is the typical blonde girl, always in a cute outfit, even if it is uncomfortable for camp. She always smells great, even after hiking and wakes up early to straighten her hair and do her makeup every day. She's the best to gossip with.

Sam dresses more like me. She is always in an oversized t-shirt and has a book in her hand. Her pin straight black hair is permanently in a low ponytail. We listen to a lot of the same music so that's how we bonded last year. Sam balances out Aly's over the top energy. I was so glad to have them both for this summer.

We dropped our bags off in the holding area and headed to the welcome meeting.

Aly was struggling to keep up with us in her flip flops but she refused to change into her sneakers. She claimed, "They don't work with this outfit." She was wearing a printed plaid skort with pink and yellow tank tops layered over each other. Her white flip flops complimented the outfit better than her white sneakers would.

Sam and I waited for her to catch up to us outside the dining hall. Sam rolled her eyes and adjusted the book she kept tucked under her arm.

"I know," I complained, "But that's Aly."

The dining hall is way bigger than the main building where all the campers check-in. It can hold all the campers and counselors at the same time for meals if needed. We have some camp activities there, like arts and crafts. When campers are here, we come in staggered waves to give the cooking staff a break. We have a lot of meetings in the dining hall, and if it is raining and we can't use the outdoor theater for skit night, we have it here.

There were voices coming from inside the dining hall before we even went in. Once we crossed through the door Aly slowly started walking along the edge of the room.

"Are we going to pick a table?" Sam asked.

"I want to see what the other counselors are looking like."

"Sizing up your competition?" I jested.

"More like scouting to see which boys are the hottest." Aly shared a look with me. "Now that you can get in on the action, this summer is going to be so much fun!"

"Yeah, I'm ready to see what else is out there." My ex's texts from earlier didn't change my attitude. This summer was going to be about what I wanted.

"Plenty of hotter fish in the sea!" Aly joked and we all laughed. "I want to be paired with the hottest boy counselors only."

"You know we don't get any control over that." I reminded Aly but she waved a hand at me.

"I know, I know. The Hamiltons decide who we all get paired with."

"Could we be paired together then?" Sam eagerly asked.

"Def!" I replied. "It's always two guy counselors and two girl counselors per age group, so we can be together. It's random how they assign it but I know they'll switch things around to pair people up who work well together."

"Well hopefully we can be together as much as possible." Sam adjusted the book under her arm.

As we walked around the room we stopped every time we spotted a familiar face to make small talk with them before saying we were going to find a table to sit at.

A roaring laugh made my head turn and I locked eyes

with the person it was coming from. "Hadley!" Aaron, my favorite counselor from last year, waved at me as he walked into the dining hall.

"Hey Aaron!"

His inviting, wide smile was beaming from the center of his light brown face as he flipped his long dreads back. Aaron and the guy he was walking with adjusted their path so they could meet up with us.

The unfamiliar face next to Aaron smiled at me. His dark brown hair flowed in curly waves on top of his head and bounced a little with each step. His face, arms, and legs were naturally golden brown and radiated in the sunlight that was coming through the dining hall windows and skylights. He was just a little taller than Aaron, with a stocky body that had softly sculpted muscles. He clearly played a sport but I wasn't sure which one, maybe football?

As he walked closer, I couldn't look away.

Aaron wrapped me in a quick hug, then moved down the line to Aly, and Sam. "Great to see you guys all back this year!"

I locked eyes with his friend and his face lit up. "Nice shirt!"

Instantly, I looked down to remember what shirt I was wearing. We both had on the exact same blink-182 tour t-shirt from 2001. It was from the Take Off Your Pants and Jacket Tour with Mark Hoppus jumping while playing bass guitar. I put it on because it was one of my favorite concert t-shirts, but never expected anyone to have the same exact shirt.

"Oh, yeah, you too!" The words fumbled out of my mouth and I hoped they sounded coherent.

He nodded then looked at Aaron.

Aaron opened his mouth, but Lucas, the Hamiltons' son, popped up from behind him. He gave him a friendly but hard pat on the back. "They let you come back here?"

Aaron chuckled and pretended to punch Lucas's arm. "I said I was friends with the kid who runs this place and that seemed to work."

"C'mon, my parents will be here in a sec." Lucas started walking to a table. Aaron looked at me. "We'll catch up later."

Aaron's friend locked eyes with me again, "See you."

I couldn't think of anything to say as I watched them walk away.

The girls closed in on me. Aly started, "Hadley, oh my god! He is so hot."

Sam continued, "That must be the new counselor, Alex. I think he's from Florida."

"Wait, how do you know that?" I asked.

She shrugged, "I saw his name on the counselor list when I checked in."

Aly squealed, "He likes you, Hadley!"

"No, we literally just have the same shirt. It's nothing." I brushed it off, but the idea got my heart racing.

"I don't know." Sam started. "He didn't say anything to Aly or me."

"Come on!" Aly grabbed then pulled us to the table across from the one Alex was sitting at. He was talking to a couple other guys but looked up at me when I sat down.

I immediately looked away.

Aly suddenly gasped. "Oh my god, Jake is more buff than last year."

A few seats away from Alex, was Jake, a counselor from last year that Aly was obsessed with. He spiked up his blonde hair, and only wore sleeveless t-shirts and board shorts, like he would somehow find a beach in the middle of Virginia. I always thought he was an obnoxious jerk, but Aly, like everyone else at camp, was in love with him for reasons I'll never understand. At first I thought it was because he's best friends with Lucas and like a second son to the Hamilton's, so I thought everyone tolerated him because they had to. But I quickly realized that some people actually enjoy his gross jokes, Aly being one of them.

I quipped, "Steroids will do that to you."

Aly snapped back. "Hadley!"

"Dude, come on, there's no way that those bulging arms are natural. Plus, he has a beer gut."

"He did turn 21 this year."

Sam sighed, "That is so sad that you know that."

"I remembered from when he told me last summer!"

I pretended to gag. "Gross."

A familiar voice asked from behind, "What's gross?"

We all spun around. Aly cried out, "Justin!"

Justin, our friend from last summer, smiled as he hugged each of us. He was wearing head-to-toe Hollister, like he had just walked out of an ad. Even his sandy brown hair was perfectly styled to look like he just came out of the ocean. Aly commented on how good he smelled and then demanded, "Sit with us!"

"Of course!" Justin took the seat next to me. He nudged my elbow, and slightly nodded across the room. "Who is that looking over at you?"

"Who?" I looked up just as Alex was looking away.

"Oh," I felt my face getting hot with blush, "I guess that's Alex? Sam knew his name since she knows everything. He's a new counselor from Florida."

"Need me to pretend to be your boyfriend?"

"Not yet."

Justin winked.

Suddenly, the whole room was quiet as Mr. and Mrs. Hamilton entered. Kelly was seated at the table closest to the door, scanning all of us counselors. She looked just like Mr. Hamilton, and you can tell her black hair was from him, even though his is peppered with gray now. Lucas favored his mother and had light brown hair, a round face, and smiled just like her. Together they ran the camp, all filling different roles to make sure everything runs smoothly.

Mrs. Hamilton joined Kelly at the table while Mr. Hamilton walked to the middle of the dining hall. His hiking boots clomped on the floor as he took center stage in front of us all. Then he clapped his hands together and cleared his throat. Everyone eagerly waited to hear what he had to say.

"Welcome to those of you joining us for your first summer at Camp Odyssey! And a big welcome back to those of you who have made Camp Odyssey your home for years. This is the 50th year the camp has been open, and each year it gets better and better. This is my 21st year in charge and I only remember this because Lucas is 21." He paused for the obligatory laughter. "Now, you young men and women are going to have a lot of responsibility placed on you. I know that some of our more seasoned counselors will understand when I say that this weekend will prepare you for every perfect situation, but there will never be a perfect situation. Make sure this weekend that you are learning and absorbing everything you can so when you are out there you can keep everyone safe but also have fun. We'll get to all the technical stuff later, for now, let's learn to have some fun!"

He clapped his hands and the energy in the room shifted from serious to lively. "We're going to start with everyone's favorite: icebreakers! You'll be working with each other and switching who you are working with each week, so you need to get to know and trust each other. To start off, you'll be sharing your name, where you are from, and your favorite camp activity with someone who..." He paused to gaze at the eager faces looking back at him. "Is wearing the same or a similar color shirt as you!"

People bounced up and immediately found partners. Justin and Sam were both wearing navy blue. Aly ran to the other girl who had a pink shirt on. A rapid roar of conversation was filling the dining hall. I looked up at Alex who was walking towards me. When he was right next to me, he gave me a crooked smile and said, "I mean you can't get more similar than the same shirt."

"For sure," I held out my hand. "I'm Hadley Sullivan."

He wrapped his hand around mine, but instead of shaking it, he gave my hand a soft squeeze. "Alex Lopez, from Florida." Sam was right.

"Florida?" I put my hands in my back pockets unsure of

what to do with them.

"Yeah, but I go to Tech with Aaron. Didn't want to go home to Tampa, so I stayed up here in Virginia."

"You chose Virginia over Florida?" I tried not to sound as surprised as I was.

He went to put his hands in his pockets, but his gym shorts didn't have any so instead he crossed his arms. "Florida gets old after a while. I'm guessing you're from Virginia then?"

"Fairfax, part of Northern Virginia."

"I've noticed everyone from Northern Virginia makes it a point to say they are from Northern Virginia."

"Yeah," I giggled. "They teach us that in school."

He laughed and I smiled, satisfied that I had made him laugh. "Okay, what else, favorite camp activity?"

"Mine is def archery."

"You know, I've never been to camp so I've never done camp stuff but archery sounds pretty sweet."

"Alright!" Mr. Hamilton boomed and the voices quieted down. "Now, find someone with the same shoes as you, same questions!"

"Well, see you around, Hadley."

I wanted to ask more but our time was up. Begrudgingly I smiled and said, "See you, Alex."

Justin came up behind me and pinched my elbow.

"Ow!" I turned around already scowling at him.

He smirked, "I didn't think you would be able to feel that!"

"Well, I did." I snarked rubbing my elbow.

"We both have Vans on." I looked down to confirm that we both had on the black and white checkered shoes. Justin's looked much newer than mine, which had gotten beat up during the school year.

"Perfect, cause I could not talk to another new person."

"You literally talked to a single new person."

"And it was a lot."

"So how was talking to *Alex*?" Justin sang each syllable of the name.

"Fine, he's totally chill."

"Is he?"

"Yeah, he's from *Florida*." I mocked Justin's singing.

He jeered back, "How exotic!"

I shook my head, "Let's get you a girlfriend before we worry about my problems."

"No, no, don't worry about me. We need to sort you and Alex out first."

I rolled my eyes.

We switched three more times. I met Kylie, who has been coming to camp for a few years but never the same week when I have. Then I managed to pair up with Aly and Sam for the last two switches so we could gossip about the other people they had met.

Mr. Hamilton yelled over everyone, "Now, if everyone can take their seats, we have a few more things to go over!"

The murmurs quickly died as people took their places back at the tables they were at before. I sat in the seat next to Justin and crossed my legs under me.

"For this weekend, you'll all be staying in the lodge. Everyone will be finishing CPR, lifeguard, and first aid instruction. Sunday will be the first laundry day, and I suggest you all take advantage of it because laundry piles up quickly in one week. The schedule of events will be the same for all the counselors. It will be a lot of hard work so you will all have Saturday night off as a reward. Sunday the kids arrive so make sure you get plenty of rest."

Justin whispered to me, "I hope we get partnered up first."

"Same! As many times as I can, I want to be with you."

"To end this, let's all huddle together." Mr. Hamilton looked around. No one was getting up. "Come on, we are all going to become close friends, so let's huddle up!"

Kelly and Lucas joined their dad. Mrs. Hamilton stayed sitting.

Others stood up, starting a ripple effect through the counselors. There were about forty of us blending together in the huddle. The heat from everyone was filling the space.

Mr. Hamilton directed, "Alright, everyone put a hand in."

Aly and Sam nervously giggled as they put their hands in. Justin and I shared a look as we put our hands in next to theirs.

"Is everyone in?"

The room filled with echoes of yes, but all I noticed was the dark tan hand that was suddenly on top of mine. I followed the hand up the arm and looked at Alex. He gave me a crooked smile then looked up, awaiting further instruction. The warmth from his hand spread into mine, making me blush.

Mr. Hamilton shouted, "Camp Odyssey on 3! 1...2...3!"

A blend of high and low voices shouted, "Camp Odyssey!"

2

All the counselors were staying in the lodge for the weekend with the boys all on one side and the girls on the other. In between the two sides there were bathrooms and a small kitchen. Everything flowed into a giant common room that had a fireplace across from a giant table pushed up against the wall. There were couches spread throughout the room for us to all relax in.

The lodge was typically used for the older campers. I'd stayed here the past few years when they combined all the high school age campers into one large group so I felt relaxed as I walked into the familiar place.

We all threw our stuff in a room that Aly had claimed before going back into the common room for dinner. The table had been pulled out from the wall and people were unstacking chairs so we could all sit.

After dinner, Kelly went over the rules for the weekend. "Some things to keep in mind: Tomorrow is a long day. Make sure you are responsible tonight, and the rest of the weekend. We need everyone here, mentally and physically. Obviously," Kelly looked hard at her brother, "We know that you will all get to know each other better. You'll play games and stay up too late. Being 'sick' and unable to work could result in us docking your pay. Miss too many days and we'll send you home.

"The rules about fraternizing between counselors are the same as always. You are not to do anything inappropriate while campers are around. We know that the rules can be a little hard to remember on Saturday nights, but if anyone is caught in a compromising position or in a bedroom with each other, then you will be sent home. If anyone needs anything just use the radios we gave you. Any questions?"

There was murmuring in the crowd but no one raised a hand. "Okay, thank you everyone. Have a safe night!" Kelly left the lodge. Everyone relaxed.

Alex took a seat on one of the green couches facing the fireplace. He looked at me and nodded his head ever so slightly towards the empty seat next to him.

Everyone was moving around me but I was frozen where I was. I looked around to see if he was looking at anyone else, but I was the only person he could have been looking at. My stomach did a somersault.

Before I could decide if I was going to sit with him or not, Aaron took the spot. The weight of my indecision pulled my face down. Alex gave me a little smile before turning his attention towards Aaron.

I turned to Aly and Sam who were walking back towards the room we were sharing with Nicole and Hannah, two counselors Aly had clicked with. When I got to the room, I pulled myself up onto my top bunk so no one would see I was upset.

Aly shuffled through her duffle bag. "I heard there is going to be a party tonight."

"When did you hear that?" Sam was grabbing something from below me. There was an odd number of us so the bunk below mine was empty and everyone had piled bags on top of it.

"Annie mentioned it to me."

"It's true," Hannah chimed in. "They do it every night the counselors are off. Apparently, Lucas lets everyone get away with it since it's his job to monitor us. Becky told me that last year Jake puked in his bed and the boys had to spend the whole night cleaning it up. They got like no sleep and Jake fell asleep during the CPR lesson. But that didn't stop them from throwing these parties every Saturday."

Sam shot up, "Wait, so this is a party party?" I didn't see what she took out from her backpack because she quickly put it in her back pocket. "I've never had alcohol."

"Relax, *chica*." Nicole, who was sitting next to Hannah,

spoke up. "Don't feel like you have to drink. It's just there if people want it. And if anyone pressures you to drink, tell one of us or the other girls and they will shut it down."

"That's good to know. BRB guys, bathroom." She let herself out.

Aly had placed two shirts on her bottom bunk. "Which one?"

I answered her, "The green one. The black shirt with lace looks like you're trying too hard." Hannah and Nicole agreed with me.

Aly quickly changed and looked at herself in the mirror on the door. "Perfect, let's get out there!"

"Go ahead," I waved my hand at her. "I'll be there in a second." They left the room but didn't shut the door so I heard the jumbled voices of people mingling in the common room.

I wasn't planning on checking my phone so soon, but after Alex invited me to sit with him, there was this familiar pang in my stomach that I was doing something wrong.

I knew that what I was feeling for Alex wasn't wrong, but I had to be sure.

My phone took forever to turn on. "Come on, come on..." I whispered to myself. It finally powered on and the home screen lit up when I heard someone behind me.

"You okay?"

I didn't look up because I immediately recognized the voice. "Yeah, Sam."

"Just came back in to change real quick."

"Oh no," There were no new messages. At first, I was disappointed. His texts from earlier made it feel like he was going to try to win me back. I thought that he might start to put in the effort he had when we first began dating. The disappointment quickly faded into satisfaction. I had told him that I would talk to him later, so he was listening to me. This lack of texting was a good sign.

"You know," Sam grabbed a new pair of shorts from her backpack. "That time of the month."

Hearing Sam sigh brought my full attention to her. "Are *you* okay?"

"Yeah, my shorts are not though."

"Shit, sorry, let me give you some privacy."

"Thanks."

"One sec." I powered off my phone again and shoved it in my bag. "I just thought that maybe someone had tried to text me."

"Your ex?"

I shrugged. Sam and Aly knew all about the problems I had with my ex during the school year. We had weekly A.I.M. sessions where we filled each other in on our lives. It was easier than trying to call each other and potentially have my parents overhear.

"My advice, as someone who has never had a boyfriend, they don't seem like they are worth all the trouble. I would just forget about him."

I sighed, "They really aren't."

Sam and I shared a quick smile before I left her to join the party.

There were less people in the common area and the sliding door was open, letting in a steady flow of voices and music. I ventured outside, seeing a few small fires going in the different fire pits several feet away.

Alex was sitting with Aaron on a log next to a bonfire. They had a lot of the girl counselors sitting with them, laughing at a story Aaron was telling. Aly, Hannah, and Nicole were all standing together giggling at Jake. Other people were sprinkled around the firepits, talking and laughing. Justin was sitting alone staring at a fire sipping on something from a red solo cup.

I smiled as I plopped down onto the log next to Justin, "Whatcha drinking?"

He seemed relieved by my presence. "Not sure. I think it's called 'jungle juice'? Aly handed it to me and I had a couple sips. Wanna try?"

I grabbed the cup and took a swig. The overly sweet

liquid hit my tongue, bashing my taste buds before the burn of alcohol came. It wasn't horrible, but it wasn't enjoyable either. Almost immediately the warmth from the alcohol found its way through my body, flushing my cheeks.

"That's…interesting." I took another sip to see if it went down easier after I got used to the taste. It didn't.

"You can have it."

"You sure?"

"Yeah, well…" Justin accepted the cup back and took a big sip. "Here. I'm not trying to be hungover for training tomorrow."

"I'm excited to actually have camp stuff to do!"

"Same, and we'll find out the pairings for the first week soon!"

"I'll be fine with whoever." I lied. I wanted to be paired up with Alex as soon as possible. The thought of him made me search him out in the crowd. The firelight illuminated his smile as he laughed at something Aaron said. I could hear Justin's voice next to me, but I was entranced by Alex.

Then he looked over at me.

I quickly looked away, covering as much of my face with the cup as I could while I took a huge gulp. I waited a second before looking back over at him.

He was looking away again.

"Earth to Hadley." Justin snapped in my face.

"Sorry, I-"

"You were staring at the cute Florida boy." Justin grabbed the cup from my hand and took a long drink.

"I-" There was no point in lying. "I totally was."

"You should go after him."

I shrugged. "I don't know. I'm still sorting shit out from the break up."

"You never did tell me what happened with all that."

"It's a long story."

He handed me back the cup. I finished off what was in it. I was definitely feeling the warmth from the alcohol but wasn't quite ready to call it a night. "Go get us another drink to share and you can tell me all about it."

I popped up, subtly looking to see if Alex saw me get up. He did.

Justin stayed put, "Take the long way back!"

I walked over to the table where a giant orange Igloo cooler filled with 'jungle juice' was. I quickly refilled the same cup then turned to walk the long way past Alex back to where Justin and I were sitting.

But when I turned around I immediately bumped into someone right behind me.

Jake.

Half of my drink had splashed all over him, making a pink stain in the middle of his white cut off t-shirt. "Sorry," I mumbled.

"Shit, I'm sorry." He swiftly took off his shirt. I had to resist the urge to roll my eyes. "Did you get any on you?"

I looked down at my white blink-182 shirt that was spotless. "No, I got lucky this time."

"Damn, let me refill your drink."

"You don't-" I started to protest but he took the cup from me and refilled it from the cooler. I looked over at Justin who was scrunching his face at me in confusion. I shrugged before turning around to see Jake filling the cup to the very top.

"There ya go."

Begrudgingly, I took my cup back. "Thanks."

"You're Hadley, right? You were here last year?"

"Yeah, I've been coming here for like 10 years."

He chuckled, "You looked super familiar."

I doubt he remembered how he untied my bathing suit in the pool last summer.

"Well, thanks for the drink. Sorry about your shirt. I can try to fix it during laundry time Sunday."

"No worries, I have a never ending supply of these shirts."

"Cool, see you around."

I started to walk away but I heard him call out, "oh, you

will!"

I was too shaken up by spilling my drink on Jake that I just walked straight back to Justin.

Before I could explain, Aly was upon us. "What did you do?"

"I spilled my drink cause he was super close to me when I turned around. No biggie."

"You got him to take his shirt off, so thanks." She giggled and I groaned.

"He's still a super creep." I took a careful sip from the overfilled cup.

"He is not! You know, I asked him about the bathing suit stuff last year, he said it was just supposed to be a joke!"

"Well, it wasn't funny."

"Lighten up, Hadley. Summer is all about having fun."

"Cheers to that!" Justin took the cup back and drank. Aly joined in finishing her cup then walked away for a refill.

"So your ex?" Justin asked as we started passing the cup back and forth.

"Long story but I'll make it super short. He's a piece of shit who said terrible things to me. We broke up months ago but he tried to text me before I came to camp."

"Did he know you were coming to camp today?"

"Maybe? It would explain why of all the days to reach out, he picked this one."

Justin's cheeks had turned rosy. "If I'm being honest with you, I never liked him."

"You didn't even know him."

"No, but the stuff you said about him made me not like him."

"Then good thing he's out of my life." Which was technically the truth.

"Hell yeah!" He joked as I finished what was left in the cup and crushed it.

"That's enough for one night."

"Agreed. Tomorrow will be a long day."

"But I'm so excited!"

"Same." We smiled at each other. My face was warm from the alcohol, the fire in front of us, and the night air.

Suddenly, I started to feel like I was going to throw up. Spit was filling my mouth and my stomach was cramping. I didn't feel like I had drunk enough to warrant vomiting but this feeling came on hard and fast. I stood up and the awful feeling in my stomach was rapidly spreading to the rest of my body.

Justin started to walk me back to the lodge. My legs felt heavier with each step. Moving my foot took all the concentration that I had left in me.

"Hang on, Hadley!" Justin's slurred words were echoing in my ears. Why was he yelling?

I could feel my vision getting blurry and I tried to open my eyes wider so I could see better, but it didn't make a difference. Everything about my body felt slanted. I could feel myself tipping over. I made it into the main hallway before everything went black.

3

I woke up feeling like complete shit. It was worse than a hangover. I felt like my body was splitting apart from even the slightest movement. Every molecule was screaming out in pain.

In agony, I slowly rolled over and dared to open my eyes. The faint touch of the sun felt like knives being shoved into my eyes. I groaned and rolled back over, away from the window.

"Hadley?" Aly whispered from below.

I grumbled in response.

"You good?"

I croaked, "No."

"Did you drink too much?"

"I guess."

Sam chimed in, "Maybe you should go to the nurse?"

"I can't."

"Just tell her you ate something that made you sick."

I groaned. "She is going to know we were drinking."

"Do you want to come to breakfast with us?"

"No, I'm just going to stay here and sleep until training starts."

"You sure?"

"Yes," I hissed and pulled my sleeping bag over my head.

I heard the door creek open then shut. The banging rattled my head and caused a ripple of pain to envelop my senses. When I winced it made my eyes hurt. Every inch of my body felt fried.

As much as I wanted to, there was no way I was going to be able to go back to sleep now. Slowly, I peeled myself out of my sleeping bag and onto the ground. I slid my flip flops on, threw a hoodie over my clothes from last night, and started walking.

"Wait up!" I tried to yell but my voice still sounded like I had screamed all night. Somehow, Sam heard me and my friends paused. Other people were managing to walk, or rather stumble, towards the dining hall for breakfast.

All I needed to do was make it to the dining hall, which was normally a quick and easy walk. I willed my legs to move by thinking about getting food in my body and feeling better.

"I thought you only had like 2 drinks?" Aly asked as she passed me her sunglasses.

I slid them on, thankful that they reduced the sun's harsh light. "Yeah, and I shared with Justin! I mean, I don't drink like that all the time but I've had more to drink before and felt fine the next day."

"Was it the drink?" Sam thought out loud.

"Maybe. I've never had, what did Jake call it, 'jungle juice'?"

"Yeah!" Aly beamed. "He said he made it himself."

I scoffed, "He probably roofied it then."

She stomped her foot, "Don't even joke about that! We'd all be feeling like shit if he roofied the entire cooler."

"I guess," It hurt to shrug. "I just need some food and lots of water to get through training."

Aly spent the rest of the walk reminiscing on the super douchey things Jake had done last night. He started a beer pong tournament with some of the counselors and won with the help of Lucas. I was glad I missed that.

About half the counselors were in the dining hall when we arrived. The three of us quickly grabbed some eggs, bacon, and I grabbed extra toast. We found ourselves seated at the table with Justin. He looked as bad as I felt.

"How're you?" He almost yelled as I sat down.

"Gross. I feel like my brain was hit by a car."

"Same, so let's hope this grease soaks it up." He shoved a whole piece of bacon in his mouth making us all laugh.

We settled into a quiet rhythm talking about what we were looking forward to today.

I felt a hand gently fall onto my shoulder.

Turning around, I saw it was Alex.

"You okay?" His face crinkled as he looked me up and down. "I was worried about you last night."

"Oh, um, yeah, I mean no, but like I'll live. I guess I had too much sauce." Why did I say sauce? No one called alcohol sauce. I hoped he would just ignore that.

"You must've because you passed out in the hallway." He gave me one more look over. "Well, I'm glad you're alright. Make sure you drink lots of water."

"Definitely. Hydrate or die-drate!" I could not stop saying the lamest things.

He smiled at me as his body shook with a small laugh. Then Alex looked at Justin, "And how're you doing?"

Justin's freckled face flushed with embarrassment. "I'll manage."

"Good, you both take it easy today. Thanks for your help last night, Sam. Keep an eye on these two." Alex gently squeezed my shoulder before turning to leave. If I wasn't so embarrassed at what I was learning about last night, I would've looked at him walking away.

"Of course!" Sam called after him.

Aly started, "What was that?" Her eyes darted between Justin, Sam, and me.

I turned to Sam for answers. "What did you help him with?"

She started, "Well, I wasn't gonna say anything, but-"

"But what?"

"Last night I heard Justin yelling so I went out to see what was wrong. You had passed out on the floor and he was trying to pick you up. I ran over to help when Justin passed out next to you. I was about to go outside and ask someone for help when Alex came out of the bathroom. He quickly scooped you up and placed you in your bed. He even tucked you in. It was actually super cute."

I shut my eyes and sunk into my chair.

She continued, "Alex told Jake to take Justin into his bed."
We all asked, "Jake?"

"He was coming into the common room as Alex was coming out of the bathroom. He offered to pick Hadley up first but Alex swooped in before he could. He told Jake to prove he can deadlift someone and get Justin into his bed." Sam chuckled at the memory.

Justin said, "So that's why I remember big, strong arms picking me up and tossing me into my bed."

"Yeah," She gave him a look but kept going, "Jake put you to bed and offered to help watch you guys but I told him I would. I checked on you both until I went to sleep. Alex even checked on you before he went to bed."

"Now that's cute!" Justin nudged my elbow with his.

"No, it's not. It's humiliating."

"It's not like you *actually* like him." Aly poked at me.

"Let's just not talk about it anymore."

They all started talking about CPR training as I pushed my eggs around the plate.

A few of the older counselors, Jessica, Becky, and Annie, strolled by us as they walked toward the table a lot of the boys were sitting at. I wasn't planning on looking up at them, but I heard Jessica's thin voice say, "Look at that. They're awake."

Everyone at our table was silent. I looked up to see Jessica sneering at me as she walked. "Couldn't hang last night, huh?"

I just shook my head.

Jessica gave a cold smile to everyone at my table before she joined Annie and Becky at the boy's table. She sat right next to Alex.

Holding back tears, I looked at Sam. "I guess everyone knows then?"

"Sorry Hadley."

After getting some food in me, I started feeling a little better. The Hamiltons split us into different groups for training but luckily I got to be with my friends. CPR training was in the morning for our group, but that was a breeze. Kelly ran us through that along with basic first aid before we broke for lunch.

I was pleasantly surprised when Aaron and Alex stopped by my groups' table during lunch. Aaron sat down next to me and stole a tater tot off my plate before saying, "Hadley, Sam, Aly, *and* Justin! You guys all planned to come back and be counselors this year?"

"Yeah!" We all said in unison.

"It's great to see you guys," He turned his attention towards me. "Especially my favorite CIT from last year."

"I can't wait until we are grouped together."

"I can't wait to cover you when you sneak your phone out to text your boyfriend at night since phones aren't allowed."

I rolled my eyes, "That isn't something you'll have to do this year."

"Really?"

"Yes. That's *more* than over."

He flashed a look at Alex across the table, then back at me. "I'm sorry, Hadley, you were crazy about him."

"Enough about him. What about you and Jordan?"

"We ended things too. It was easy to get through the summer, but harder to get through freshman year of college."

"Sorry, dude. Breakups suck."

"Only when there is no make up." He suggestively raised his eyebrows and I playfully hit his arm. Alex coughed, forcing us both to look at him.

He pointed to his watch then stood up from the table. "We gotta go get ready for lifeguard training."

"Shit, is it 12:30 already?" I looked over at Sam, Aly, and Justin, who were confused at my sudden burst of frantic energy.

Aaron put his hand out. "No, it's only noon. We're going to be the ones running lifeguard training so we need to go get everything ready."

"They're letting you run it?" I asked sarcastically. Alex laughed when Aaron's mouth dropped open in fake outrage.

"Well, I ran it last year and Alex here is from Florida so the Hamiltons assumed that means he knows how to swim."

Alex became playfully defensive. "I *know* how to swim. I learned to swim in the ocean, which makes me a better swimmer than you."

"He's so full of shit." Aaron rolled his eyes and started getting up. "See you all in a bit."

Alex lingered at the table and quietly said to me, "Glad to see you are feeling better. You look good now…I mean better than before."

"Breakfast helped." I said, holding his gaze just a bit too long as he ran his fingers through his hair. We all exchanged goodbyes.

As soon as they were out of the dining hall, I turned to my friends.

Aly started, "Aaron is a good wingman."

"Wingman?"

She scoffed, "That was clearly for Alex's sake."

"What do you mean? We barely spoke just now."

Justin leaned in, "He needed to make sure you were single. That's why Aaron brought up your ex."

"That's just Aaron. I talked to him about all my boy troubles last year. We bonded over it."

"And he could've picked any other time to come ask you those questions, but he did it in front of Alex, right before we all get in the pool together."

"Oh." The realization of what they were saying was sinking in.

"Yeah." Justin and Aly said in harmony.

I slid down my chair, while Aly started going on about how cute and funny Aaron was. Sam and Justin were nodding along.

Alex was making sure I was single.

This was the first time that I felt single since the breakup.

Before I just felt alone. My ex and I had such a horrific break up that I had only recently shaken those haunting feelings. This was the first time I had felt happy about not being tied down to another person, because now I could do whatever I wanted with whomever I chose.

An eagerness swirled in my stomach as we headed to the pool.

Lifeguard training was harder than I anticipated it being. Not the actual training and maneuvers for rescuing people from the water, that part was easy.

The hard part was feeling Alex's eyes on me. He kept his shirt on and never got in the pool, but I was totally exposed to him. Initially, I felt self-conscious in my bikini. I was worried about the parts of my body that I hate jiggling and shaking with each step I took into the pool.

Once we were in the water, it was easier to forget how much I hate my body. I made sure to pay attention to everything Alex was instructing us to do. He even complimented my form while I was 'rescuing' Sam.

When training was done, I slowly got out of the pool, careful not to move too fast and sucked in my stomach. I dared to look up and over at Alex, who let the whistle drop from his mouth as he looked me up and down.

My stomach tightened under his gaze. Insecurity forced me to turn away and wrap myself in a towel.

After lifeguard training, we all got dressed and took a giant tour of the campgrounds. As we all walked around, it was weird seeing how nothing seemed to change about Camp Odyssey. The paths between buildings were more worn down, and the paint on some buildings had started to fade, but everything still looked like it had since I started coming here.

Everyone was tired as we sluggishly moved into the dining hall for dinner. While we were eating, everyone was whispering about the party that was going to happen back at the lodge before we all moved into cabins. I promised myself not to drink too much and told Justin to hold me to it.

As we were walking back to the lodge, full but ready to have some fun before the kids arrived, lightning flashed into the sky. A few seconds later, a loud clap of thunder followed, and immediately following that was a curtain of rain.

It was a mix of shrieks and giggles as we all ran the last 100 yards to the lodge. Aly immediately started whining about her hair getting frizzy. I happened to scan the crowd, spotting Alex pushing his wet hair back.

When he looked over at me and caught me staring, he winked.

Quickly, I looked away as I felt my face flush and the warmth spread down my neck and onto my chest.

I ran after Aly and Sam who were already changing in the room.

"You good?" Sam asked when she saw me.

"Yeah,!" It took a moment for me to relax my whole body. Aly was still complaining under her breath about her frizzy hair, no matter how many times we assured her it was fine.

We all quickly changed into dry clothes and headed to see what everyone was doing. People were trickling into the common area of the lodge. The couches were filling up so people were clumping together in different corners. Jake and Lucas were trying to set one of the tables for beer pong, and Kelly was shutting them down.

When I scanned the room, Alex was finishing pouring himself a drink. His gaze floated around the room until it landed on me. He held my eyes over the brim of his red solo cup as he took a sip.

We nodded in acknowledgment at each other.

"Let's go get drinks!" Aly dragged us over to the table that Alex was still next to.

"Hello ladies," He put his own beer down on the table and grabbed a few new red solo cups from the stack. Then he took a can from a backpack under the table. "It's Bud Light, is that cool?"

"Sure!" Aly said, a little too excited. Sam and I shared a

look. He poured a few beers and then immediately put the cans into a black trash bag. He must've noticed my face because he shrugged and told us, "Kelly told me to hide everything so that's what I'm doing. Make sure you throw your cups away when you're done. We have to take the trash out before we all go to bed."

We all nodded and took our cups from him.

"I'm gonna go give this to Justin." Sam grabbed Aly's hand and pulled her away from us.

I took a step to follow them, but instead I turned around to talk to Alex. This was the perfect opportunity to talk to him now with no one else around. Nervously I mumbled, "Thank you."

"For what?"

"For the beer, for cleaning up, and…for last night."

"It was no trouble at all." He gave me a crooked smile before taking another sip of beer.

I needed him to keep talking, "So, you said you go to Tech. What year are you?"

"Just finished my freshman year."

We both took sips, then I continued, "What brought you to Virginia?"

"I've lived in Florida my whole life and" He lifted a broad shoulder, "I just wanted to experience something different. I might try to work in the government post-grad so I don't know, it just seemed like a good place to be."

"Cool," I was scrambling trying to think of something to say. "Your whole family lives in Florida?"

"My mom did, she moved back to Peru."

"Peru?"

He swirled a finger in front of his face. "That's where I get all this from."

"You know how to speak Spanish then?"

Alex chuckled, taking a long drink, "Yeah."

"Can you say something in Spanish?"

He smirked as he looked down, "Nah, I'm not gonna do

that."

There was a tension suddenly in the air like I had said something insulting. "I'm sorry! I shouldn't have asked." I hoped my apology would recover the moment. I was ready for him to brush me off, or chastise me, just like my ex would do whenever I said something upsetting to him.

Instead, Alex shook his head, "No worries, just like it's a language not a party trick, ya know? Besides, you won't understand anything I say."

"I took Spanish all of high school." I joked trying to lighten the mood.

"Then you say something."

"Uh," I could feel the embarrassment spread across my face as I blurted out, "*Hola, como estas?*" The most basic thing was all I could come up with.

"*Buen trabajo.*" The words smoothly rolled off his lips and into my ears. I wanted to hear him keep speaking Spanish, but I guessed he wouldn't like that. He looked at me smiling, waiting for me to register what he said, but the little bits of Spanish that I had happened to learn in school had slipped away. He leaned in close to my ear and whispered, "Good job."

As I was floundering for something to say, Justin interrupted us. "Sorry guys, have you seen Aly? She wanted me to get her when we started our card game."

"She was with Sam." I replied.

"Well, Sam is over there." Justin pointed to where she was sitting alone.

Alex scanned the crowd then pointed towards the start of the boy's hallway. "There she is, talking with Jake."

Justin groaned. "I should've known. I'll leave her be then. Sorry to interrupt!" He walked away.

Alex looked at me with a crooked smile, "Are you gonna go save your friend from Jake?"

I sighed, "I probably should. But I thought you guys were friends?"

"Nah, guy gives me a try hard vibe. I don't trust him."

"I don't either!" I said it a little too enthusiastically so I reeled it in. "Aly is obsessed with him and anytime I'm critical she blames the bathing suit incident."

"The what?"

"Oh, it's nothing." I waved my hand to emphasize this point but he raised his eyebrow asking me to continue. "Just last year when we were CITs for a week, Jake undid my bikini top in the pool. I freaked out on him but he denied it, even though Justin told me he saw him do it. I wanted to complain about it but I knew it would be useless. Lucas and Jake are best friends so they get to do whatever they want here. And it was just that one day and he never did it again, but he's still a creep in my book."

Alex stood up straighter, and the cup he was holding was crunching as he clenched his hand into a fist. "So nothing was ever done about that?"

"Well, no, but like it's whatever now."

He shook his head. "No, it's not whatever."

"Please don't do anything." I didn't want a scene to be caused because of me on the second day of summer.

Alex turned and looked me in the eyes. "If he does anything, and I mean anything even remotely creepy please tell me. If your stomach turns even the littlest bit because of something he does tell me. I'll handle it."

"I don't need you to do that…" I looked down, nervously twirling a loose curl.

"Someone should handle him. So let me know, please."

"Okay," I looked back up and our eyes met.

His eyes were deep, dark brown that almost looked black. It was easy to get lost in them. I wanted to keep looking into them, but Alex nodded back towards Jake. "You really should go save your friend."

"You're right." Nodding as I twisted to walk away. Alex grabbed my hand to stop me and I turned back to him.

"We'll finish this later." He gave my hand a light squeeze before letting go.

"We will." I bit my lip as I walked towards Aly.

Jake had one arm on the wall next to Aly's head. She was smiling like an idiot at him as he told her the story of the time he lifted 350 pounds or some shit like that.

"Hey girl, can I steal you for a sec?"

Jake sneered at me. "We're talking."

"And now you're not, cause I need to talk to her."

She smiled up at him, "I'm sorry. Girl code."

"See you later, ladies." He smirked and went off to grab another beer.

I pulled Aly into the bathroom and told her what had just happened with Alex and how it made me feel. It was the quickest reason I could think of that was worth stealing her away from Jake.

She squealed with delight, "A summer love! So exciting!"

"I guess."

"No it is! Are you ready to go back out?"

"Almost, you go ahead."

"Okay!" Aly walked out and left me alone.

After what happened between Alex and me, I wanted to check my phone and see if my ex had texted. I just needed reassurance that I could fall into these feelings.

I scurried back to the room, powered on my phone, and plugged it in to charge. Tomorrow we were moving into cabins and I might not be able to charge it while there. As I waited for the phone to turn on and load all the messages, I thought about how things had been between Keith and I before I left.

The last six months I've been committed to forgetting about what happened between us, but it was hard when I saw him every weekend. He still worked at the same restaurant that I was a hostess at. Recently, he had become a bartender and even though I got him that job to begin with, everyone thought he was so cool now. He told everyone he caught me cheating on him so they all thought that I was the one who did something to wrong him.

But I didn't do anything wrong.

The same bitterness towards him started to creep up my

throat. If he did say anything to me I wasn't going to be in a place to be receptive now.

I had a text message!

It was from my dad asking for a check-in text. I quickly sent him a grainy picture of my sleeping bag with my thumb in it for proof of life.

The rest of the night was alright. I just hung out with Sam and Justin. Towards midnight people started making their way to bed. As we were getting ready, Hannah rushed into our room. "Hey, Aly passed out in the bathroom."

"Shit." Sam and I said in unison.

We rushed across the hall and into the girl's bathroom.

Hannah led us to the stall she was in. Aly was slumped over the toilet, luckily she had managed to get all the vomit in there and not on her.

"Alright, I think all three of us can move her." I looped my arms under hers, Sam went to grab her legs, and Hannah helped grab her abdomen. We all nodded at each other before lifting Aly up. She wasn't heavy, but her awkward deadweight was hard to lift and then walk with. We ended up placing her back down on the floor just outside of the stall.

"This is going to take forever." Sam groaned.

"I saw Jake outside." Hannah said. "We can ask him to help."

I bit back the insulting thing I wanted to say about Jake. "Yeah, he'll be able to lift her up and into bed."

Hannah nodded before disappearing out of the bathroom. She came back seconds later still explaining to Jake what happened. "We just need you to move her across the hall."

"You guys need to learn to handle your booze." He effortlessly scooped Aly up. "Just need someone to get the door."

Hannah obliged and then Sam and I rushed ahead to let him into our room. He practically dropped Aly down on her bunk.

"Thanks, Jake." I grumbled.

"Whatever." He huffed before storming out.

We propped Aly on her side in case she threw up again then all went to bed.

4

The next day we all felt the hurried rush to get things done before the kids arrived. We had to take turns getting our laundry done, get together with our groups for the week, and make sure all the cabins were ready.

After breakfast, I headed to the laundry room. I had the 8:30 laundry slot but I arrived a few minutes early to get some alone time and think things over. Going into the laundry room for the first time felt like peeking behind a curtain into somewhere I wasn't supposed to be. It's underneath the lodge that we all stay in while we're not in cabins with kids. There were 5 washers and 5 dryers so we can all crank out our laundry in a few hours. Even though I had only worn two outfits since I arrived at camp, I wanted to have all my clothes clean to start the week off.

I dumped the contents of my drawstring mesh bag into the washing machine, added a scoop of laundry detergent, then guessed at what combinations of buttons started the machine. As the sound of water starting to swirl inside the machine filled the room I released all this tension I didn't realize I was holding in my body.

I thought about leaving my laundry and coming back in 30 minutes when it would be ready to switch. At home I always leave the laundry in the machine and come back hours later to switch it, but I didn't feel like I could do that here. I decided to stay put.

There was a bookshelf filled with the lost or forgotten books from the last 50 years. Lots of Stephen King novels and an incomplete set of the Harry Potter books were the standouts for me. My hand grabbed an older edition of *The Shining*. As I was reading the back cover, the door to the laundry room slammed shut.

Startled, I turned around and saw him.

"Shit, sorry!" Alex mumbled as he stood frozen in front of the door. "I didn't think it would shut that fast."

"It got me too."

"You're at 8:30 also?"

"Looks like it."

"Cool, I know you won't steal my clothes."

"You do have some cool band tees."

Alex smirked, "I knew I couldn't trust you."

I smiled back unsure of what to say so I defaulted to looking back at the book as Alex loaded his laundry into an open washer. He added soap, pressed the button, and soon his machine was humming along with mine.

He broke the silence as he took a seat on the worn out couch facing the machines. "Great book!"

"Yeah, I read it last year. I forgot the book I'm reading now in my bag so I just grabbed this."

"What are you reading now?"

"Making my way through *The Lord of the Rings* series. I figured this summer would be a good time to get through them."

"Loved those books too, and they did a great job with all the movies."

"That's what got me into reading them. My dad had the books but I was never interested in them until I saw the movies."

I put *The Shining* back in its place on the shelf and dared to take a seat next to Alex on the couch. "Since you like *The Lord of the Rings*, do you also like *Star Wars*?"

"Nope," He said with a straight face. "Actually I hate it."

"Oh," I anxiously tried to mend the sudden awkwardness with words. "I'm so sorry, I just everyone I know likes both but like-"

"Chillax, Hadley." He gently placed his hand on my leg. I could feel my face instantly blush despite internally screaming at myself to just be cool. Alex pulled his hand back but kept his crooked smile on. "I'm just messing with you. I love *Star Wars*."

Floundering, I tried to recover. "Good cause I need someone else to talk about it with. I was banking on Justin to talk to me but he's got such different ideas about what they are going to do in Episode 3 that it gets hard to talk to him. I need someone to speculate properly with."

"Now that conversation would last way longer than our allotted laundry time."

"So we'll save that for next time?"

"It's a date."

I could feel the redness pooling in my cheeks again but there was nothing I could do to stop it. I couldn't think of a funny quip to say back to the idea of a date with him so I just said, "Sounds great to me."

The screen door to the laundry room burst open with a kick and Jake walked in. "What's up, boners?" He kept his sunglasses on as he loaded his clothes into the laundry.

Alex rolled his eyes towards me before putting on a friendly smile, "Sup Jake?"

"You guys have laundry now too?"

We both nodded.

"You know you don't have to stay here the whole time, right? You can come back."

"Yeah," Alex retorted, "I thought that at Tech too then I got my shit stolen."

"Whatever," Jake started the washing machine. "See you later, chodes."

We awkwardly waved bye as Jake left.

"Fucking loser." Alex grumbled under his breath, then asked, "When do we find out who we're working with this week?"

My body relaxed at the change in subject. "They'll tell us at lunch. We bring all our bags and stuff with us to the dining hall, then once they tell us who we are with, we have to go to the cabins and make sure they're ready for the kids. Oh, and make sure you have your burgundy camp shirt on. We're all supposed to be uniform when the kids arrive so we are easier to spot."

He nodded. "Got it."

"I'm glad we'll change who we are with every week cause I don't want to be stuck with some people more than I have to."

"So we could get paired together?"

"Yeah," My heart skipped a beat. "Possibly."

"Good, cause I have no idea what I'm doing as a counselor." We both laughed and leaned into the scratchy couch across from each other.

Another guy came in, mumbled hello, threw in his laundry and left.

"That's Matt." Alex shrugged. "He was pretty quiet last night too but he said he's been to camp a lot."

"What made you come to camp? I know you came with Aaron, but there's got to be other cool stuff you could've done."

"I could've gone home and worked at my old job but I don't know, I wanted something new, ya know?"

"What was your old job?"

"Nothing special. I just worked at a restaurant."

"I work at a restaurant back home too."

"Then you know how shitty it can be." We both laughed then he asked, "What about you? Why did you want to give up your whole summer?"

"This has been my dream for years! I've always loved camp. I've been coming here since I was 8 and I was a CIT last year so it was an easy decision to come back as an actual counselor now that I've graduated."

"What's a CIT?"

"A counselor-in-training. For a week instead of being like a regular camper, you can be a CIT and help the counselors run the show."

"When does that happen?"

"It's only for a specific week in the summer that they do the CIT program. It's usually towards the end of the summer when camp is busiest and they need the extra hands. Otherwise, it's just counselors."

"How do you know all this?"

I shrugged, "From coming here so many years. You hear things and it's not exactly a secret how this place is run. Kelly loves talking about the logistics of camp. Last year I just asked her tons of questions about camp to get out of cleaning vomit from the pool. She made someone else do it so we could keep talking."

"Well played, Hadley."

I did a little pretend bow. "Thank you."

"But really, it's the summer before you start college. You didn't want to spend it with your friends?"

"Not really. I miss my best friend, but otherwise..." I sighed before admitting, "I needed to get away from people back home."

"I understand that."

"You do?"

Alex nodded, "There are people back home that I never want to see again."

"Well, if you ever want to commiserate..."

"We can do that on a different date." We shared a smile.

The door slammed and Sam rushed into the laundry room. "I couldn't find my laundry basket!"

She threw her laundry frantically into the washer and started the machine. "Relax, it'll be fine!"

"Now everyone is gonna be behind."

Alex added, "Everyone will get their laundry done."

"Okay." She plopped herself down on a chair next to the couch we were sitting on.

I didn't mind Sam being there. It was nice to have someone to placate whatever was going on between Alex and I. We all talked about what we were looking forward to while we finished doing laundry.

As I was leaving to go pack up, he said, "Don't forget about our *Star Wars* date."

"I won't!" I called back.

Every week everyone did the same activities, but the order we do them changed depending on the group we're in. We each had a turn doing archery, horseback riding, high ropes, canoeing, and a nature hike where we walked through the woods and a creek to the little waterfall nearby. In between all that we had swim time, arts and crafts time, and sing-a-longs after dinner each night before cabin bonding back at the campsite. It's a lot but there was never a dull moment.

For this first week I was paired with Justin, Maggie, and Brandon. We took the kids to the cabins we would be staying in for the week. Just as we got the kids settled, it was time to trek to the dining hall for dinner.

Some of the campers were starting to feel homesick. They were 10 and 11 years old and while they loved to say they don't miss home, their faces told a different story. We played trivia games at dinner to help lighten the mood and keep them distracted.

After dinner, it was back to the cabins to hang out a bit before lights out. We made a bonfire in the fire pit and let the kids take turns telling scary stories. Maggie had us all get the kids back into the cabins promptly at 9:30.

The cabin was surprisingly roomy inside considering how small it looks from the outside. There are 12 bunks, 6 on each side with a bathroom that splits the cabin down the middle. The counselors always took the bunk closest to the door.

The girls were all settling into their sleeping bags and getting ready so I snuck a peek at my phone underneath my own sleeping bag.

There was a text from Keith: **Talk on phone?**

I texted back: **IDK 2 much 2 txt**

Instead of a text back, he called me. Quickly, I silenced the call and frantically looked around. The girls were none the wiser, all of them either already in their sleeping bags or finishing changing for bed time.

"Maggie," I said just loud enough for her to hear.

"What's up?" She chirped back from below me.

"Do you mind if I go make a call really quick? It can't wait until morning."

"No prob! Just be back before I call lights out!"

Outside the sound of crickets had become louder as the sun had gone down. It was pitch black except for the flood lights on all the cabin doors that were illuminating the paths and areas just outside them. In the middle of the two cabins was the small common area that had covered seating, next to an open fire pit with benches around it. During the day we used it to get the kids all gathered up, or play games during down time, and do s'mores at night. I thought about sitting there, but felt like I just needed to get this over with and if I sat down it would take longer.

I walked a few feet away from the cabin but still within the light and called him back.

"Hello?"

His voice made my heart jump. "You wanted to talk?" I sounded more annoyed than I was, wanting him to think I was doing him a favor by even talking to him. Entertaining whatever he was trying to do was a favor.

There was a long sigh and then, "He came clean."

"What?"

"Brian came clean about what he did to you."

Suddenly, I was shaking with anger. "So now you believe me?"

"Yeah!" He sounded so proud of himself. It made me want to throw the phone.

I snapped back, "You didn't believe me when I told you."

"You were on top of him. What else was I supposed to think?"

"You were supposed to believe that I, your girlfriend, was telling you the truth."

"Baby, you gotta understand, it's my brother-"

"Your step-brother, that you hate."

"We've been getting closer-"

"Cause he gives you weed."

He groaned, "Can you just let me talk?!"

I stayed silent.

"Look, I'm sorry I didn't believe you. I know what Brian did, or tried to do, and it's fucked up but he's sorry too."

I stayed silent expecting him to say more. More apologizing, more groveling, more pleading, more anything. But that was it. Just a quick sorry that was worthless now. I finally mumbled, "So?

"So we can get back together."

"That's not how that works."

"Yeah, it is."

"No, Keith, you screamed horrible, awful things at me when you literally threw me out of your house because you believed your step-brother over me. You've known how miserable and depressed it made me and you've done nothing about it."

"I know! I fucked up and I'm sorry."

I scoffed, "You don't sound sorry."

"Look, do you want to get back together or not? Cause I thought that's what you wanted?"

There was the Keith I remembered. The reason we could never have a conversation was because it always turned into an argument. His attitude would clash with mine and we would bring out these horrible sides of each other. Then he would want the fight to be over so he would just say whatever he thought would end it and we could move on. I thought this time would be different. "This is why you called me? To talk to me like this?"

"I thought you would be more agreeable. You said you wanted to get back together so I thought this would make you happy."

"I'm not happy. I'm still angry and hurt by what you and Brian did to me that day."

"Baby, it's been months, c'mon."

"Seriously?!" I almost screamed out of frustration.

"You can't ice me out forever. I know you still love me."

This insane cycle we were on was going to end. I was sick of the awful feeling he gave me in my stomach, like I had to be on edge or hyper aware of everything I was doing so I didn't upset him and start a fight. I didn't want to start that again after months of not doing it. I would never get back together with him.

"No," I said firmly. "I don't love you anymore."

"Call me back when you want to get back together." Keith hung up the phone. I could see his face at me from the other end, wearing the smirk that he always had when I would just say whatever he wanted to hear so he could win and the argument would be over. I groaned and shut my phone closed, kicking at the ground in frustration.

5

High ropes has always been my least favorite camp activity and today was no different.

The high ropes course consisted of all these platforms built higher and higher up in the trees connected by different wires and ropes that the kids took turns climbing through. There was a hard side or an easy side, and we guided our group of kids one way or the other at the split after the first obstacle. Once the younger kids got over their fear of heights, they always had a great time. And the older kids enjoyed trying to be the fastest across whatever part of the track we were on. It ended in a giant zipline back down to where we started.

Everyone had to wear a helmet and harness. I always hated wearing the harness but it's a must even if it does feel super uncomfortable. I just felt like the harness straps squeeze my stomach and thighs so it spills over giving me the worst muffin top.

But it was required and so we all had to wear one.

Which was why I always volunteered to be the caboose. No one would be behind me staring at how tight the harness was on my stomach or how my whole thigh was exposed now that my shorts have ridden up. If I went last, no one had to see that until I'm ziplining back then I could take my harness off as soon as I landed.

All the kids quickly got their harnesses on and had started making their way up the ladder onto the first platform. I volunteered to be the caboose. Justin, Maggie, and Brandon were all spread out through the line of kids we had. The last camper, Lisa, was slowly starting to make her way up the ladder.

As I was getting ready to climb up the ladder, Alex came

into the clearing leading his group.

There was barely enough room for me to climb as I scurried up the ladder. Lisa had stopped moving and was staring back down at the ground.

I tried to encourage her, "Lisa, girl, you got this. This isn't even the challenging side of the high ropes course. You can do it!"

"No, no, no, Miss Hadley." She squeaked back, "I don't got this. I want to get down."

Looking back, I could see Alex's head tilt in confusion.

"It's too late, you've got to go."

She shook her head, "Not if I don't move."

"Lisa," I said through gritted teeth. "I will give you whatever you want if you just get up that freakin' ladder."

She thought for a second, "More dessert?"

"Sure! As much dessert as you want!"

Alex was leading his group over to the shack to get their helmets and harnesses on. It would only be a matter of minutes before he was over here.

"Okay!" Lisa eagerly reached for the next rung on the ladder. She was too confident in moving her foot up the rung, slipped, and slid back down onto me.

Lisa managed to stay on the ladder.

I fell off.

My harness tightened and the rope caught me before I hit the ground.

I was dangling just a few feet off the ground as Alex walked over.

He quietly joked, "You have a knack for getting in trouble."

I immediately recognized the movie he stole that line from. "Am I Spiderman in this situation? Or Mary Jane?" I mumbled, trying to spin myself back around to the ladder.

"Well, *you* are swinging from a harness."

"Then *you* said the wrong line."

Alex chuckled as I continued to spin.

I could feel everything start to radiate heat from the full body blush of embarrassment. It was mortifying. I had been on this high ropes course every summer for almost a decade. I knew how to climb up that ladder and scale across this thing, even if I hated being up there. But here I was, swinging from the safety rope like some shitty Peter Parker.

"Mind if I help?" Alex said as he gently put his hands on my hips and finished turning me to the ladder.

"Thanks." I mustered up a smile before quickly climbing up to the platform.

Lisa was still there waiting to go across the tightrope. She loudly asked, "Why are you so red?"

"Just go. The next group is waiting."

"I still-"

"You still get your dessert."

She clapped in excitement before getting up on the tightrope.

I was waiting for her to finish getting across as Alex arrived onto the platform.

"These things have no give." He joked while pulling at his harness.

"Yeah, they're meant for safety not fashion."

"Why, are you saying it's not a good look?"

"No," I jested and tried not to look down at his crotch. "You pull off the bunched up shorts look." We both shared a laugh that eased the tension a little.

"Your girl is waving you over." Alex pointed to where Lisa was frantically waving from the other side of the tightrope. I smiled before starting across.

We kept making awkward small talk and running into each other for the rest of the high ropes course. He didn't mention having to help me back onto the ladder, but I knew he was thinking about it. I looked so stupid in front of him.

He made the high ropes course look easy. It was effortless how he scaled up the ladder and tiptoed across the different ropes. His arms looked strong as he maneuvered around every obstacle. I wished he'd wrap those big arms around me.

The rest of this week flew by because every day was packed with activities. Despite searching for him on the down low every time we went anywhere, I didn't really get to see or interact with Alex the rest of the week until skit night.

Every Friday, each age group always did a skit and sang some songs as a last hoorah before the kids were picked up in the morning. Maggie asked the kids what skit they wanted to do and they came up with the amazing idea to do Hulk goes to camp like if Bruce Banner went to camp but had to hide he was Hulk so he didn't start smashing everything. We all got dressed up in green and purple. The kids did great and it was pretty cute.

Just when I thought I couldn't like him more, Alex played guitar during his group's skit. I was enraptured by the way his arm muscles flexed as he moved the guitar pick up and down on the strings. Justin at one point elbowed me to stop looking over at him.

"You're drooling." He joked.

"Shut up." I rolled my eyes but immediately looked back at Alex.

I couldn't help it, even when I tried to look anywhere else, my gaze would pull back to him like a magnet.

Once everyone was done with their skits, it was announced that Sam's group won skit night putting on an Intro to Camp skit. They were awarded the trophy, cheering as they led everyone out of the pavilion.

While walking back to camp, Justin suggested, "Go talk to him."

"About what?"

He threw his arms up, "Literally anything. You've both been at camp all week."

"No, no, I'm not going to force it."

"You'll stare at him all night but you won't go talk to him?"

I gasped from indignation but he was right. I wanted to talk to him, but this wasn't the time. "Not right now!"

"Oh my god," Justin rolled his eyes and turned around. "Alex!" He shouted loud enough to get his attention.

Alex jogged up to where we were walking. "What's up?"

"What are your thoughts on Nickelback?"

"I don't know, man. I don't mind them, but I don't love them. Why?"

"We were debating if Nickelback is rock or pop?"

"Good question," His face scrunched as he was thinking. "I guess they would count as rock."

"Thank you," Justin looked over at me. "Hadley, he agrees with you."

There was no choice but to go along with it. "Thanks for proving my point." I smiled and tried to act as naturally as I could following Justin's lie.

Alex asked, "Do you like Nickelback?"

"Oh no," I giggled. "Not my cup of tea."

"Me either. I need more angst in my music."

"Same."

That's when I realized that Justin had lagged behind, leaving us alone.

Alex leaned in close and whispered, "A few of us are going to go into town tomorrow to get stuff. Do you want anything?"

I took a second to think but I was never picky about free booze. "Nope, whatever you guys grab will be fine!"

"Cool, see you around." He turned and joined his group walking to their cabins.

I hustled back to Justin. "What was that?"

"That was me, being exhausted by your pining over this boy, and wanting you to do something about it."

"Justin!" His name came out in a long groan.

"Look, summer is short. You only have eight more weeks so if you want him, go after him."

6

In the morning, we all woke up feeling glum because it was the end of the first week with campers. All of the kids hugged each other, some exchanged phone numbers so they could keep in contact, and there were a lot of tears. These kids set the standard for the rest of summer and I was going to miss them.

With the kids gone, there was a lightness in the air that I hadn't felt all week. During lunch, everyone was sitting with their friends and catching up on the week. Justin, Sam, Aly, and I all sat together going over our weeks. Aly was complaining that she had to be paired with Henry, who she doesn't think is cute at all but she had fun practicing flirting with him. Sam, Justin, and I simultaneously rolled our eyes. She got up to gossip with some of the other girls and we were alone.

Until Aaron slid into the chair next to me while Alex took the chair Aly had just vacated. "We're going to run into town." He nodded over to Alex. "You guys want us to pick up anything for you?"

"What are you getting?" Justin asked.

Aaron turned to look at him, "Whatever you want."

Justin's eyes widened but he coolly said, "We'll just take whatever, right Hadley?"

I nodded.

"Told ya." Alex smiled at Aaron like he won something.

"Alright, we'll get you guys a bottle of whatever then." They got up from the table.

Once they were far enough away, Justin spoke. "Are we supposed to give them money?"

Sam nudged my elbow. "I think Hadley is arranging

payment in another way."

"No!" I blushed. "At least, he hasn't said anything about it."

Justin said, "They must have fakes, because they aren't twenty-one yet."

"They do." Sam confidently said. We looked at her and she added, "Aaron showed me his while I was with him this week. It looks legit too."

"I've always wanted a fake." Justin sighed. "But I don't think anyone will believe I'm twenty-one."

"I wouldn't." Sam joked and I laughed. But Alex and Aaron could pull it off. I'm sure when they went up to the counter to buy whatever booze they picked, they were confident enough that they wouldn't even need to show their fake IDs.

Everyone already had their bags packed and we all moved in waves back to the lodge for the night. It was easier if we all packed up and moved out before switching into new cabins depending on what people we are grouped with.

Now that a week of being with campers was done, I was starting to feel like a counselor. I was able to stay here and be a part of the bonding experience that I had heard rumors about all these years. It was better than what I had imagined from the whispers I had caught and pieced together.

Kelly and Lucas brought pizzas out to the lodge at night and everyone came together in the main room. After the pizza, the drinks carefully came back out. It was subtle at first, some of the older counselors handing off water bottles that had been filled with a combination of booze and Gatorade. But once Kelly left, the drinks were becoming more obvious as Lucas and Jake moved the party outside.

Aly managed to sneak us a water bottle full of liquor before sauntering off to flirt with Jake. Justin, Sam, and I claimed a log by the fire.

Once we sat down, I took a sip. Whatever clear alcohol that was in this water bottle had a horrible burn to it. It was something cheap that had a vague taste of watermelon. "What is this shit?" I passed the plastic water bottle I had been offered to Justin.

"I don't know." He shrugged. "Aly didn't say."

We looked over at Aly who was giggling and touching Jake's arm as he flexed to crush a beer can. I dared to ask, "What do you guys think of Jake?"

"He's just a meathead." Justin shrugged, taking another sip.

Sam laughed, "I think he's too stupid to do anything."

I scowled in his direction. "I *really* don't like him."

"You don't have to. Aly *really* likes him. And we know you *really* like Alex." He teased before handing me back the bottle. I took another swig and the burning sensation was getting easier to take.

"That's besides the point."

"I'm not his biggest fan, but everyone else seems to like him. Even Aaron gets along with him so how bad can he really be?"

"Alex doesn't like him either."

"So start a club and get matching t-shirts. You're not going to change everyone's minds, especially with Lucas and him being joined at the hip."

"He's right." Sam cut in before I could say something back. "I know you hate him because of what he did to you last year, but he was able to downplay that then and he'll do the same now. Just let it go."

I gritted out, "Fine." Then took a big, burning sip from the bottle.

Sam sighed, "I'm actually feeling pretty tired."

"You sure? It's just past ten!"

"That's all I can do after a long week."

Justin hopped up after her. "I'll walk you to your room. I

need to use the bathroom anyway."

I looked into the fire as they both walked away. I dared to take another burning sip and noticed that the more I drank, the less it burned. This was dangerous.

Alex suddenly plopped down on the log beside me, "Excited for laundry tomorrow?"

"Yeah," I smiled at him, "Except I won't be able to get any reading done."

"I mean I can let you have some quiet reading time."

He looked like he was going to leave so I said, a little too excited, "No, I think I'd rather have a conversation about reading." He took a sip of his beer before scooting closer to me on the log.

Alex nodded at the bottle. "Whatcha drinking?"

"Not sure. Aly handed it to me."

His eyebrows shot up. "Where did she get it?"

"Don't know actually." I giggled and felt the heat of the booze spreading to my cheeks.

"Party foul, Hadley. You never drink from anything that wasn't opened in front of you."

"Thanks for the sage advice, old man." I held his gaze while I took another sip.

His eyes were serious as he said, "Just be careful."

The booze was fueling my attitude, "I usually am."

"Usually?" Alex smiled before taking another sip of beer.

"Well," I lowered my voice, "Are you always careful?"

"No." He subtly shook his head. "Not always."

We started to lean closer to each other. His hand landed on my thigh, and this small touch sent waves through my whole body. The distance between us was closing with each slowly passing second.

This was it.

I was about to kiss Alex.

His fingers tightened on my thigh.

Both of us sucked in a breath.

My lips parted in anticipation of his meeting mine.

Suddenly, I heard clacking flip flops coming towards us. I assumed it was Justin coming back from the bathroom and he would stop once he realized he was interrupting something.

But it wasn't Justin's voice that let out a soft, "Damn."

Alex pulled back and I turned to glare at the person who decided to interrupt this moment.

Aly squeaked, "Sorry to interrupt, but we're starting a game of spin the bottle with the high school counselors."

I shook my head. "I'll pass."

"No, c'mon we want everyone to play!"

I shot back. "Sam isn't playing."

"She said she would before bed!"

If Sam was going in on the fun, then I had no excuse, other than the obvious, to not join in. I wanted to stay with Alex, but Aly's foot was tapping impatiently. "Please! Pretty please with sugar on top!"

She wasn't going to stop until I gave her what she wanted. I groaned, "Fine!"

"Yay!" She clapped her hands together before reaching out for mine.

I looked over at Alex whose face was scrunched with disappointment. "Sorry, she's a brat." I sighed as she pulled me up.

"No worries, we can finish our talk later. Have fun." He managed to give me a half-smile before finishing his beer.

"Thanks," I mumbled and followed Aly. Once we were out of ear shot I hissed at her. "Aly we were finally…talking."

"I know but we're doing this now." I had stopped following her so she would turn and look at me. She saw the disgruntled look on my face and threw her hands up. "I'm sorry but you guys can go back to just talking after this."

I huffed. "We were about to kiss."

"If he was really about to kiss you, he would've taken you somewhere else more private. That's what everyone else has been doing."

"I don't care. I don't want to play."

"Please, just play a quick game? I'm going to try to spin the bottle so Drew and I can kiss."

"I thought you were all into Jake?"

"I am, but that doesn't mean I can't explore other options!" Aly winked then pulled me inside the common area of the lodge.

I just needed to get through this game quickly, and then I could go finish my talk with Alex.

So I sat down in the circle, took a deep breath, and prepared myself to just randomly kiss whoever I needed to. It wouldn't mean anything. This was just a game kiss.

Looking at the other options, I wasn't thrilled. The boys were all cute in their own way, but not as cute as Alex. For a split second, I thought about backing out of the game and finding him. But I was already here and Aly had her eager hand on the empty vodka bottle in the middle of our circle.

Aly went first and ended up kissing Henry, not Drew. I felt bad for Henry because Aly wore her disappointment on her face when the bottle stopped spinning in front of him. Henry still had a softness to his cheeks and not a single hair growing on his face. He nervously pushed his shaggy blonde hair away from his face before Aly quickly pecked him on the lips.

They sat down and it was Drew's turn next. He spun it and it landed on Sam. She looked at Aly who was visibly upset but didn't say anything. They quickly touched their lips together. I wouldn't even call it a kiss.

On Sam's turn she spun and it landed on Matt. She seemed a little excited about kissing him. It looked more legit than what her and Jackson did.

Then so on and so on. More people paired up. Some were happier than others about who they had been matched with.

Finally it got to me and I landed on Justin. I breathed a sigh of relief. I could kiss Justin with no problem.

We both giggled as we quickly pecked each other on the lips.

With the game finished, some people split off to go hook

up. It was obvious after this first week that people were starting to like each other. The drama of summer was just beginning. With hookups starting, that means breakups and makeups were just around the corner.

Sam waved bye as she quietly went back to the room to read.

"Wanna go back outside?" Justin asked as he helped me off the floor.

"Yeah, I could use some fresh air after that."

"Nothing like kissing your best guy friend."

I nudged his arm with mine. "I'd kiss you over those other guys any day."

Outside was a very different vibe than the one we had just been in. The playful but slightly anxious feeling was now heavy and charged with booze. I scanned around to see if I could find Alex. Everyone seemed to be paired up and off in their own little world. I saw Jake and Becky flirting, Aaron and Ashley together, then most other people were clumped together in their own groups. Even with the crowd spread out, I couldn't see Alex.

Justin suddenly, nervously demanded, "Let's just go back inside. I'm getting tired now."

"Why?" I suspiciously peered around Justin to see what he had.

Alex was sitting with Jessica.

Jessica, who was beautiful, tall, and blonde. A girl with college experience and no tragic backstory like me. They made sense together.

We didn't.

I breathed out, "Oh."

"C'mon let's go." He started pulling my arm but I couldn't move.

I watched Alex smile and lean closer to Jessica. She grabbed his shirt and pulled him in for a kiss. He grabbed her back and the two of them were fully making out on the same log we had been sitting on together.

"Okay, creeper, time to leave." Justin picked me up by my

waist and carried me back inside.

"I can fucking walk." I hissed before he set me back down. I tried not to blow up on Justin. He didn't realize that he had grabbed me just like my ex had done all those months ago. My mind flashed back to how I felt, crying as my ex hauled me out of his house then threw me onto the ground.

I stomped back inside and ran into my room. Justin followed and shut the door behind us.

Sam was already in the room reading. "What happened?"

I broke down crying.

Justin informed her, "Alex was kissing Jessica, the bitchy blonde counselor."

She shrugged, "Makes sense, Jessica is hot."

"Not helping Sam!"

"Sorry, but like, what did you expect? He's a guy surrounded by girls. He's probably just trying to hook up with as many as he can before the summer is over."

I hung my head and groaned, "You're probably right." When we didn't kiss, he just moved right on to the next girl.

"I'm sorry, Hadley. I know you really like him."

"He probably doesn't even like me anyways."

Justin and Sam shared a concerned look.

I wiped the tears away, forcing myself to stop crying. "Let's talk about something else. How's your book, Sam?"

We spent the next hour talking to each other about books and literally anything else but boys, especially Alex.

As we were winding down for bed, we heard faint crying coming from the bathroom. I went out to see what was going on and saw Nicole and Hannah in one of the stalls. Hannah was holding back Nicole's hair as she puked and sobbed.

"Oh my god! Are you okay?"

Hannah answered for her, "She must've had too much to drink."

"I only had like two drinks!" Nicole mumbled out between gags.

"I don't know what to do." Hannah pleaded.

"Hold on, let me go get Justin to help you get her into bed." I left and started rushing down the hall over to the boy's side of the dorm when I ran right into Alex.

"Woah, slow down, fast and furious." He laughed but I was dying inside.

"Everything good?" Jessica asked. I hadn't seen her next to him until she spoke up.

"No," I quickly answered her, then turned back towards Alex. "Nicole is in the bathroom and doesn't feel good. Can you go help her get to bed?"

"Shit, yeah, I got you." He took a step forward. "Jess, go get her an *actual* water bottle."

"But Alex, we were," She looked me in the eyes as she grabbed his arm. "Busy."

"This'll only take a few minutes, just go."

"Fine." She groaned and gave him a quick kiss. I turned away so I didn't have to see it.

When she was done with him, Alex walked into the bathroom and Jessica walked away. I heard her voice call out, "Jake, stop giving those little girls booze. They can't handle it."

I stood there at the edge of the hall unsure what to do. I started to head back to the bathroom when the door flung open and Alex emerged carrying Nicole. Hannah was rushing behind them as they disappeared into the room they had bunked in with Sam, Aly, and me.

I followed them in, staying out of the way as Hannah filled Sam in.

"Thanks for your help, Alex." Sam let out a light laugh. "We need to stop meeting like this."

He breathed out a laugh, "I know you'll take care of her but come get me if you need anything."

She nodded and crawled back into her bed. When Alex turned to leave he stopped right in front of me.

He ran his fingers through his hair before starting, "Hadley, can I-"

Jessica burst through the cracked door. "It took forever to

find a water bottle!"

"Thanks." He took the bottle from her hands. "I'll be out in a sec."

"Hurry up." Jessica looked at me, "You guys need to get it together. Alex won't always be around to babysit you." She crossed her arms and left.

Alex swallowed and when he handed me the water bottle, our eyes locked. "If you need *anything*, come get me."

I looked away from his eyes, "We'll be fine."

He didn't say anything as he let go of the bottle and left.

After a beat, Sam coughed, and I gave the water bottle to Hannah. Then I climbed up into my bunk bed, attempting to sleep.

My sleeping bag slid against the bunk bed mattress as I tossed and turned. Selfishly, I kept replaying that kiss between Alex and Jessica. How a smile split his face before Jessica grabbed him. How he had grabbed her back. I needed that jealous pang to hit my heart over and over again until it didn't hurt anymore. If I made myself hate him, or at least dislike him, then that would be the end of it. It's the same way I got over my feelings for my ex. It had to work again.

Guess that's why it's called a crush, right?

7

I woke up early and did my best to avoid Alex, but there would be nowhere to hide during laundry and I knew it would be awkward. My plan was to get there first then leave before he arrived, but I wasn't quick enough.

The screen door creaked open just as I was finishing up loading my clothes into the washer. Instinctively, I looked up but then focused my gaze back on the machine.

I heard his nervous voice say, "Hey Hadley."

"Hey," I quickly threw the laundry detergent in and turned on the washer. With as much fake enthusiasm as I could muster, I added, "See ya!"

"You're not going to wait for your clothes?"

"Nah, I'm gonna go play cards with Justin and Sam."

He started to say something.

I rushed out the door, blurting out, "Bye!"

Once I was outside the laundry room I released the breath I was holding. He seemed upset that I wasn't going to stay with him, but I wasn't going to give in. I needed to get over this crush.

Everyone was hanging out in the common room playing card games. It was too hot and muggy from the early morning rain to be outside longer than we needed. I sat at the table with Justin where we talked for a few minutes until Sam joined us.

"Alex was in the laundry room all alone." She suggestively nudged my elbow. "Are you going to go hang out with him?"

"Not today. I'd rather be with you guys."

Sam asked, "You good?"

I nodded.

Justin leaned in, "You sure? After last night-"

"Which is why I'm not hanging out with him this morning."

They shared a look before we settled into a game of Slaps. It always takes me a second to remember the rules. We started placing cards down and Sam immediately slapped my hand. I gave up the cards without an argument.

Justin informed us, "Nicole got super sick last night."

"I know. I saw her."

"But did you hear that Ashley and Taylor got sick too? They like passed out in their rooms and woke up with vomit on their sleeping bags."

"Oh shit!" Sam and I said in unison.

"Yeah, I guess they had too much to drink."

"I thought Taylor doesn't drink?"

He shrugged, "I guess she does?"

"Did any boys get sick?"

"T. J. apparently threw up too. He was hooking up with Annie so Becky told me she thinks they gave each other the stomach bug."

Sam shook her head, "That's not how the stomach bug works."

"Well, that's what Becky told me."

"Interesting." I grimaced.

"What?"

"Why did Becky tell you all of this?"

"She said I had a face that 'people want to tell stuff to' so she talked to me after breakfast when Aly and her were talking."

"Anything else get mentioned?"

Justin sighed but he gave me the answer I was looking for. "Becky told us that Alex and Jessica spent the rest of the night together."

Hot, jealous tears started to form but I refused to let them fall. I didn't know why I was getting so worked up over Alex. We hadn't done anything other than flirt with each other. He didn't do this to hurt me.

So then why did it hurt?

"Sorry, Hadley, but-"

I shook my head, "It's cool. I already knew it."

"We're here if you need us." Justin put his hand on my back.

"Could be worse!" Sam tried to joke.

"How?"

"You could be hungover on top of it."

We finished our card game in relative silence after that.

When 30 minutes had passed I went back into the laundry room. Alex was there reading *The Shining* so I didn't say anything when I walked in.

He obnoxiously coughed, making me instinctively turn around. "No hello?"

"Sorry, I wasn't trying to interrupt your reading."

"It's cool."

I gave him an awkward smile and switched my laundry.

He startled me with a sudden question, "Are you mad at me?"

"No." I kept putting my laundry into the dryer, refusing to turn around.

His tone was demanding when he called my name, "Hadley?"

I spun around to look at him.

Alex put the book down, got up, and walked over to me. "Are you mad at me?"

"No!" I said too emphatically. "Why?"

He took another step closer. There was only about a foot separating our bodies. "You're just, I don't know, acting differently now."

"I'm not...I mean..." I sighed, "I'm just pretty tired after this first week."

"Yeah, same dude."

That was all he said before he walked back over to the chair and picked his book up. An accusatory silence was building between us. There was no way he didn't believe I wasn't somehow a little pissed at him. I wondered if he would call me out, but instead he kept up the ruse.

When I had finished moving all my clothes to the dryer, I turned to say to him. Our eyes locked. The hardness of his face didn't match what I saw in his eyes, which seemed sad, but his jaw was tight. I was distracted by his hand scratching the black stubble speckling his skin. Once I broke the stand off we were having, there was no point in trying to say anything else now.

I mumbled, "Be back later," before leaving again. This time I didn't go back to Justin and Sam. I decided to sit outside and think at an empty picnic table.

Alone, it was easier to sort through my thoughts and feelings. I was pissed that he kissed another girl. It felt like we were about to kiss last night and that the spark between us could've turned into something. If Aly hadn't pulled me away then it could've been me making out with Alex on that log.

But then is that all it would have been? Would this just be a convenient hook up for the summer?

Hooking up was never something I was into. I wanted a real connection, and I thought I could have it with Alex.

That's why watching him kiss Jessica hurt so much. I knew it made more sense for him to be into her. He probably just wanted to make out with whoever he could. I just offered myself up to him as easy pickings, and when I left he just moved on to the next one.

And I wasn't sure if I was really ready to like someone again after what happened to me. My ex dominated and then destroyed my life. Almost every memory I had of high school contained him in some capacity. There really hadn't been anyone or anything before him, and figuring out life after him hadn't been easy.

This was the first time since my ex and I had broken up that I felt something more than friendship for a guy. That realization shook me. I liked Alex. I liked him too much.

But I wanted to make this summer to enjoy my friends and myself and not worry about a boy. As long as I can remember, I've had a crush on some boy in my class or a celebrity or even a few times a cartoon character. I didn't need a boyfriend or even a potential boyfriend. I needed to make this summer about me and my happiness.

Doesn't mean I should be a jerk or be awkward to Alex. I could still flirt but there's no expectation and no pressure. This would just be clean, simple, flirty fun for the summer.

With a clear mind I went to grab my laundry. I braced myself for another awkward interaction but was surprised instead.

Alex was gone.

I checked and his clothes still had 10 minutes left in the dryer. I shuffled back and forth, holding my warm laundry bag against my chest. It made me think of the warmth I got all over my body when Alex and I touched. No, I needed to shut those thoughts down.

Part of me wanted to wait until he came back and apologize to him. If I could just explain why I was being rude to him and cleared things up, we could at least be friendly the rest of the summer.

Another dryer next to the one that had Alex's clothes beeped to signal that it was done.

The sudden noise startled me, so I headed towards the door. I chickened out, but there would be another opportunity to fix things with Alex.

Everyone was gathered in the dining hall for Mr. Hamilton to announce the new groupings for the week. Aly was already buzzing next to me because she was going to be with Drew, the guys she had wanted to makeout with. Justin and Sam had been called and they were working together.

"For the next 10 and 11 year old group, we have Becky, Owen, Jessica, and Alex."

My jaw fell open.

Justin grabbed my hand, Sam sucked in a breath, and Aly whispered, "Damn!"

I looked over at Jessica, who was grinning like a cat at Alex.

My eyes moved to Alex, who was stoic. Aaron gave him a pat on the shoulder.

"Moving onto the 12 and 13 year old group, we have Hadley, Emily, Henry, and Aaron."

A relieved sigh left my body when I heard Aaron's name. He'd keep me sane this week. Maybe I could pick his ear about the whole Alex thing? He would know better than anyone.

When I caught Aaron's gaze, he gave me a thumb's up and I returned the gesture. Out of habit, I flicked my gaze over to Alex, who looked down instead of looking back at me. When I looked back at Aaron, he rolled his eyes.

I didn't have time to ask Aaron what that was about. We split off into our groups and spent the rest of the evening wrapped up in talking with the campers and our co-counselors.

We found out on Monday that we have the same pool time slot as Alex's group. Just when I thought I'd be able to take a break from my crush that admittedly, was inching closer to an obsession, I was going to see him all week. And not just see him, but see him shirtless, wet, and in a bathing suit.

I had seen glimpses of Alex in his bathing suit when we all had training. But this was the first time that I would be able to see him shirtless. And it was for the whole week. As I expected, he's got those soft abs that you get when you're an athlete. Whatever sport he plays, he must be good at it.

He has two tattoos, a big clipper ship on his ribs and then this weird loopy thing, that I think is a signature on his chest over his heart. I wanted to ask him about them but after how awkward things were doing laundry I didn't even know how to start a conversation with him.

Luckily, Aaron broke the ice. "Who is up for a game of basketball? Hadley, c'mon. You're on my team." He grabbed my hand and pulled me into the pool.

Some of the bigger kids swam over to line up in front of the basket. We split up into teams and the game got started. Everyone was having fun but taking the game very seriously. I got the ball and turned around to try to shoot but Alex was looming over me.

"Go on." He taunted. "Take the shot."

I shook my head then twisted as Alex reached for the ball. He grabbed my waist to try to stop me. I lost track of everything around me, except for Alex's skin touching mine. He was warm, even in the cool water, and I could feel goosebumps starting to pucker as his arms moved around my waist trying to keep me from moving. Panicking, I quickly threw the ball over to Aaron. Alex immediately let me go and swam over to guard him.

A few minutes later, I got the ball back and threw it easily into the hoop.

"Nice one!" Alex whispered as he moved past me.

When the game was over I got out. I couldn't handle being that close to him or letting him wrap his arms around me again.

I was sitting on the edge of the pool when a couple girls asked me to play mermaids with them. It was a much welcome distraction but every now and then I would catch Alex looking over at me. Nothing could keep my mind from wandering back to him, the way he moved around in the pool, his arms flexing with each shot he took, or how the water flew over his hair as he whipped it back.

One of the kids, Steven, had an asthma attack after we

finished horseback riding. We weren't sure what triggered it, but all of a sudden he dropped to the floor and was grabbing his throat.

Since my little brother has asthma, I figured out quickly what was going on. He looked exactly like John did the first time he had an attack. His face was creeping towards blue as his lungs struggled to take in air.

I started to panic as the other kids' screams filled my ears, but after a deep breath I remembered what to do.

My hands patted his pockets until I found his inhaler and helped him take a few puffs. After the drugs worked into his system, he could take deeper and deeper breaths. Henry and I took him to the nurse to get him checked out while the other kids went to arts and crafts.

Luckily he was fine. Shaken up, as we all were, but fine.

Everyone was impressed with how quickly I acted. Kelly even came and found me at dinner. "You did a great job out there today." She said, giving me a pat on the shoulder.

"It was what any counselor would have done." I tried to sound modest, but I was pretty proud of myself.

"But you were the one that did it."

I was riding the high that Kelly's words gave me, when Alex sat down across the table from me.

Even though we've had the same dinner slot all week, he had been avoiding our table. The past few days, he's only waved at Aaron before settling down at his group's table in the dining hall.

He held my gaze for a second too long before looking to his left, "Good thing Dr. Sullivan was there to save your camper, Aaron."

"Seriously, man! You should've seen her!" Aaron nudged my arm.

"It wasn't that big of a deal. I just got a kid's inhaler out of his pocket."

Alex gave me a crooked smile. "Nah, it's a big deal. Own it, Hadley."

My face was erupting with bright red blush as I looked down at my mac and cheese. "Well, then...thanks."

"I'll see you guys later. Gotta go get the table ready."

"See you!" Aaron called after him but I said nothing.

I tried not to think of Alex's attention the rest of dinner, that night, or the next day. But it didn't work. Every time I saw Aaron, my brain made the connection to Alex. There wasn't a good moment to talk to him about it yet. We'd been making small talk with our other counselors, discussing college plans or things we want to do with the rest of summer when camp is over. There was never an opportunity for the heavy kind of conversation I wanted to have with Aaron. We were never alone long enough for me to talk to him. Emily, Henry, or campers were around us all the time.

Until archery on Wednesday.

Aaron and I were standing next to each other while the kids were lining up across from their individual targets. I wanted to take a couple shots, but there weren't any extra bows to use so I was forced to the sidelines. Emily and Henry went to get the next activity ready while we led the kids through archery. So it was just us two, *finally*.

"Alright, loose!" Aaron called out. Most of the arrows curved down and landed in or on the ground. A few actually managed to hit the targets attached to hay bales.

"Make sure you pull back so your palm is by your ear!" I shouted as the kids got their next arrow ready.

"Loose!" The next round of arrows went out, more hitting the targets this time.

"Good job, guys!" I wasn't sure how to bring up the subject of Alex organically. I didn't want to just blurt out my feelings for him and I didn't know how to bring him up in conversation.

As the kids were getting their next arrows ready, Aaron asked, "So Hadley, this is the first time I feel like I can just like talk to you. How have things been? How was Senior year?"

I actually sighed in relief that he turned the conversation

this direction.

"Good, I guess."

"You guess?"

"Yeah, I'm excited to start college in the fall, but everyone keeps going on about how hard it is."

"Loose!" Aaron shouted then turned back to our conversation. "For sure. School gets way harder once you're in college. But the freedom of college is sweet."

"I bet it is."

"Loose!" Another round of arrows flew into the air. "Good thing you're single now. You can really enjoy your freshman year now."

All I could manage was a clipped, "Yep."

"What happened with all that? Sounds like it was bad."

"It was, but I don't want to rehash that right now. Not because I don't want you to know. We can save that for another time."

"Loose!" Aaron shouted then lowered his voice to me. "Shit, I'm sorry, dude. I know all about bad breakups."

"You and Jordan?"

He nodded, "Yup, I caught him cheating."

"Oh," My shoulders sagged. "I'm so sorry."

"It happens." He shrugged. "Loose! Anyone new?"

"Nope."

His eyebrows shot up. "Got your eyes on anyone here?"

"I mean, there's some cute guys here."

He suggestively nodded his head, "There are."

I felt bold enough to say, "Especially some of the new counselors."

Aaron gave a tight smile, confirming what he already suspected. "Loose! Like Justin?"

"No!" The kids all turned their heads to see why I had yelled. "All good! Loose!" I turned back to him. "Not Justin."

Aaron floundered at my outburst. "But you guys are together all the time. And you kissed him the other night during spin the bottle."

"No," I breathed out, shaking my head. "Justin and I are just really good friends. I don't like him like that."

"So then," He crossed his arms. "Who do you like?"

"Don't make me say it."

His lips curled into a grin. "Say it, Hadley."

"Loose!" I shouted for the kids to fire another round of arrows.

He leaned in close and whispered, "Just say it. I need verbal confirmation from you."

I covered my face as I whispered back, "I like Alex." Once the words were out of my mouth, I peeked through my fingers to look at Aaron.

His face said what he didn't, that he knew it all along.

"But it doesn't matter." I protested. "He doesn't seem like he likes me back."

"It's not that complicated."

"Yes it is. He hooked up with someone else."

"Loose!" Aaron chuckled, "I mean, does that really matter? We're not paired up for the summer based on who we hook up with the first week."

I scoffed, "So just hook up with a different girl every week then? That's the game?"

"No," He shook his head, "not that. I mean for some people it is, but that's not what most of us care about. Being here is different. It's like all the drama of school but intensified because we're all around each other all the time for nine weeks. Everyone has to sneak around to avoid the Hamiltons finding out on top of everything. It gets messy every summer."

"I didn't want a messy summer hookup. I don't know…I thought he actually liked me."

"Loose!" Aaron sighed but smirked, "He does."

I felt all the tension release from my face. A lightness rippled through my whole body and then was immediately replaced by a surge of adrenaline. Alex likes me. I just got verbal confirmation from his best friend that he likes me. A satisfied huff left my smiling lips.

Aaron smiled before turning to the kids. "Alright, go collect your arrows! Do not fire any shots until we tell you to!"

Shaking off the euphoric feeling, I focused on the task. We helped some of the kids get their arrows back into the quivers and set them all back on the line.

Per Camp Odyssey tradition, I told the campers about the Archery Dessert Round Rules. "We're going to keep score this round. A bullseye is worth 10, anything in the red rings is worth 7, anything in blue is worth 5, and finally the black ring is worth 3 points. After that it is considered off target." I shouted. "Winner gets an extra dessert tonight!"

The kids excitedly whispered among themselves before getting serious and concentrating.

"This time you all fire off your arrows at your own speed. Wait until everyone is done to collect them. Ready? Loose!" Aaron shouted and the arrows started flying.

I was still reeling about what he had said when he jumped back into the conversation. "Just talk to him. He thinks you hate him now."

"I mean, I am pissed."

"I get it, but you kissed Justin."

I rolled my eyes, "That doesn't count."

"Why not?"

"Cause he's just a *friend*."

"Like I'm just a *friend*?" He was hinting at something that I wasn't sure of. Aaron had always been a friend to me in a brotherly way. Last year when I would sneak out to try to call my ex, he would give me advice or listen to me complain about him. I was reluctant to take his advice at first, but when I started saying what Aaron told me to say to my ex, things did get better. Until I had gotten home and our relationship just reverted back to what it had always been. So in a way, Aaron and Justin were the same kind of friend to me.

I clarified, "We're just friends."

Aaron smirked, "And so are Alex and Jessica."

A girl shouted out in excitement that she hit the bullseye!

He continued, "He's into *you* and if you're into him too, you'll have to forgive him for hooking up with someone else when you were kissing someone else."

"I guess you're right." I didn't exactly agree with it, but he had a point.

"You figured it out."

"Figured what out?" I asked out of confusion.

"I'm always right." He winked then went to go help the kids with their arrows.

8

That Thursday was the special celebration and pool party for July 4th. The campers had free reign over the pool and the fields next to it. The counselors all split up and helped watch all the kids together.

Since we didn't have to stay with our assigned groups, I went right to my friends. Sam, Justin, and I had just laid our towels down. "How's it been going?" Sam asked first.

Justin and I both replied, "Good!"

He leaned in close to me, "How's Aaron?"

"Actually, he told me some pretty interesting information yesterday."

"Did he?" His eyes grew with anticipation.

"Yeah, he basically told me that Alex likes me."

Justin's jaw dropped. Sam pursed her lips.

"Oh no," I responded to her reaction. "What now?"

"I wasn't going to tell you."

"Well, now you have to tell me."

She let out a long sigh, trying to put off the inevitable.

Justin came to her aid. "She wasn't going to tell you that she caught Alex and Jessica making out in a shed while they were supposed to be organizing the life jackets after their kids had been canoeing."

I slowly blinked trying to gather my thoughts. "Did you tell anyone else?"

"No!" She pulled away offended that I suggested it. "No, just you and Justin. I know better than to tell Aly this kind of stuff."

If the Hamilton's found out about Alex and Jessica doing something like that where campers could have seen, they could have been kicked out.

"You saw it with your own eyes?" I knew Sam didn't lie, but I didn't want to believe this.

"Yes, Jessica had him pushed up against the wall. He looked mortified but she looked almost proud that I had caught them. I don't know what happened after that because I backed out of the shed and ran."

"When did that happen?"

"Yesterday."

My heart sank. "Shit."

"I'm sorry, Hadley. Maybe he's still into you and just doesn't know how to end things with Jessica?" Sam offered, trying to comfort me.

"It is what it is now. " I shrugged and picked up my copy of *The Hobbit*. Justin and Sam mirrored me with their books and we just sat there in silence. I re-read the same line over and over again, unable to process the words. My brain was too busy trying to process my emotions.

Aaron told me Alex liked me but he probably didn't know the extent of what Alex and Jessica were doing. And I had confessed to him that I still very much liked Alex. Aaron wouldn't use the confession in a bad way, but it was one more person who knew how I felt about Alex. Shit, Alex didn't even know how I felt about him. I shook my head to try to wipe away the conflicting thoughts in my head.

Someone made a shadow over my book.

I looked up. The pool water was dripping off his dark tan skin as his arms hung lazily by his sides. I could feel my mouth hanging open at how low his bathing suit was on his waist. My gaze worked up his chest until I found his dark brown eyes.

Alex gave me a crooked smile, "Hey Hadley."

I managed to say back, "Hey Alex."

He pointed to the pool behind him, water still dripping off his toned arm. "We could really use you. Aaron's team keeps smoking us."

"You sure? Cause I only made that one basket last time."

"Yeah, you would make a big difference."

"Okay." I shrugged, trying to pretend not to be too excited. I was going to use Justin and Sam as an excuse to not go anywhere near the basketball hoop but even they were waving me away.

Since we were on the same team, he didn't get close enough to guard me, but he found a way to compliment me every move I made. When Alex shot the winning basket for our team, Aaron decided it was time to take a break from basketball.

With the game over, Alex went around high-fiving everyone. When he finally got to me, he gave me a high five and then his fingers slid in between mine. Our hands stayed connected as he lowered them back into the pool under the cover of the rippling water. He pulled me closer to him to softly say, "Told you that you'd make a big difference."

The warmth of his hand combined with the closeness of his body made me break out in goosebumps. Why was he doing this now? Jessica was literally on the other side of the pool, seeing us talk, she probably saw our hands touch and fall into the water together.

I couldn't think of anything to say back. My eyes frantically moved from where our hands were to his gaze on me.

"See you later, Hadley." He gave my hand a squeeze under water before pulling it away.

"See you." I waded away from him and promptly got out of the pool. I rushed over to Sam and Justin, and silently laid back down on my towel.

"Did you guys win?" Justin asked.

I frantically nodded.

"Why do you look shocked?" Justin's question forced Sam to look up from her book.

"Alex just like…held my hand in the pool?"

Both of their mouths dropped. He continued, "We just saw you guys high five. When did the hand holding happen?"

"Literally after the high five."

"We couldn't tell, it just looked like you were talking."

"Good. I was worried Jessica would see."

Justin crossed his arms and scowled in Alex's direction. "Why is he holding your hand when he's been making out with Jessica all week?"

"Maybe," Sam chimed in. "He realized he doesn't actually like Jessica, and really does like Hadley."

"Then he needs to cut shit off with Jessica."

She shook her head. "I was with Jessica last week. She's a giant bitch. I bet Alex is just doing what she wants so he doesn't have to deal with her while they work together for the rest of the week."

"He's probably just a playboy trying to string Jessica, Hadley, and whoever else along for the summer."

"I don't think that's it." Sam turned to me. "What do you think?"

I looked over at Alex, who was in a corner of the pool talking with Aaron. When Aaron moved his head emphatically, my eyes followed the direction he had signaled to see Jessica lying out with her friends.

My gaze returned to Alex, who was now shaking his head. Aaron's head then nodded in my direction. Both of their eyes connected with mine and I instantly turned around, hoping they hadn't realized that I was watching them.

"Hadley..." Sam called me back to her question.

"I think..." I dared one more look over at Alex and Aaron, but it was impossible to figure out what either of them was saying now. If Alex was really just a playboy, then he was damn good at it. It contradicted what Aaron told me, but maybe Aaron was in on it too? I thought I could trust him, but obviously our short camp history is trumped by the fact that Alex is his best friend and roommate. Sam's suggestion that he was just trying to get through his week with Jessica gave me hope. If he was into me, and not her, then I still had a shot. I just needed them to be done before I could shoot it. "I think I'm done talking about this. Let's go find Aly. I want someone else's boy drama to be the focus."

They both shrugged, but together we all gathered up our pool stuff and went to find Aly, who was with Hannah and Nicole.

Shortly after the basketball game, the cookout started. The Hamiltons grilled tons of burgers and hot dogs for everyone. The dining hall staff set up a giant serving line outside for everyone to make their way through. Everyone got to eat together outside instead of in the dining hall. It was chaotic but fun to watch the kids all run around enjoying the party.

Since we didn't have to sit with our kids, I ended up at a picnic bench with my friends and a few other high school counselors. I didn't appreciate this nickname the college counselors had given us. We were all technically counselors, but there was definitely a separation between the ones who had already been to college, like Aaron and Alex, and those who had just graduated high school, like me and my friends.

The small group of us were all talking about the different counselors and who everyone thinks is cute. Aly of course, made a strong case for Jake and I rolled my eyes instinctively.

She snapped at me, "What is your problem?"

I spat back, "He's a disgusting creep."

"You just don't know him."

"I don't need to know him. He's gross. He's twenty-one and hitting on someone who just got out of high school. Like who does that?"

"But if he was nineteen it would be okay?" She scowled.

Everyone got quiet, waiting to see what I would say.

I could feel a heaviness cloud my thoughts. I was right about Jake. He was a creep and always would be a creep. Aly failed to see that. I had failed to see it before and I wasn't going to let that happen again. I managed to get out, "Yeah, because from what I can tell, he's not going to hurt me or anyone else."

"How do you know? How do you know he won't? I've known Jake longer than you've known Alex. Besides, it's not like you're the best judge of that kind of thing after what happened to you."

My jaw dropped.

Justin came to my defense, "That's fucked up, Aly. Apologize. Now."

"What? I'm sorry but it's true. Just because something tragic happened to you with an older guy, doesn't mean it'll happen to me!"

Hurt flared through my chest. All my thoughts were smashing themselves into the forefront of my mind. I told Aly what happened to me in confidence and she threw it in my face. But this pain was making my thoughts sharper. I rose from my seat, leaning into Aly's space across from me. "That's the thing, Aly. You don't think it'll happen to you. You think you can trust people because you *know* them. But you never know who would or could do something terrible to you."

She met me with her indignation, "So you just can't trust anyone?"

"No." I sat back down. "I trust myself. And my gut is giving me that same feeling I got around my ex's step-brother but I ignored it for months."

"You're just biased against-"

"Aly," Sam glared at her. "Stop."

Aly looked around for help. Hannah, Nicole, and the few others around us were silent.

After a few beats, she looked down in defeat. "I'm sorry." She kept her head down. "It's just really been bugging me how much shit you talk about Jake. I know you don't like him, like it's crystal clear that you hate him, but I don't, so please just stop. At least stop saying it to me."

Was telling Aly what I really thought about Jake a shitty thing to do? I didn't think so. I felt like I was protecting her from something terrible happening to her. I wanted her to listen to what happened to me and recognize the glaring warning signs in every situation so she would never have to experience what I went through. But clearly my approach wasn't working. It was only making her cling to Jake more, which is the opposite of what I was trying to do. So for Aly's sake, I needed to be better.

I nodded. "I'll cut back the shit talking."

She finally looked up and smiled, "Thank you."

"But, please, be careful."

"Always." Aly waved her hand in the air, a sign this conversation was done.

Justin cleared his throat and forced an awkward conversation about the food. It felt like a bandaid put over a gash. It didn't help but it made ignoring what just happened easier.

When the sun finally set, the Hamiltons had Lucas and Kelly set off some fireworks. The kids got so into it, screaming and cheering, which turned into a contest to see which group of kids could cheer the loudest. Justin's group won and ended up getting extra ice cream.

Everyone was exhausted from all the fun today and we herded them all back to their bunks. Aaron and I were at the back of our group, making sure none of the kids wandered off.

Aaron knocked my elbow with his, "Did you have a good day?"

I hesitated.

"Yes, Aaron I had a great day." He tried to mock my voice by making his own voice higher. "That was the response I was looking for."

"Well, it was a very confusing day."

"Confusing?"

We shared a look. He was clearly expecting me to mention Alex holding my hand, but I didn't want to start that conversation with him. Not after what happened with Aly. That dredged back up a slimy memory that would take some time to drown again. I told him enough to answer his question. "Just drama with Aly kind of ruined the whole feel of today."

He must've sensed that whatever she did really messed

with me. "Well, summer is just getting started. You've got plenty of time to have great days."

"I hope so."

9

On Friday, I got my first care package and it was full of my favorites: Goldfish, Reese's, and Starbursts. There were also notes from all my siblings. It made me miss them all so I wrote each one a letter back letting them know I got their messages.

We ended up winning skit night for our Camp Odyssey's Got Talent where the kids took turns showing off their skills or lack thereof for comedic effect. Their little faces lit up when Mr. Hamilton said that they had won. We got to walk back to our cabins with the golden skit night trophy and proudly put it on our table during the last breakfast. They couldn't stop smiling and during pick up, they all showed their parents what they had won.

As the last kid was picked up, I felt the familiar pang of grief for the end of another week. They were a great group of kids, but I was ready for the freedom that Saturday night offered.

Aaron and I were walking back to the lodge after the final cabin inspection. It took so long because of how messy our campers left everything. Kelly had to come back after dinner to check us off, it was that bad. Emily and Henry had rushed back to the lodge, but Aaron and I lagged behind.

He asked, "You excited for the party tonight? This would be a good chance to catch up with people you haven't really talked to all week."

I shrugged, "I guess."

"See how you feel after a drink or two. I bet you'll have the courage to talk to him then."

"Who is getting all this booze anyways?"

"Jake and Lucas have a handle of vodka for each week that they mix with the powdered Gatorade from the dining hall to make their crappy 'jungle juice.' Then it just depends, some people pick stuff up from town when they have the chance to go in. Some people brought other stuff. I have a bottle of Sailor Jerry's if you want some?"

"What is that?"

"Cheap but good rum!"

"I'll try it!"

"Hang tight."

He went to fetch it from his room while I waited in the hallway outside of the boy's room side of the lodge. I caught a glimpse of the bit of mess that was already on the floor of their room.

He came back out, shutting the door behind him. "Do you drink a lot?"

"Yes and no. I don't have a fake so I can't go out or drink every weekend but I definitely can throw them back. My friends and I usually get a bottle from someone's parent's stash and drink in their basement."

He took a swig straight from the bottle and then passed it to me.

"Bottoms up!" I joked as I took a sizable sip. It didn't burn as bad as I thought it would. It had a subtle spice to it like all rum does with just a dull burn at the end. "This is actually pretty good!"

"Right, take another sip."

With this next drink, I could feel the warmth from the booze spreading into my cheeks.

"How do you feel?"

"Good!"

"Good!" Aaron held his hand out for a high five and I, probably too eagerly, smacked it. "Thatta girl. Now talk to him."

"And say what?"

"Just go." He turned me around and pushed me out into the main room where everyone was sitting. Aaron went to sit next to Alex with his bottle of rum. It was being passed around the counselors who were sitting next to each other in a closed circle. No one noticed I had entered the room.

Or so I thought.

Alex was looking right at me even though Jessica had her head leaning on him. Without the campers or the Hamiltons around, people were being much bolder with their public displays of affection. It stung watching Jessica cuddle up closer to him. She was laughing at something Becky had just said before she took a sip from the bottle. Alex looked away to take his drink before passing it along. He mumbled something to Jessica before getting up and walking towards me.

I tried to move to avoid talking to him but he was quicker. He blocked my way around him with his tall, stocky frame. I looked up, ready to ask him to please move, but he quickly whispered, "Follow me."

"Why?" I started to call after him but he didn't stop. I followed him as he went back into the room I had just stood outside of with Aaron.

"Alex?" I called through the gap but refused to go inside.

"It's cool, come in."

I pushed the door further open and saw him digging through his duffle bag looking for something. The sleeping bags had been haphazardly thrown onto the bunks and not made, the duffle bags were either on the floor or the beds, and someone's clothes were thrown all over the floor. There was the distinct odor of different body sprays mixing together to make a new, overpowering odor. I was eager to get out of the room as soon as possible.

"Here!" He exclaimed, pulling out a ziploc bag that had different small bottles in it.

"What the hell is this?"

He proudly smiled, "When I asked you if you wanted anything from the liquor store you said get whatever, so I just grabbed airplane bottles of different stuff."

"You didn't have to do that." My heart started racing from the excitement. When I told him that, I didn't actually think he would get me anything. That's how it usually went with my ex if I ever told him to just get whatever. This actually meant more than he realized.

"I didn't know what you liked so I figured this would cover all the bases and you could share with those friends of yours."

I grabbed the bag from him, beaming at how much thought had been put into this. "Thank you, Alex. Let me pay you back for it?"

"No worries, consider it a peace offering now."

"A peace offering?"

"So you'll be nicer to me during laundry time."

I hung my head, "Sorry about that."

He shrugged but smiled, "It's all good."

I wanted to say something else to him about why I was mad at him before but I didn't know how to say it without sounding crazy. Luckily he said, "Go enjoy tonight with your friends."

"I will." I held up the bag. "Thank you again for this!"

I started walking out and he followed. "Let me know which ones you like and I'll get more next time we can go into town."

"Def!" We walked back into the main room and Alex sat back down next to Jessica. She immediately threw her arms around him but he scooted away from her. Before they could notice me looking, I walked over to where Justin and Sam were.

I made a quick scan of the room as I sat down on the couch next to Justin. "Where's Aly?"

"Actually, good question." Justin answered. "I don't know. She said something about a game of never have I ever and walked back down to the girls hallway."

I shrugged but held up the bag of airplane bottles. "You guys want some?"

"Hell yeah!" Justin smiled and grabbed the bag. "I love Tito's." He reached in and grabbed a little bottle of vodka with a metallic pink cap.

Sam asked, "You do?"

"Yeah!" He laughed before downing the whole thing. "My b-" He shook his head. "My friend and I drink it back home all the time. My mom always has it in the house. She makes vodka sodas like every night with it. It's stupid easy to steal it from her."

Sam and I shared a look and I took the bag back from him. I pulled out Fireball, one of the few that I recognized from the assortment Alex had given us.

She hesitated. "What'll go down the easiest?"

I looked at the rest of the bottles in the bag. "This one." I pulled out a brown bottle that said Kahlua on it. "The label says it's a liqueur so it's not as strong as actual liquor."

Justin and I watched her open the bottle and take a cautious sip. "Actually..." She took another sip. "That's not so bad!"

There were still 6 left and I wanted to share with Aly but she wasn't there and I didn't want to carry these bottles around with me for the rest of the night. "Alright, what do you guys want next?"

Sam finished off the Kahlua. "I'm gonna call it a night. You guys have fun. Come get me if you need me!"

"Night!" Justin and I chimed in unison. Together we went through the rest of the bottles, trying each one. Soon all the airplane bottles were back in the ziploc bag, but they were empty.

We were feeling the buzz from drinking and giggling in the corner together. We started doing impressions of the other counselors trying to see if the other could guess who we were talking about, cracking ourselves up.

I kept catching Alex looking over at me. Every time our eyes would meet I would quickly look away, and when I would look back over to see if he was still looking at me, he had turned away.

The booze was making me feel bold and I kept my gaze on Alex, willing him to turn back around and look at me.

Instead, I watched as Jessica placed herself in his lap so she was facing me. Our eyes locked before she lifted Alex's chin up and planted a kiss on his mouth. Everyone in their circle started cheering and making noises, until Aaron started shushing them.

That jealous sting was the worst one yet. I wanted Alex to know what this felt like and I needed a distraction from the ache in my chest.

"Justin," I whispered but it was probably louder than I thought.

"Hadley?"

"I have an idea."

He chuckled, "That's never good."

"Shut up." I playfully smacked his shoulder before leaning in closer. "Do you want to hear it?"

"Sure."

"Let's kiss."

"No." He pulled away.

"Please, it'll make Alex jealous!"

"I thought you said you were going to be done with all that."

"I thought so too until he gave me the little bottles and I keep catching him looking over at me. And that doesn't even factor in what Aaron told me-"

"Alright, let's do this."

Justin was starting to lean in, but out of the corner of my eye I could see Alex wasn't looking. "No! Not yet."

"Hadley!" He groaned and grabbed my face so I would focus on him. "Listen to me. I'm only kissing you because you're my friend and I want to help you. If we're going to do this, we're going to do it right and it's gotta be hot." His eagerness surprised me and all I could do was nod.

"Okay," He started to lean in. "Now giggle."

My boozy laugh filled the space between us.

Alex glanced over.

"He's looking." I breathed just before Justin's lips met mine. My eyes closed as I committed to the part I was briefly playing. I let him take the lead and he expertly maneuvered my mouth with his own. Justin was a surprisingly good kisser. His lips moved against mine and his tongue snuck into my mouth. We made out for a few minutes before he pulled away.

"Shit." I breathed out. I had never really thought of Justin like that before, but that kiss, that kiss just made me realize that he was actually pretty hot.

He laughed, "I know what I'm doing."

"I'll say." When I looked over at Alex, his spot on the couch was empty. And Jessica was gone too.

"Come on," Justin grabbed my hand and started to pull me away. "Let's get you to bed."

When we got to the door, he went to hug me goodnight. I don't know if it was the booze or the kiss, but I leaned in towards Justin, my mouth pursed for another kiss. He put his hands on my shoulders and pushed me back.

"Shit, my bad." I mumbled. His face was contorted into something that looked like frustration and awkwardness.

"I don't-"

"I'm sorry. I shouldn't have-" I started to walk away but Justin came after me. We walked further into the hall and I was about to go into my room when he caught up with me.

"It's not like that."

"No, I know you don't like me like that. I just...after that kiss...I thought maybe-"

"It's not that I don't like you."

"I get it, you don't have to-"

"Damn it, Hadley, listen to me!"

His words froze me. Grabbing my arm, he pulled me down to the end of the hallway.

"What's going on?"

He took a deep breath and then stated, "It's not that I don't like you."

I leaned in closer to him.

Cautiously, he whispered, "I don't," He took a deep breath before quickly saying, "I don't like girls like that."

"Oh." I breathed out.

"Yeah..."

"Oh, Justin." I gave him a huge hug.

"I wanted to tell you at the beginning of summer, but I didn't know how to bring it up without making it like a whole thing. But I'm gay." He breathed out and looked away, visibly relieved.

"I feel so silly thinking back on all the shit I said to you."

"It doesn't matter now. I was waiting for the right time to tell you and I guess this was it."

"Thank you for telling me." We shared another hug. "But how did you get to be such a good kisser?"

"I kind of had a boyfriend this year."

"Was that who you were drinking Tito's with?"

He nodded, "But it was hard sneaking around all the time and I was coming here for the whole summer so we called it off. I'm hoping we get back together when I go back to school but..." His shoulders lifted. "It is what it is." His hand grabbed mine and squeezed. "Thank you for being so cool about this."

"Were you worried I wouldn't be?"

"A little. But that has less to do with you and more to do with what's happened to me. You'd be surprised how many people seem like they would be cool with this but end up being awful about it."

I was going to say something to comfort Justin but we heard voices coming around the hallway.

Jake and Becky were laughing about something when they saw us. "Oh, sorry!" Jake slowly turned around and pulled Becky with him.

We shared a look before I said, "That was weird."

"It's late, everyone who is going to hook up is trying to claim an empty room so they can do what they wanna do quickly without getting caught. Maybe that'll be you one week." He winked.

I rolled my eyes. "We should be getting to bed."

We said goodnight and went our separate ways.

When I got into my bed, everyone else was already

asleep. I didn't think Justin and I were up that late, but it was already past midnight. I replayed the kiss between Jessica and Alex, over analyzing it for signs that Sam's theory that he was just going along with whatever Jessica was doing was correct. Alex didn't seem like he was as into her as he was last week. But maybe I was just projecting what I wanted to see onto what I actually saw?

I forced my thoughts onto happier things, like what happened just now with Justin. He trusted me with one of the most important parts of him. I've never had anyone trust me like that and I would never do anything to betray that.

10

The next morning, I was alone in the laundry room. I had expected to see Alex here, but it wasn't until my machine had started filling with water that he walked in. He looked rough, like he had barely slept and was still in his gym shorts and t-shirt from the night before.

I dared to ask, "Hey, are you good?"

"Uh-huh." His raspy voice replied. I watched as he painstakingly dumped his clothes into the washer and went to turn it on.

"Wait!" I cried out, gently pushed him aside. "You forgot detergent." I opened the washer back up and put a scoop of my detergent in.

"Shit." He grumbled, pressing the buttons to start the machine. "Thanks Hadley."

"No worries."

Alex slumped onto the couch and closed his eyes.

He looked so rough. Even if I was still annoyed or jealous or whatever the name for this emotion was, I still felt like I needed to help him. "If you wanna go to sleep, I'll watch your stuff for you."

"No, no." He sat up and scratched the stubble on his face. "It was just a long night."

"Yeah?"

He yawned, "Yeah."

Sam came in to drop off her clothes. "Mind watching them? Justin thinks he can beat me at UNO."

I replied, "I got you!"

"Thanks!" She finished setting her laundry then waved herself out.

Once she was gone, I sat down next on the couch facing him. I didn't need to ask him anything, he just started venting to me.

"Last night was too much. This whole week was too much." Alex shook his head as he yawned. "It wasn't even just how much attention she needed from me. When we did try to talk, we had like nothing in common. And when I didn't say stuff, she would bug me about being too quiet. It was like no matter what I did, it was wrong. The only time I really felt like she liked me was when we were hooking up."

I nodded for him to go on but internally I was screaming with joy that he said they had nothing in common.

"But what really got to me was that she kept trying to make out any second we were alone. I kept freaking out that a camper would see us but she didn't care. Aaron told me the Hamiltons are actually pretty strict about campers seeing counselors hooking up in any capacity and I don't want to get kicked out of here. So I told her I didn't want to be tied down for the summer and there wasn't really a point of getting invested in each other when we would go our separate ways at the end of this." He sighed and yawned at the same time, "She did not take that well."

"Well, no girl would." There it was. The perfectly good reasons why we wouldn't be able to get together either. My heart sank but I tried my best to keep my cool. "That sucks to hear when you like someone."

"Yeah, but Hadley, I'd rather be honest, even if I'm hated for it. Her and I don't click and I don't want to be with someone just because they're hot."

"If you explained it to her that way, then that's not so brutal."

He leaned back into the couch and let out another long yawn. "She kept me up most of the night because she was crying so much and I felt bad but like I wasn't going to change my mind. When Jake and Lucas went to bed at five, I finally told her I had to get some sleep."

"Shit."

He hesitated for a moment. "Sorry, I didn't mean to unload all this on you."

"No worries," I softly smiled at him. "You can talk to me."

Alex gave me a crooked smile, "Enough about me. How was your week?"

"Oh, my week was totally chill."

"Aaron said he had a great time with you this week."

"We had some really good conversations."

"I heard."

I dared to lean in closer to him. "I'm excited to see who I'm with this week."

"Same." His hand softly landed on my thigh.

"I-"

A loud bang interrupted me and Alex pulled his hand away. We looked up to see Jake rolling in with his clothes. He called out, "Morning asshats!"

Alex grumbled, "Shut the fuck up, man."

"All tired out from your lover's quarrel?"

"Jake," I spat. "Do you even know how to spell quarrel?"

He waved his eyebrows suggestively. "You and Justin seemed pretty cozy last night."

I shot back, "So did you and Becky."

"Yeah, we were." Jake humped the air before loading his laundry into the washer.

"Gross." I looked over at Alex who was fighting a yawn while glaring at Jake. He turned his back to us to start his laundry as Matt came in. He paused in the doorway before slowly walking towards the washers.

"Hey Boy Scout." Jake stomped over to Matt and knocked the laundry basket out of his hands, sending clothes onto the floor. Alex shook his head before sinking back into the couch. He looked more exhausted than when he had first come into the laundry room.

"See you later, chodes." Jake laughed himself out.

Matt's face fell as he went to pick up his clothes.

When Alex started to get up, I held out a hand to stop him. Matt's clothes fell closer to me, so I got up and collected them. "Sorry about Jake. He's the worst."

"I'm used to guys like him."

"Matt, right?" He nodded. "Is this your first year?"

We stood together then carried his hamper to the last washer that was open. "I've been coming here for a few years now."

"Really? I've never seen you at Camp Odyssey before."

He shrugged. "Wasn't meant to be."

"How are you liking things here?"

"It's been fun. Parts of it are great, parts of it suck. But that's how everything goes."

"I guess it is."

I could tell by how he turned away from me that the conversation was done so I moved back to my spot on the couch.

Alex's eyes were closed, and I decided I would wait for Matt to leave before picking up on our interrupted conversation.

Matt finished starting his laundry and waved to me as he left. The door quietly shut behind him and I turned over to Alex.

He started snoring on the couch.

So I grabbed a random book and started reading.

I was only a couple chapters into a beat up copy of *Jurassic Park* when my washer signaled that it was done. I expected the noise to wake Alex up, but he was sound asleep. Quietly, I switched my laundry then sat back down.

Alex's washer went off a few minutes later. Again, I looked over at him, expecting him to wake, but he didn't even stir.

My first thought was to wake him, but after what he told me happened last night, I wanted him to get sleep, especially since we were getting new kids today. I got up to switch his laundry myself, but then paused. Was that too forward of me? It was one thing to add detergent for him, it was a totally different thing to handle his clothes and make sure they got into the dryer.

If I was in his shoes, I would want someone to switch it for me and let me sleep.

I opened the lid to the washer and moved his clothes over to an empty dryer. Instantly, I recognized his blink-182 shirt. Then I got curious and started looking at his other shirts, like his black Linkin Park shirt or the ones he had from playing sports in high school that were faded and fraying. His burgundy camp shirt was the same color as the Tech shirts he had. The rest of his clothes were a mix of gym shorts, socks, and boxer briefs.

I started the dryer, sat back down, and then Alex stirred.

I froze waiting to see what he would do before reacting. He slumped onto his side, tucking his legs so he was curled up on the couch. His dark, unkempt hair was tickling my thigh, but I didn't move.

Alex's snoring picked back up when Sam returned. Her eyebrows came together as she pointed at him.

"Apparently," I whispered loud enough for her to hear, but not wake him. "He was up super late last night ending things with Jessica."

She smiled and held up a finger. With a quickness I wasn't used to seeing from her, she switched her laundry over then sat down in the chair next to my side of the couch. "Okay, explain."

"He was telling me he didn't really get to sleep because when he was breaking up with her, she kept him up most of the night crying and making him feel bad."

Despite our whispers, I could feel her excitement. "Hadley, this is it!"

"I guess."

"What do you mean you guess? He's single, you're single. He likes you, you like him. It's gonna happen now."

"You think?"

She nodded.

"Let's get through this week and see how Saturday goes."

"I don't know if I can take another week of you two not being together."

I rolled my eyes and looked down at Alex.

I didn't think I could take another week either.

The conversation needed a change. "How's it going out there?"

Sam rolled her eyes. "Aly is all butthurt because Jake and Becky hooked up last night. Justin is doing his best to console her without you."

"I'd come help but..."

"Don't worry about it. Aly will live."

Alex started to stir on the couch. Sam and I held our breaths, but he just adjusted his head and kept sleeping.

"I'll let you get back to your *reading*." Sam smirked then let herself out.

We were alone again, but I went back to the book I was reading so he could keep resting.

Matt came in and quietly switched his laundry from the washer to the dryer. Jake, per usual, was late and obnoxiously opened and slammed the door when he came in.

"Yo, what the fuck?" He pointed at Alex.

I was so done with his shit. I hissed, "Be quiet for once in your fucking life."

"Bitch." Jake scoffed but quietly switched his clothes. On his way out, he opened the door wide while looking at me.

My whole body tensed in anticipation of what he was going to do.

He smirked as he slid himself through the doorway and let the door slam shut behind him.

Alex's head shot up, "*¿Que fue?*"

"It's okay!" I put my hand on his back. "It's okay."

When he looked up at me, his eyes were still cloudy with sleep. He managed a nod as he yawned, letting his head drop back to the couch. I held my breath. Part of me was hoping he would go back to sleep, but another part of me wanted him to wake up so we could talk.

I was waiting to see what he would do when his hand snuck up and gently grabbed onto my leg just below my knee.

Without opening his eyes, he lifted his head, used his hand to pull himself closer, and then rested his head on my thigh. "*Mejor.*" He breathed out before yawning again.

The sound of my pounding heart filled my ears. I had to focus on breathing to help myself calm down. Slowly, I pulled my shaky hand away from him, picked up the book, and tried to start reading again. I kept as still as possible while he slept not wanting anything to ruin this moment.

My eyes were reading the book in my hands, but none of the words were registering. All my brain could focus on was how Alex's chest rose then fell, or the few words in English or Spanish that he mumbled as he slept, or the feel of his hair and skin touching my thigh.

I thought back to what Sam said earlier. Alex and I are both single now. We could try to do something about how we felt, but it would have to wait until Saturday. Another week of fleeting glances and quick conversations with Alex. I could do it though. I could make it through another week if the promise of finally being together on Saturday was dangling between us.

My dryer buzzed that it was done, but I didn't get up. I waited until Alex's laundry was done before I reluctantly called his name. I didn't want to end this, but we would need to get the rest of our day going and more people would be coming in to do laundry soon.

He didn't move.

I said his name a little louder.

Still nothing.

My hand dared to move to his shoulder, giving him a gentle shake. That forced his eyes open. He sucked in a deep breath, looked up at me, then down at my thigh that was warm and red where he had just been laying on it. Slowly, he lifted his head up, rubbing the sleep away from his face as he went. "Sorry."

"Don't be." My skin where his face had been was already missing his warmth.

"Shit," He looked down at his watch. "I never switched

my clothes."

"I switched it. Hope you don't mind." We both stood up and walked over to the dryers that held our clothes. I opened the one that had his, motioning for him to take them out before starting on my own.

"I can't thank you enough, Hadley. I'd be screwed without you."

I shrugged but smiled, "It was no problem."

"Seriously," He finished throwing his clothes into his basket, turning to me. "I owe you one. Big time."

I looked up at him, "I'll remember that."

Alex took a step closer to me when Sam came in. "Hadley, I don't know how much more of Aly I can take alone." She hoarsely whispered but then started talking normally when she saw Alex was awake. "Oh, I thought you would still be asleep."

He shook his head, "I was about to head out. Thanks again for everything, Hadley. I'll see you around."

"See you, Alex." I watched him leave before turning to her.

She was smirking as she put her clothes in her basket. "Looks like you had a better time than I did."

"He fell asleep on me."

"How? He was passed out when I was in here earlier."

"Jake slammed the door and woke him up, so then Alex like adjusted himself so he was sleeping on my thigh."

"Holy shit." She enunciated every syllable. "C'mon, let's go tell Justin!" We grabbed our baskets and headed out just as the next wave of counselors were coming in to do laundry.

Later that day we were all gathered for lunch and assignments. I walked in with Sam, Justin, and Aly. We had spent the last few hours getting ourselves packed up and ready to greet campers then move to our new cabins. I let Justin and Aly in on what happened in the laundry room and they both shared Sam's enthusiasm.

Aly pulled my hand and sat us down at the table closest to where Alex and Aaron sat instead of our normal table.

"Aly..." I let the look I gave tell her how I felt about moving tables.

"What?" She grinned, purposely leaving the chair that was facing where Alex was sitting open. Sam and Justin quickly sat down at the other seats so I had to take that one.

Sighing, I sat down before looking over at Alex. His gaze was on me, but it wasn't intense this time. Instead, there was a sweet smile curving his face. I smiled back before turning my attention to Mr. Hamilton reading out the names for this week.

I liked hearing who everyone is going to be with for the week. As Mr. Hamilton called out the names, I looked around to gauge their reaction. Some people were more excited than others about who they were working with.

"Moving on to the 8 and 9 year old group," Mr. Hamilton's voice rose as he turned the paper with everyone's names on it over. "We have Annie, Alex, Hadley, and Jackson."

I looked at Justin to double check I heard that right. He reached over to pinch my arm but I slapped his hand away. I wasn't daydreaming. This was real.

Alex and I were going to be together all week.

My smile was a little too big when we locked eyes with each other. He winked back at me.

Containing my excitement as we broke off into our counseling groups was hard. I wanted to run over and hug him, but that would've been crazy. Instead we, Annie and Jackson included, all high fived and prepared to meet the kids for that week.

The kids had a lot of energy after dinner so we made a

bonfire while they all ran around and played outside the cabins. Alex sat right next to me on the bench, our knees just barely touched while we stared at the fire.

"I'll call lights out this week." Annie declared. "But they need to get this energy out first."

"Camp is fun!" I chimed in. "Let them have fun."

She doubled down. "They'll be cranky in the morning."

"Then they're cranky and they go to bed easier tomorrow."

Alex jumped in. "She's got a point."

"This is your first year, right?" Annie's question was directed at me. Her tone wasn't bitchy, just more of a you-should-listen-to-me-because-I-know-what-I'm-doing vibe.

"First year as a counselor, but I've been coming here forever."

"It's different being a counselor."

"It shouldn't be. We should all be having fun too."

"I'm just here to avoid going back home or paying for a dorm over the summer." Jackson snorted.

"Heard." Alex lifted up his arm so they could fist bump. "What school are you at Jackson?"

"O.D.U. I'm a bio major."

"Nice." He looked at Annie. "Lemme guess, U.VA?"

She scoffed. "No, I got to Tech."

"Shit, I've never seen you around."

They kept going back and forth, trading different facts and stories about life on campus. Jackson told them about O.D.U. while Alex and Annie compared their years at Tech and I could tell he really liked being there. I had nothing to contribute.

Alex nudged my leg with his, bringing me back to the conversation. "Where will you be in the fall?"

"Roanoke."

Annie asked, "Like Roanoke College?"

"Yeah, I wanted to get out of NoVa."

"Heard that." Jackson held out a fist and I bumped mine to his.

Alex looked at Annie as he asked, "Roanoke, that's the little college close to Tech, right?"

She rolled her eyes. "Yes, they always come to Tech for the parties and football games cause they don't have any."

Alex turned to me, "Don't listen to her. You can come see Tech games whenever you want."

"Thanks." I looked down to hide my blush.

Annie's watch beeped. "9:30, let's wrangle these guys up and get ready for lights out."

We all nodded and started shouting for the kids to follow us into the cabins. Annie started taking the girls to our cabin and Jackson led the boys to theirs on the opposite side of the bonfire. I stayed with Alex and helped make sure the fire was completely put out with a combination of water and dirt.

Alex smacked his hands together to get the dirt off them. "Thanks for your help with *everything* today."

"I didn't forget about that I.O.U."

Our eyes locked. He asked, taking a step closer to me, "And what are you planning on using it for?"

I took a step closer to him. "Not sure yet."

Our bodies were dangerously close. He wrapped his arms around me and gave me a tight hug. "Goodnight."

I hugged him back, "Goodnight."

He let go first and we peeled ourselves away from each other. When I got into my bunk, I hugged my pillow like I had just hugged him.

11

We did the easy high ropes course for our first activity of the week. I almost went to the front of the line just to avoid Alex seeing me up close in my harness again. I still felt super self conscious about how I look in that thing, but after falling off the ladder that first week, I couldn't embarrass myself much more.

Alex and I ended up at the end of the line together so while the kids were taking turns getting onto the obstacle course, we started talking.

"So, what are you studying at school?" I asked, "I didn't catch it last night."

"Engineering, still not sure what kind yet."

"Makes sense why you're at Tech then."

"Yeah," Alex smiled. "My grandpa was an engineer and we were really close when I was younger so it's one of those cheesy 'I want to be like him when I grow up' kind of things."

"No, that's sweet."

"What about you? What's your plan for school?"

I groaned, "I want to go to school for writing, but my parents want me to major in education even though I told them I don't think I want to be a teacher."

"What? Why not? I think you'd be a great teacher."

"That's what everyone says so I kind of don't want to do what everyone expects from me, ya know? Plus, being a teacher isn't just getting summers off. It's a lot of work for a little bit of pay. At least that's what I've heard from my parents. They're both teachers."

"Isn't writing the same gig? You do all the work and then maybe have a shot at making it?"

"Yeah, but I love it."

"Then do what you love."

I just stared up at him, touched by the sincerity of his words.

One of the kids cried out in pain. We both looked over and saw that Timmy had fallen and scraped his knee.

"I got it." Alex gave me a reassuring smile before getting up and grabbing the first aid bag. I watched him as he calmed Timmy down, explained everything as he cleaned, and covered his scrape. He even gave Timmy a big pat on the back after he helped him up.

We got all the kids through the high ropes course without any more injuries.

During arts and crafts, I did my usual friendship bracelet making and some of the girls tried to join in. I had just gotten the last girl's bracelet started for her when Alex sat next to me.

"Could I make one of those?"

I smiled, "Anyone can."

He looked at the friendship bracelets I had on my wrists. In my downtime I had already managed to make myself two, and one for each of my friends, in addition to the ones the kids asked me to make. It has always been one of my favorite things to do to pass the time at camp.

He pointed to the diamond patterned one, "How do I do that one?"

"Oh, that's a hard pattern."

"You think I can't handle it?"

"We'll see." I spread the string out in front of him. "Pick two colors, it's easier with two."

He grabbed red and black. "My favorites."

"Mine too." I said as I cut the string and handed it to him. "Now what?"

"Fold them in half and tie a knot so there is a loop at the top." He completed that step easily.

"Since we're sitting at the table, we'll tape it down, but as long as you can attach it to something, you can work on it."

He started taping the whole thing.

"Not the knot." I corrected him. "Keep the tape above the knot."

"Okay..." I could tell he was starting to feel out of his element.

"Ready for the next step?"

He nodded.

"You need to make sure the colors end up alternating. Start with black and tie two left side knots on the next red string. Take the one on the left and make it look like a four."

Alex froze trying to compute what I had just said. Then he gave me a crooked smile and asked, "Would you just make one for me?"

I giggled. "I can def do that."

Leaning in close, he whispered, "I'll buy you something for your troubles."

I felt my whole body get hot at the deep tone he was talking to me in. "It's really no trouble. I make like five of these a week."

"I can't wait for mine then." He casually got up and went back over where the boys had started a game of touch football.

Later that same day, Justin and I were sitting together by the pool and I filled him in on the friendship bracelet deal.

He groaned, "Just kiss him already."

"I have to wait until Saturday."

"You can just sneak one this week."

"What if we get caught? I don't want to sneak around like everyone else does. I want the timing to be right. I want the first time I kiss Alex to mean something."

It would be the first kiss since everything happened.

I needed it to go right.

I watched as Alex moved around in the water, keeping the basketball away from the other boys before leaning back to shoot a basket. As his arms stretched up, I saw his ship tattoo on his ribs. Everyone watched the ball sail into the hoop. Aaron smacked the water and he went to retrieve it.

"You've only got like 6 more weeks to figure this out. But you gotta do something soon, cause if you don't, we might have another Jessica situation."

"I know that." I grumbled.

"Here's an idea: Ask him about his tattoos. Boys with tattoos love that shit."

"How do you know that?"

He grinned, "I just do. Look, he's getting out of the pool. Perfect opportunity."

"Our pool time is up." I quickly got up, thankful for the easy excuse out of this conversation. "I'll catch up with you later!"

I gathered up my stuff then fell in step with Annie, Alex, and Jackson who were corralling the kids out of the pool.

Alex and I were walking next to each other. He had his shirt slung on one shoulder, his towel on the other. I had my towel wrapped around me, my pool bag under my arm. My wet flip flops were squelching with every step and each time it happened, Alex laughed. "You gotta get some slides like these." He lifted up his foot to show them off. "These don't make that noise."

"But I got these at Old Navy to specifically match my bathing suit."

"Well, then don't sacrifice fashion for function."

The squelching was filling the silence between us again so I asked, "Your tattoos," I pointed at the ship on his ribs. "Like what do they mean?"

"That I had money to blow and I thought it looked cool." He laughed and I did too even though I didn't exactly get the joke. "No, but this one-" He pointed to the tattoo on his chest, "This is my mom's signature."

"Really?"

He nodded, "For a long time it was just me and my mom

so when I went away to school I brought her with me."

"Wow, that's super sweet. Was she mad you got a tattoo?"

"I already had the ship." He lifted his arm up and used his other hand to trace a line down the ship. "She was pissed about that one. I got it done by a friend's cousin, who is an actual artist, but it was done in a basement so it's not the greatest. There's tons of scarring."

"No, it looks good!"

Alex took my hand and brought it to the tattoo. The warmth of his skin was shocking against my finger tips. "You feel that?" His hand guided mine down the hull of the ship. The skin there was slightly raised compared to the rest of it. "It's all scarred up. Luckily, you can't tell unless you feel it."

I swallowed, calmly pulling my hand away from him. My nerves were fried and all I could think to say was, "Yeah, I couldn't tell."

"What about you? I don't see any ink on you."

"Oh, I want tattoos but I'm too indecisive. It's something I'm working on this summer."

"If you had to pick something right now, what would you get?"

There was something I wanted. "Have you ever read *A Series of Unfortunate Events*?"

Alex shook his head.

"They're some of my favorite books and there is a secret organization where all the members have this like eye tattoo on their ankle so I'd get that."

"See, you know what you want."

"Okay," I blushed. "But that's just one idea and I have a million more but only a limited amount of skin so-"

"Just focus on the one you really want."

I bit my bottom lip. We were getting close to the cabins and I didn't think I could handle any more flirting after touching Alex's ribs. "I will," I shook my head, "but not until I'm out from under my mom's roof. I don't want to deal with her wrath."

"I understand that."

The conversation was cut off when we got back to the cabins and split up for showers.

After dinner, we started another small bonfire and let the kids run around while we talked. We were sitting in the unofficial but official spots we were in before. Alex's leg was even closer to mine tonight.

"Alex," Jackson asked, his voice low. "Did you end shit with Jessica?"

I deflated at the sound of her name.

"Yup." He tried not to sound annoyed.

"Why? She's so hot!"

"So?" He spat out.

"So? C'mon man, I'd love to have a shot with her."

His words were sharp. "Then take one."

"Okay, easy for you to say."

Annie cut in before it turned from a conversation to a confrontation. "She's telling everyone you dumped her and making it into this big deal."

"I just told her I didn't think we were a good fit."

Jackson shook his head and Annie shot him a look.

Alex looked at them. "Tell Jessica to stop talking about this before we both get kicked out of camp."

Annie started, "The rule is about getting caught-"

"I know what the rule is." He snapped. "You know why the Hamiltons don't seem to give a shit if we hook up at the lodge? Because there's no campers around. If we do or say shit like this where the campers can hear it, then it's a problem. So the more we talk about this, the chances of a camper hearing get higher. Stop talking about it."

They nodded in agreement.

Alex turned his gaze to me, and I watched it soften. I felt like I should say something to him, but I just stayed quiet.

He shot up. "I'm calling it. Goodnight, Hadley." Then he went to the cabin.

Annie, Jackson, and I sat in awkward silence for a few minutes, listening to the sounds of the kids playing tag.

"Way to go, Jackson." Annie smacked his arm.

"What? How was I supposed to know he'd react like that?"

I dared to ask, "Why did you bring it up?"

They both looked at me then to each other, clearly they knew something I didn't.

Jackson shrugged, "Let's just say, Jessica is not happy Alex ended things with her."

Annie's watch beeped to signal it was time to get the campers ready for bed. They went to do that while I put the fire out alone.

12

After that night, Alex and I spent every day laughing and quoting different movies to fit whatever situation we were in. We stayed behind to organize the life jackets after canoeing. Together we helped the kids with archery. His excuse was always, "Hadley knows more than I do, so I need her to show me how to do it right."

But Annie and Jackson knew there was something up other than us being good friends. I caught them sharing looks whenever I laughed at his jokes or we finished each other's quotes.

Towards the end of the week, I tried to just quickly turn on my phone to do my weekly proof-of-life check for my dad but I had seven text messages and three voicemails from Keith.

"Annie, mind if I go outside real quick? I need to check something." I subtly wiggled my phone so she knew what I was talking about.

"You're good, just come back when I call lights out."

I stepped into the cool, dark night to quickly check the messages but they said the same thing. He missed me, wanted me back, promised it would be different, and all the other bullshit he thought would get me to come back.

I started deleting them all in frustration when I heard Alex's voice behind me. "Hadley? You good?"

Faking a smile, I lied. "Uh-huh."

He shook his head. "No, you're not."

I sighed, "It's nothing."

He didn't let up, closing the distance between us. "What's wrong?"

Taking a deep breath, I confessed. "Long story short my

ex keeps harassing me over text to get back together."

"The ex that Aaron was talking about?"

I nodded, "I told him I was done and over it. But he keeps texting and calling me. He thinks that if he tries hard enough we'll get back together because it worked before but it's not going to this time. It's not. I just want him to leave me alone."

He smirked, "Give me your phone."

"Why?"

"Because the only thing that'll get rid of a guy that won't leave you alone, is another guy. Shitty but it's true."

Handing him my phone, I asked, "What are you going to do?"

He pressed a few buttons and opened up my phone's camera. "We're going to send him a picture of us." He moved to me and hunched down so our faces were next to each other. "Get in close." Our cheeks were touching. I was smiling from ear to ear as the camera flashed and took our picture. He turned it around to examine it before showing it to me.

"Oh, that's cute!" My voice made it obvious how ecstatic I was.

"Let's try one more." He hunched down again and we pressed our cheeks together. As I started to smile, Alex turned his face and planted a kiss on my cheek. I was so taken by surprise that I scrunched up my face while giggling.

He turned it around to show me. The picture looked like we were an actual couple.

"That's better, but I think I'll send him both." He started to scroll through my phone. "What's his name? Nevermind, it's this number you have like twenty text messages from. Attaching the pictures and," His fingers made quick work of typing out whatever he was saying. "Done." He handed my phone back to me.

I started to open the text but instead I asked, "What did you tell him?"

"Fuck off."

"Damn."

"No one should have to deal with that."

My phone started buzzing, "He's calling!"

He chuckled, "Do not answer it."

I nodded and sent it to voicemail. Maybe it was the nerves or the excitement, but we both started laughing at what we had just done.

My phone immediately started buzzing again. "Gimme." I handed him back my phone and he answered, sounding super polite. "Hadley's phone."

I could hear Keith yelling through the speaker, "Who the fuck are you?"

Alex stayed so calm, smiling the whole time. "Doesn't matter."

"It does if you're taking pictures with my girlfriend like that."

"She's not your girlfriend, dumbass, so leave her the fuck alone." He hung up on Keith. I could picture him in his room seething at the idea that I was with someone new.

"Block his number."

"You can do that?"

"Yeah, it's easy. You want me to?"

I nodded. He pressed a few more buttons. "Done." Once again he handed my phone back to me.

Humbly, I whispered, "Thank you, Alex."

He touched my chin and lifted it so my eyes met his. "You deserve someone that respects you. Don't ever let a guy talk to you like that again."

When our eyes met, I felt this pull towards him. His hand slid up my cheek where he gently stroked his thumb. My lips parted as I closed my eyes and leaned in for a kiss.

The rough vibrations of my phone shook my hand. Instinctively, I looked down to silence the call and ignore it.

I put my hands on his chest and we both leaned in towards each other.

"Hey!" Annie hissed and we both turned to look at her. "Didn't you hear me calling lights out?"

Alex smirked while I flushed with embarrassment. "Sorry, I'll be right in."

"Get inside now." She shook her head and headed back towards the cabin.

"Fuck." Alex breathed out and let his forehead fall until it gently touched mine. I wanted to lean forward and quickly kiss him. My body was screaming at me to just do it, but my mind didn't want our first kiss to be rushed like this.

I sighed, filling the space between our lips. "We need to go."

He smiled, stroked my cheek one more time, then leaned back and took his hand away. "Go get some sleep, and keep that phone off. I'll see you in the morning."

"Okay," I bit my lip. "See you."

We walked in opposite directions and my phone started buzzing again. It was Keith's home phone calling me but I ignored it.

After sneaking back into my sleeping bag, just as I was going to power off my phone, Sarah called.

I had to ignore the call but quickly texted her that I would call her when I could.

Annie double checked everything was locked. Some girls were already asleep, some were still whispering and giggling to each other.

"I knew that phone thing was just an excuse." She chided at me while she got into bed.

"It wasn't."

"C'mon, Hadley. I know what I saw."

"It's not...I really did check my phone. Alex was just helping me block my crazy ex."

She scoffed. "I think he was doing a lot more than that."

"Well, nothing happened."

There was a pause before she gently warned, "You two need to be more careful."

"I know."

At breakfast the next morning, Alex sat down next to me and asked, "Heard anything else from my best friend?"

He normally sat next to me during meals, but this time, he put his leg right next to mine. I swallowed before answering, "Yeah, he tried to call me from his house phone but I ignored it."

"*Buen trabajo!*" He held up his hand for a high five.

I clapped his hand with mine and then our arms fell back down.

Alex's leg was still pressed against mine under the table, but all I could feel was his gym shorts. I wanted to feel the warmth from his skin on mine so I moved my left arm so that it was touching his right.

His eyes flicked down at our arms and then back up to look at me.

I grinned, "I'm going to need you to help me block his home number too."

"I can do that."

"Oh, and I gotta remember to call Sarah back." It was more of a reminder to myself then trying to share with Alex.

"Sarah?"

"She's my best friend from back home. She tried calling last night too, so I promised to call her back tonight to fill her in."

"Let me know if we need to take more pictures to send her."

"I will." I blushed, looking down at my waffle.

He turned and started asking the campers what they were excited for today.

As he was listening to them, he kept his right arm against mine awkwardly using his left hand to eat.

After breakfast we all trekked to the stables for horseback riding. All the kids complained about the smell, but Logan, who had been whining all week, kept going on about it.

He shouted, "I'm not getting on some stinky horse!"

"Logan," I pleaded, "Once we are on the trail, it doesn't stink. It's just the barn where the horses live. The trail is awesome. I think you'll really like it."

"No, I won't go!"

"Fine then I'll sit out with you."

"No!"

I groaned and threw my hands up in the air as Logan huffed over to the corner of the barn.

Alex walked over to him, "Come with me."

Logan kicked the ground but followed him as they walked out of sight. I helped the rest of the kids get on their helmets and start getting on their horses. There were enough horses for our small group of campers and all the counselors to ride the trail if we wanted.

We were close to heading out when Alex and Logan came back into the barn, both of them smiling. I shot Alex a surprised look that he returned with a confident smile. They quickly got ready and onto horses so we could start the trail ride.

Annie and Jackson led the group, with Alex and I in the back. He looked really uneasy at first, almost sliding off of his saddle.

"Did you not do this the last two weeks?" I turned around to ask as we were weaving through the woods, the horses expertly avoiding the trees.

"Nah," He adjusted himself as the horse swerved to avoid a low branch. "They never had enough horses or I volunteered to sit out."

"Then why did you come today?"

"I told Logan that I would try it if he would." He smiled but quickly focused back on staying on his horse.

"What did you say to him earlier?"

Alex grinned, "Took a bit but he basically said he's really homesick and thought if he was bad enough his mom would come get him. That's what happened at the other camps he went to this summer."

"Oh," Suddenly, I felt bad for all the times I was upset or

frustrated with Logan.

"Yeah, that kid really loves his mom, which I get. So I told him I would go with you guys and try this out because I hadn't done it yet because I was scared. I told him if I had to be brave then he did too. He could be brave by sticking camp out a few more days, his mom would be really proud of him. You know, that kind of stuff."

"You're amazing." The words slipped out of my mouth.

"I know." He smirked.

I was having a hard time seeing the rest of our group in front of us. "We gotta pick it up."

"How?"

"You gotta give her a little kick." I called back to him.

"I don't think she'll appreciate that."

"It'll be fine!"

"Okay..." He hesitantly called out. When he kicked his horse, she gave a little whiny and picked up her speed. She ended up going around my horse.

We caught back up to the group and finished off the trail ride. I was so proud of him and the kids were all super excited they completed the trail together. Even Logan was going around high fiving all the other kids!

I finished the friendship bracelet for Alex just before our final dinner. It took me a little longer than normal to complete it because he wanted such a complicated pattern that needed to be perfect. We were relaxing in the common area while the kids were running around playing games before dinner. Some had cards out, some were playing tag, and a group of girls were playing M.A.S.H. together on a picnic table.

Alex was sitting on top of another table just watching the kids to make sure none of them got hurt. I went over to him, presenting the friendship bracelet.

"Sick!" He quickly hugged me. "Thanks Hadley, this is awesome!" He tried to tie it on his own wrist, but was unsuccessful.

"Here, let me." I took the bracelet back. My fingers brushed against his wrist as I tied it. The familiar warmth of his skin against mine sent electricity through my fingers as I finished the knot. "There you go."

"I'll cherish it forever." He nodded for me to sit down next to him and I happily took the invitation.

His focus stayed on the kids as he said, "This has been the best week of camp so far."

"Why is that?"

He turned to look at me, "I think you know."

I adjusted my hand so that my pinky finger was on top of his. "I do."

A silence settled between us but I didn't feel the need to fill it. It was nice to just sit there next to him.

We only had one more night to get through and then we could try to figure out what all this flirting was going to amount to.

Logan came up to us, "Mister Alex, can you play soccer with us?"

"Soccer?" He over exaggerated his disgust. "I don't like soccer."

"Please!" Logan put his two hands together. "Mister Jackson is playing on the other team so we need a grown up too."

"Normally I refuse to play, but since you asked…" Alex stood. "I'll break my rule this time. Just for you." He gave Logan a big pat on the back and they walked over to the grassy area where they had paused the soccer game. The kids who were playing cheered when Alex joined.

Annie filled the empty spot next to me on the picnic table.

"I told you to be careful." She warned under her breath.

I put my head in my hands, "I know, I know. I don't want to get kicked out-"

"It's not just that."

I looked up to see her staring at the kids.. "What is it then?"

"You didn't hear this from me."

Leaning in closer, I nodded.

"Jessica has been telling anyone who will listen that if she finds out that you and Alex are hooking up"Annie rolled her eyes. "She's gonna make you pay. Her words."

"Make me pay? What the hell?"

Annie double checked no campers were in earshot. "I don't know, that's just what Becky told me. I think Jessica is a dumb bitch, but I do think that she'll try something if she gets the chance."

My face hardened, "Good thing Alex and I aren't hooking up."

She studied my face for a second. "So all this flirting and tension between you two, and you still haven't kissed or *anything*?"

"Nope."

"I'll let Becky know. She can tell Jessica to cool it on the threats."

"Thanks."

"No worries." Annie's watch beeped. "Let's go to dinner everyone!"

I spent the rest of the evening trying to enjoy my last night with Alex as my co-counselor, since I didn't know when or if I would get paired with him again. He sat down next to me and his leg slid over to touch mine.

But Annie's warning was in the back of my mind. What could Jessica do to hurt Alex and me? If anyone caught us, they could get us kicked out of camp. But that could only happen if we did anything beyond putting our legs next to each other. I loved these little touches that we were sneaking, but I wanted more. It was worth the risk of Jessica's wrath or getting in trouble just to finally kiss Alex.

After dinner we had thirty minutes before skit night

started.

"Guys," Annie shouted to get the campers' attention. "We put it off as long as we could, but we need to figure out what to do for skit night. Since we don't have a lot of time, we are doing the 'Is it time yet' skit and calling it a day."

Logan shot his hand up.

Annie was ready for a complaint, "Yes?"

"Can I be first?"

"Yeah!" She answered enthusiastically.

Logan must've known that the first person on the bench is the best role to have. Alex and Jackson set up two benches, long enough to fit all the kids. Logan sat down first and each kid that came on stage asked the next, "What time is it?" Finally, when Ben, that last kid came on stage, Logan got to say, "It's time!"

And then all they do is switch which leg they have crossed. It's super simple, but the kids got really into it.

We got back from skit night late and weren't able to do one last bonfire with the kids. They were a little disappointed so we let them play 15 minutes of flashlight tag before sending them to bed. Annie and I reffed while Alex and Jackson were captains of the two teams. No surprise, Alex's team won.

Once we had most of the kids settled in the cabins, I checked my phone. Sarah had sent me eight texts demanding an explanation about yesterday. I turned to Annie, "I swear I need to make an actual phone call this time."

"It can't wait until tomorrow?"

"I would really rather do this now."

She nodded but tapped her watch as a warning.

Once I was far enough away I called my best friend. Sarah answered the phone practically screaming, "Hadley!"

"Hey," I whispered back.

"What is going on? I got this angry call from Keith that you had a new boyfriend? I have barely heard from you all summer but you're texting that dick?"

"I only really check my once or twice a week to let my dad know I'm alive and Keith kept sending me these harassing messages about getting back together so my friend helped me tell him off for good."

"He was freaking out that you have a new boyfriend."

"Well, I want him to think that, but it's not true."

"Hadley...I can hear the lie in your voice."

"Well, it's not true yet. I'm hoping tomorrow will change that."

"What's his name?"

"Alex Lopez. He's from Florida. Like how cool is that?"

Sarah squealed on the other end of the phone, "Tell me all about him!"

"So he is super hot and we have so much in common. I really like him and..." Out of the corner of my eye, I saw Alex waving and walking over to me. "Shit, he's on his way over to talk to me so I have to go."

"Fine but text me please! Love you!"

I hurriedly whispered, "Love you too! Bye!"

Alex's face crinkled in confusion, "Who was that?"

Hoping he hadn't heard anything, I tried to play it off, "Just my friend, Sarah. She wanted to make sure I was okay."

"The one you were supposed to call?"

"Yeah, but it's fine. I can talk to her later." I slipped my phone into my hoodie pocket.

He motioned over to the girls cabin, "Annie called lights out, did you hear?"

"No, shit I missed it. Thank you."

"I figured you didn't, that's why I walked over here."

We both stood there for a second, looking at each other. I had just started getting lost in his dark brown eyes when he leaned in and whispered, "And I thought I heard you say my name."

"Oh...I...um...yeah...I..." Sounds were coming out of my mouth but nothing was forming into words.

How much had he heard?

My face was exploding with a blush that was rapidly spreading to my whole body. I had to look away from him before

I died of embarrassment.

Alex took a confident step towards me and I forced myself to look back up at him. His grin was dark as he whispered, "We can talk about what I heard tomorrow."

A loud coughing noise interrupted us. I didn't need to turn around to know it was Annie.

He gave me a crooked grin and walked backwards towards his cabin. When he spun around to walk forward, I turned to face Annie.

She threw her hands up in the air. "Again?"

"It wasn't-"

"Save it. It's the last night. You two can not make out or make out or whatever it is you want to do tomorrow when there are no campers around."

"I'm sorry, Annie. I didn't mean to put you in this position."

She just huffed and locked up the cabin.

Tomorrow night couldn't come soon enough.

13

The next day, after the kids were gone, we went through the usual motions of cleaning and catching up with other counselors we hadn't seen. Justin filled me in on Aly's newest obsession with Nate, one of the other high school counselors. She would fall in love with whoever she was paired with that week, telling us she didn't realize how cute and funny he was once she got to know him. But her obsession with Jake would always rise back up once that week was over. It was a cycle at this point.

As soon as we got into the lodge, I was determined to finally get my moment with Alex.

I went into the room that I had been sharing with Sam, Aly, Hannah, and Nicole the last few weekends. "Aly," With all the sincerity I could muster, I asked. "Make me look hot."

Her face lit up. "You are already hot, we're just going to enhance your assets!" Before I could reply she was rifling through her duffle bag and pulled out a bright pink tank top.

She offered it up but I shook my head. "I still want to look like me."

Her mouth scrunched as she thought, "Oh!" Her pointer finger shot up with an idea. "I have a black v-neck! Find your cut off jean shorts!"

Throwing on the clothes, I pulled the v-neck shirt down as low as I could while keeping my bra covered and pulled my cut offs up to expose the bottom of my ass. Sam, Nicole, and Hannah watched in awe as Aly used the little bit of makeup I brought to camp to make my blue eyes pop. She ran her fingers through my loose curls to ruffle them a bit then stepped away.

I couldn't stop looking at myself in the mirror. "Shit,

you're good, Aly."

"I know." She brushed her shoulders off. "Let's go."

We all went out to see how the party had been unfolding while I was getting dolled up. The warm air was flowing through the sliding door that was left open. It was one of those summer nights that felt warm and refreshing instead of hot and sticky.

Justin was sitting around a fire pit with the rest of the high school counselors while the college counselors were in their own separate bonfire. I could tell they were playing 'ride the bus' based on the questions that Aaron was asking everyone.

Alex's dark, wavy hair was easy to spot and I moved my gaze down until I locked onto his eyes. He broke our eye contact to look me up and down. When our eyes met again, he shot me a crooked smile.

"Let's go get some 'jungle juice!'" Aly slid her arm around mine. When I turned to stop her, she whispered, "Make him come to you."

I didn't want to wait, but I followed Aly and the other girls to the cooler. We each grabbed ourselves a cup then made our way to the bonfire with Justin. We slipped into the circle, joining into the conversation they were having about what game to play.

"Spin the bottle!" Aly cried out before she had even sat down completely. The debate continued but I wasn't paying attention. I was too focused on sneaking my gaze to the side and catching Alex staring back at me. He was clearly losing at the game they were playing because he finished one drink then Aaron promptly handed him another.

"Earth to Hadley." Justin waved a hand in front of my face. I tore my gaze away from Alex and looked at him. "How was your week?"

"Amazing." My eyes wandered back over.

"She's a goner." Sam quipped to Justin.

Aly's voice interrupted my thoughts, "Who is down for never-have-I-ever?"

Some wanted to play a drinking game and some just

wanted to play a regular game. Aly got up, "Okay, whoever wants to play never-have-I-ever, come to the picnic tables with me!"

Matt stood up, "And whoever just wants to play Mafia, stay here."

Some people got up to follow Aly, but Justin and Sam were staying in the circle. Unsure where to go, I stood but didn't move.

Alex saw me and nodded his head over to the cooler.

I looked down at my still very full cup and decided to chug it. It was easy to gulp down the sweet drink. "Going to get a refill." My hand shook the now empty cup.

"Have fun quenching your thirst!" Justin laughed.

Alex met me at the cooler. His hand smoothly took the empty cup out of mine and he started to refill it. "Are you going to play games with your friends?"

"Not sure yet. Why?"

"Just didn't know if you wanted to have some alone time with me. I was spoiled having you around all week."

He handed me the cup. I took a sip to help me think of what to say. "What would happen if I was alone with you?"

"We could finish our conversation from last night." He flashed a smile that made me feel warmer than the booze did.

I dared to ask, "The one about what you overheard?"

"Yeah, but," He locked eyes with me. "We won't be talking."

My heart started racing. I wanted to find the most secluded place in the whole lodge so we could 'not talk' to each other and finally kiss.

I leaned in closer to whisper, "Come inside in a few minutes. Don't make it obvi." He smiled and started to finish his drink.

I sauntered away into the lodge.

From what I could tell, everyone was outside so we would be completely alone no matter where we went. I started walking to Alex's room but the rooms had too much potential for people to walk in. I stood in the boy's hallway unsure which direction to move.

Alex caught me in my indecision.

"Where should we-" Before I could finish my question Alex had me pinned up against the wall.

He brushed a soft brown curl behind my ear before gently pressing his lips to mine. Eagerly, I kissed him back. His hand wound into my hair as his hips pushed into mine. Our mouths moved together as his tongue slipped between my lips.

I wanted more.

I could feel the restraint in the rest of his body. He started to pull away, his lips just barely on mine. My hands found his shirt and pulled him in closer to me. I snaked my tongue into his mouth, which he eagerly accepted. Our kisses started to slow down, the initial desire that had exploded between us simmering to a steady fire.

Alex pulled away, giving me one more soft kiss.

I breathed, "Wow."

He whispered, "You have no idea how many times I wanted to grab you and kiss you this week."

My head was spinning. "I wouldn't have stopped you."

He leaned in for another kiss but we heard someone's voice calling to people back outside. The sound of flip flops clacking on the floor was getting closer. A shrill laugh echoed in the common room.

"Fuck." Alex swore, frantically looking around. His hands were still on my waist but they slid down to my hips and guided my body to the left. He pushed the boy's bathroom door open then shoved me inside. "Wait here." His eyes were dark as he pulled the door closed behind him.

Alex just shoved into the bathroom.

The pulse of panic was thrumming in my brain.

The last time a boy shoved me into a bathroom, something terrible happened to me. I needed to get out of here before I had a full blown panic attack. As I lifted my heavy arms up to open the door, I heard why Alex freaked out.

"Alex!" Jessica's voice rang out so loud I could hear her

perfectly through the solid wooden door.

"What's up?" He sounded like he was still just outside the door.

"I spilled beer all over Aaron's cards, and he sent me to get some more. You have cards, don't you?"

"Yeah, give me a minute and I'll bring them to you. I just need to go to the bathroom."

"I'll wait for you so we can go together."

I heard him sigh before his voice perked up. "Nevermind. Let's go get the cards."

"You'll play with us, right?"

"I'll come play a round with you." Alex's voice was getting quieter as he walked away. The last thing I heard was a loud giggle from Jessica.

Alex left.

He shoved me into the bathroom and left me.

I started to remember the last time something like this happened.

Phantom foreign touches were pressing into my hips, moving up my stomach, and settling on my chest. The pulsing panic that had been subdued while I was listening to the conversation on the other side of the door was finally free to flow through my whole body.

It felt like the more air I tried to breathe in, the less I was able to. My lungs weren't filling properly. A fuzziness was creeping into my vision. I threw my hands over my face and pressed my eyes shut, but that just made it easier for me to hear the voice that I had been trying to forget.

I took a few awkward steps away from the door. When my back hit the cool tiles on the wall, I slid down and landed with a thud.

I couldn't stop the awful thoughts from scrolling through my mind. Uncontrollable sobs shook my body. I tried to focus on breathing, but when I breathed in deeply, I got a whiff of the bathroom cleaner and remembering where I was just made everything worse.

The door started to slowly open.

I didn't have the energy to hide. Whoever was going to find me in here was going to see how pathetic I was.

I just didn't want it to be Alex. I didn't want him to see me like this.

"Hadley..." Justin's worried voice floated through the door just before he popped his head in. His eyes grew wide when he saw me. "Oh shit!"

"He...he..." I tried to choke something out between sobs, but I couldn't take a deep enough breath.

"Let's get you to your room." I let Justin lift me up from the ground and I curled into his side. We walked together as fast as we could to avoid being seen by anyone.

When we got to my room, Sam instantly perked up from her bed where she was reading. "What the fuck?"

"I don't know." He laid me down on the bed next to her. She gently moved my tear matted hair away from my face. I silently sobbed while Justin explained. "I was outside talking to Aaron when Alex came outside with Jessica. He broke away from her to quickly tell us that Hadley was alone in the boy's bathroom and someone needed to go get her. I took off and just found her on the floor panicking."

I sat up, the panic suddenly replaced by rage at how Alex had pawned me off on someone else. "We were making out until Jessica came inside and then he shoved me into the bathroom and left me to be with her!"

"He shoved you in the bathroom?" Sam asked.

"Yes! He just used me and then pushed me in there and left me." My crying was slowly stopping, but more from exhaustion than actually being over what had just happened.

Sam rubbed my back to help calm me down. "It's not like that. It's not like what happened."

Justin looked at her, "What happened?"

She shook her head.

He put a comforting hand on my back. "Please don't take this the wrong way, okay? I get being shoved into a bathroom by a boy is shitty, but you were just having a full blown panic attack. That's...that just doesn't add up. Did Alex do something else to you?"

"No!" I said a little too aggressively.

"Then what's going on?"

I looked at Sam, who shook her head. "You have to tell him. It's not my story to tell."

"What story?"

"I was..." I struggled to get the words out. "I was sexually assaulted by my ex's step-brother a few months ago and what just happened with Alex brought all that shit up again."

Justin's face fell.

"My ex's step-brother shoved me into a bathroom when he did it. So when Alex did it just now, it fucked me up." I tapped the side of my head for emphasis.

"Does he know what happened to you?"

"No!" I shook my head. "I don't want to tell him. He'll think I'm damaged goods or something."

"We've all seen how he looks at you, Hadley." Sam patted my back. "Alex likes you a lot. He'll like you even if you tell him this."

I wiped the last few tears from my face. "I'm not ready to tell him."

We sat there in a heavy silence then Justin shot up. "I'm going to go let Alex know I got you out of the bathroom safely."

"Please don't-"

He held up a hand, "I would never tell him what you told me. I'm just going to let him know you're okay. I'll be right back." He slunk out of the room and closed the door behind him.

I looked over at Sam. "Sorry I cried on your bed."

"I'm just glad you stopped. I've never seen you like that."

"It's been months since I've had a panic attack."

"You know Alex didn't mean to trigger one."

"I know. I just...I don't want to see him while I'm still like this."

She breathed out a laugh, "You do look rough."

I managed to laugh back. "Thanks bitch." I got off of her bed, changed into my pajamas and took what was left of the makeup off my face. Justin came back into the room just as I had gotten into my bed.

"It's done."

I sat up in my sleeping bag. "What did you say?"

"I went over to Alex. It took a minute for me to get his attention. Jessica was all over him. When she finally freed him I told him that I found the bottle he told me about and put it back where it belonged."

"Good code!" Sam added without looking up from her book.

I sighed and rolled over. "Thank you for everything, Justin."

"Of course. If you guys are good, Aaron invited me to play poker with the college counselors."

I mustered all the enthusiasm I could, "Someone should have fun tonight."

"Sam, if you need me just come get me!"

She saluted without looking up from her book as Justin left.

After what just happened I was drained. My eyes were shut but my brain was still too wired to sleep. Frustrated, I tossed and turned in my bunk.

Sam offered, "I can turn the lights off if you want to sleep?"

I kept my eyes closed as I responded, "No, it's fine. It's not the light."

"Wanna talk?"

"I wanna think."

"Lemme know if you change your mind about the lights or the talk."

I wanted to change my mind about other things. All I wanted was to kiss Alex. After the awesome week we had together, I expected our first kiss to be like the cherry on top. I wanted our first kiss to be perpetual bliss.

Even though I had felt like that when we kissed, all that was being eclipsed by the panic attack I had right after it. I know he hadn't meant to cause it. I know he probably didn't even realize that I was so upset. How was I going to talk to him about this at laundry in the morning? Should I be mad at him? Ignore him? That wouldn't work, he would find a way to talk to me. I could just explain myself and why what he did was a bigger deal than he realized. Or should I just wing it?

14

I purposely got to the laundry room early to avoid seeing Alex, but when I whipped open the door, I saw him in his usual spot on the couch. He had been reading but quickly put the book down, standing up when I arrived. "Hey." There was a caution to his tone that I hadn't heard before.

"Hey." As soon as I saw him, all the words I had rehearsed the night before fled my mind. I didn't even know how to start a conversation now, so I turned and silently loaded my clothes into the washer. I took my time pouring in the detergent and setting the dials. As the washer started whirring, I slowly turned around and was face to face with him.

I hadn't even heard him move.

He tried to joke, "Are you just going to ignore me now?"

"Well, I would run into a bathroom but there isn't one nearby." That came out harsher than I meant it to.

His arms went to either side of me to hold onto the washer, caging me in. He hung his head low before saying, "I'm really sorry about last night."

I sucked in a breath and waited for him to say more.

Dark eyes met mine. "I just didn't want us to get caught, especially not by Jessica. She's got it out for us and if she saw us together," A smile flashed across his face. "It would be hard to deny what we were doing."

As much as Alex's words were helping, I was still feeling the aftershock of my panic attack in my body. I needed him to know that he couldn't do what he did to me again. So I retorted, "That doesn't make what you did okay."

"I know it doesn't. I tried to go back to you after I gave her the cards but she insisted on sticking to my side. I would've gotten you myself but I couldn't find a good enough cover up. That's why I sent Justin in. No one would question you and Justin doing anything together."

I nodded.

"Don't tell him I told you this, but…" Alex lifted his hands from the washing machine and slid them down my arms. When our hands met, he laced his fingers into mine. "Later on last night, Justin let it slip that you had a panic attack. I promised him that I wouldn't say anything about it, but I was really worried about you. I went to check on you before I went to bed but Sam wouldn't let me in the room. She said you needed to rest." He took a step closer so that our hips were touching. "I'm sorry that I made you have one."

"It happens." I shrugged. "It was more about something totally unrelated to you."

"Still, I fucked up."

The pressure that had been in my chest all night was gone. Now I just wanted to get back to feeling good with Alex. I teased, "It just fucked up our first kiss."

He slid a hand up to my face and gently brushed his thumb over my bottom lip. "Let me make it up to you. I still owe you from last week."

"Someone might catch us." I whispered as he slowly closed the space between our mouths.

"Right now, I don't care." Alex let out a breathy chuckle. His hands grabbed onto my hips and tugged until I was flushed against his chest. Slowly, he whispered, "Do you care?"

"I don't." I breathed before my lips met his. I wrapped my arms around his neck as his arms went tighter around my waist. Our kisses started out soft and slow. The passion that had bolstered our kiss last night was still there, but it needed a few sweet kisses to build on. His mouth worked mine as his tongue explored. My fingers went into his dark, wavy hair to gently tug.

We heard voices and footsteps getting closer to the laundry room. I panicked, aggressively pushed him back, then turned away from Alex to make it look like I was starting my wash.

He scoffed before grabbing his clothes from the dryer. He had been here so long that his laundry was already completely done.

"Hey!" Sam called before opening the screen door.

"Hey!" I called back as she came in.

She grinned as she made her way to the washers. "Alex, what's up?"

"Not much." He didn't look up at her.

She noticed how off he was acting and shot me a look. I just shook my head. Once she had finished loading her clothes, she turned to me. "We're about to start an UNO game. Wanna join?"

"Yeah, I'll be out in a sec."

"Cool." She didn't say anything more as she left.

Once we were alone again, I desperately looked over at him.

Alex didn't look up from his laundry. "So this is how you felt?"

"Pretty much."

"Feels...shitty."

"It does."

We stood there in a tense silence. Alex started folding his laundry, something I hadn't seen him do the last few weeks.

"I'm sorry-"

Matt opened the door just as I started talking. With a quiet huff, I parked myself on the couch and waited. Thankfully, he read the feeling of the room, not saying anything to either of us as he loaded in his clothes. He did give me a little wave as he left.

The tension between us rose back up once we were alone again.

Alex still wasn't looking at me so I got back off the couch to lean against the dryer next to the one he was folding his clothes on. I took a deep breath and started again, "I'm sorry I pushed you away. I really like you Alex, and I don't want to ruin this or get caught."

He finished folding his t-shirt and looked at me. "I really like you too, Hadley. And I can't get kicked out." He let out a defeated sigh as he shook his head. "So we keep this on the down low then?"

I nodded.

"And you're okay with that?"

I nodded again.

"Good." He sighed and I thought he was going to kiss me again but instead he said, "You told Sam you were going to play cards."

"I don't have to. I doubt we'll be paired up again this week."

Alex caught on to what I was doing and grabbed my waist. "How will I manage without you all week? I'm not going to have anyone to talk to."

"I'm not worried about talking."

His hands slid down my waist and landed on my thighs. Before I could object, he lifted me up onto the dryer. "Alex!" I squealed in protest, but I was silenced by his lips that knew exactly how to move against mine. When he thrust his tongue in and around my mouth, I could feel myself melting into him.

His fingers started to sneak under my shirt. The light touches moved higher and higher up my stomach. I pulled away, recoiling at a resurfacing memory. It wasn't Alex's hands that bothered me, it was the way my body responded. I felt a sudden violating feeling consume me. I wanted to be out of my own skin and far away from this feeling. I tried to focus my thoughts on happy things to calm me down, but I couldn't focus on just that. My thoughts were like a tv flipping between channels, unable to settle on just one. Instead, I turned my attention to trying not to cry from the memory and embarrassment.

Alex cupped my face, "You okay?"

I nodded. "Yeah, everything you're doing is good."

The pads of his thumbs stroked my cheeks as I blinked back tears. He delicately pressed his lips to mine before pulling back just enough that I could look into his deep brown eyes. Despite how my body reacted when he touched certain parts of it, this feeling of being so close to Alex was good.

I smiled up at him like a fool.

He shook his head as he smiled back.

The sound of the laundry door bursting open broke us apart. I was still sitting on the dryer but Alex took a step to the side just as Jake walked in.

"What's up..." Jake's mouth fell open as he looked between us before walking over to the washing machine. He chuckled, "I didn't think you had this much game."

Alex refused to look at Jake as he clapped back. "Don't know what you're talking about, dude."

"Don't worry, I won't tell Jess."

"There's nothing to tell." He spat, finally looking at Jake. Alex's knuckles were white from how hard he was clenching his fists around one of his shirts.

Jake finished putting his clothes in and added detergent. He took his time adjusting the dials on the washing machine. I looked at Alex, who kept his dark gaze on Jake the whole time. Once the washing machine was whirring, Jake walked over to me leaning against the dryer I was still sitting on. "So Hadley, you're still fair game?"

Alex's arm flinched like he was about to hit him but he had stopped himself.

Jake ignored him and looked at me expectantly. I pushed my disgust down before replying, "I'm free to do whatever I want..."

His eyes widened.

I finished, "But the last thing I want to do is you."

"We'll see." He grinned before finally turning his attention to Alex. "Down boy." With that last taunt, he left the laundry room.

As soon as the door was shut, Alex said, "If it was possible to beat his ass and not get kicked out of here, he would be dead."

"Maybe the last day of camp?" The joke helped release all

the tension in my body.

He breathed out a laugh, "Maybe." He visibly relaxed before positioning himself back in front of me. He wrapped me up into a tight hug and I squeezed him back. Then he pulled back, "You should go play cards with your friends."

"You're trying to get rid of me?" I teased, trying to bait him back to my lips.

"No, I want to stay here with you but I have to get some things done before camp starts."

"Like what? We've got plenty of time before the campers come."

"I have to meet with Kelly at 11."

An instant flash of panic, "Why?"

"Nothing bad." He quickly clarified. "I need to make an international phone call and Kelly said I could use the phone in her office."

"An international phone call?"

"Yeah, today is my mom's birthday and she's in Peru. I need to leave now so I can run into town and buy one of those prepaid cards first. So go play UNO with your friends. I'll see you at lunch." He gave me a crooked smile.

I whispered, "I'll miss you this week."

"I'll miss you more."

We shared one more quick peck before he helped me down from the dryer. I held the door open as Alex took his laundry basket out. He went back up to the lodge to grab his keys while I went to where I saw Sam and Justin at the picnic tables.

I walked into the dining hall for lunch with Sam, Justin, and Aly, who was filling us in on the gossip she had heard while laying out this morning.

As soon as we crossed into the dining hall and my eyes adjusted to the change in light, I looked for Alex, instantly spotting him next to Aaron. All the boys at their table were laughing at the story Aaron was telling.

We all grabbed food then followed Aly to the table we had sat at last week. Aly was still rattling off whatever gossip she heard but I had tuned her out the second we walked into the dining hall.

Mr. Hamilton made his way to the front of the room. His hair looked like he had run his fingers through it. He clapped his hands and the room went quiet.

"Thank you." Mr. Hamilton cleared his throat. "Another week done! We are a third of the way through the summer." He paused while we all clapped. "You all have done an amazing job so far. The campers are all raving about their counselors and we've already had several parents reach out about sending their kid another week this summer. I couldn't be happier with how camp is going so far."

Mr. Hamilton sighed, "Which is why I know that when things don't go as planned, you all will be able to adjust with ease. We'll be down a counselor this week and the rest of summer, which shouldn't be a problem. Instead of doing two teen groups, we'll combine to have one group and house that group in the lodge with seven counselors. This is how we'll be running the teen group for the rest of summer. In the lodge we'll have Mike, Nick, Lucas, Matt, Brittney, Sam, and Hadley."

I looked across the table at Sam. We both smiled at finally getting to be together for a week.

Mr. Hamilton finished reading the names and Alex was with the youngest group. He was with Aly, Aaron and Hannah. Once Mr. Hamilton had finished reading out the names, everyone started murmuring as they realized whose name wasn't called: Kylie.

Kylie, for whatever reason, had left for the summer.

I hadn't really talked to her since camp had started. We hadn't been paired together yet but from the few conversations we had had, she seemed sweet. It was her second year as a counselor but I really didn't know a whole lot about her.

Normally, everyone stays in their little table groups for lunch, especially after learning we might not get to see our friends for the rest of the week. But after everyone started figuring out that Kylie had left, people were up and roaming around to different tables to see what others knew. Aly confidently walked over to the table of girls Kylie normally sat with, using her friendship with Hannah as an in.

Alex and Aaron came over and sat with us after they had cleaned up their food trays.

Aaron asked, "Do you guys know why Kylie left?"

"Not for sure. We're waiting for Aly to get back." I nodded over to where she was leaning in, listening to Hannah.

"I think I heard someone talking about it this morning." Justin chimed in. "Someone in her family died and she was going home."

I nodded, "I heard one of the other girls say someone missed their family too much and wanted to go home."

"That's such a lame reason to leave." Aaron scoffed.

"People get homesick." Alex shrugged and adjusted his leg under the table so it was right up against mine.

Sam jumped in, "She was in the clinic this morning."

We all looked at her to continue.

"I went there to get a band aid." She held up her bandaged pointer finger. "Nasty paper cut. While I was waiting, I saw that Kylie had signed into the clinic literally right when it opened for an 'unspecified injury.' The nurse came out of the room Kylie was in to get me a band aid and I saw her but she didn't look injured."

"Weird." I said and everyone seemed to nod in agreement.

Aly perked up from the other table and walked back to us. She parked herself back in her chair before saying, "They don't know anything. Kylie left this morning and just said she needed to go home."

"Well, you were my best shot at getting the gossip." Aaron said as he started to stand up and Alex followed. I instantly missed the feeling of his leg next to mine.

"Sorry we weren't more helpful." I sarcastically joked back.

"It's fine. Have fun with all the teenagers this week. At least you have Sam!" Aaron gave Justin a slap on the shoulder. "You're all by yourself this week."

"I'll manage." Justin said as a very soft blush was spreading across his cheeks.

Aaron grinned before turning his attention to Aly. "C'mon, you. I know you're going to make one of us carry your bag so let's just get it over with."

"Give me a second, I haven't finished eating!"

"All anyone ever does is wait for you!"

She huffed, "Then go on without me! I'll get my bag myself."

"I'll get your bag." Alex conceded.

"This is why you're the best, Alex." Aly smirked at Aaron.

"Right in front of me? Rude." He playfully smiled and started to walk away. "See you *soon!*" He put extra emphasis on the last word.

"See you." Alex gave my shoulder a little squeeze as he went to follow Aaron.

"See you." I called after him.

We finished eating and cleaned up. Aly went to meet Aaron, Alex, and Hannah in their cabins while Sam and I hiked back to the lodge with our stuff.

Mike, Nick, Lucas, and Matt were already on the boys side of the lodge getting their stuff put away. Matt gave us a nod of acknowledgement and went back to his room. He was the only one I knew out of all the boys we were with.

"Hadley and Sam, right?" Mike came over to where we had walked in with our duffle bags.

I answered for the both of us. "Yeah, Mike?"

"Mikey, actually. We haven't been grouped together yet."

"Well, there are a lot of us." I adjusted my duffle bag on my shoulder.

"Nice to get to talk to some new faces."

"We see each other every Saturday." Sam retorted.

"Mikey!" Nick called from down the boy's hall. "You need to get your ass in here and help us!"

"Duty calls." Mikey grinned before slowly jogging back to the boy's hall.

Sam and I shared a look before moving over to the girl's hall. After we put our bags down and had chosen bunks, Brittney came in. From what I'd heard, Brittney is a bit of a gossip and friends with Jessica. I was thankful to have Sam as a buffer for us this week.

"Hey bitches!" Brittney squeaked as she threw her bag on an open bunk. "Ready for a fun week?"

"Totally!" Sam mocked her.

"Okay," Brittney picked up on the sarcasm. "What about you, Hadley?"

"Yeah, having the teens will be fun. Especially all together like this."

"And we won't even need to move our stuff out on Saturday!"

"Bonus!" I tried to be excited with Brittney. Her energy was a little contagious.

Sam subtly rolled her eyes before heading for the door. "Bathroom."

With her gone, Brittney took a step closer to me. "So, you and Alex?" She smiled and gave an over exaggerated wink.

I was taken aback by her abrupt question, "What do you mean?"

She looked at me like I was dumb, "You guys are like together, right?"

"No, who said that?"

The way she giggled sounded like an insult. "No one had to say anything, it's pretty obvious."

I'm not sure why I started getting frustrated or upset, but I could feel my body start to tense and heat rise up to my cheeks. She didn't do anything wrong by asking, but it felt like an intrusion.

Jessica must've put her up to this. "Alex and I aren't like a thing. Do I think he's hot? Yeah. Would I hook up with him? Yeah. But it's not like that. He doesn't want a relationship this summer."

She huffed, unconvinced. "Maybe you should act like that then."

"Thanks for the advice." I ended the awkward conversation by offering to restock the bathroom supplies.

15

We got all our campers checked in then hiked to the lodge. They were excited to have the whole air conditioned lodge to themselves and quickly spread out choosing rooms with the people they had connected with when they arrived. Almost all the bunks were taken in a matter of minutes.

Being in the lodge under these circumstances felt different, but in a good way. Watching all the kids get along and enjoy their first night made me feel proud.

At high ropes the next day, I didn't care so much about what I looked like in a harness, but I still volunteered to be the caboose. Everyone else made their way up the ladder and to the platform, passing by me on their way.

Mikey practically pushed Sam up the ladder so he could be alone with me. She kept shooting us glances until she was too far into the high ropes course to see us.

And once we were alone Mikey whispered, "You look good in a harness."

"Weird thing to say."

"No, I mean it in a good way! It shows off your ass."

As much as I hated it, if I flirted with Mikey, it would help convince certain people I wasn't into Alex. So I teased back, "I bet you say that to every girl."

"I don't." He took a hungry look at my ass in the harness and I wanted to shrink.

Mikey tried again later that day at the pool while Sam and I were laying out. He grinned a little too wide. "Hadley, I can rub the sunscreen on your back if you want?"

Sam, who now knew what happened at the high ropes

course, snapped, "I got her."

He threw his hands up and walked away.

I shook my head but kept my gaze on Mikey as he got in the pool. We had just finished putting on sunscreen and leaned back onto our towels to read when a giant splash of water hit us.

Sam was livid as she shot up, looking for whoever just got her book wet. Mikey grinned up at me from the edge of the pool closest to us. "Sorry! I wasn't trying to get you wet!"

Instead of rolling my eyes like I wanted to, I giggled. It felt so fake but I hoped it sounded real enough to convince Brittney, who was laying out nearby.

We lost track of time at the pool. Normally Sam keeps us all on track, but she was so upset about her book getting wet, she hadn't noticed that we had gone over our swim time. We only realized this when the next group showed up, all of us jumping up and rushing out of the pool.

I couldn't stop the smile that split my face when I saw Alex leading his group into the pool. He looked confused to hide the smirk on his face. "You guys lose track of time?"

"Yeah, sorry." I wrapped my towel around myself and threw my stuff into my pool bag.

He walked closer to me, "All good."

Aaron gave me a pat on the back as he herded little kids into the pool. They looked so small next to the mass of teenagers leaving.

Aly gave us quick hellos as she and Hannah brought in the rest of their kids.

It hit me while I was standing in front of Alex that I missed him more than I even realized. We lingered in each other's presence for a beat before he spoke. "Hopefully, I'll see you around."

"Hopefully." And without realizing I was doing it, I wrapped my arms around him for a hug. His body tensed as he awkwardly put his arms around me. When I pulled away, I was red with embarrassment and his eyes were wide with fear. To make the whole exchange look less like a public display of affection, Alex wrapped his big arms around Sam. She cringed at the unwanted contact and gave his back an awkward pat. He let her go and we both scurried away.

"What the hell was that?" Sam hissed once we were far enough away from the pool.

"I don't know, I just got overwhelmed and hugged him."

"So I had to get hugged too?" She shook her head, "You're lucky I love you. You know I hate being touched."

"I know, Sam. I'm sorry."

"That better be enough to make sure no one suspects anything."

It needed to be.

Later that night, Mikey slid in next to me on the couch and casually threw an arm around me. Sam had just gotten up to go to the bathroom, leaving me alone.

"What do you say after lights out, you and I go for a late night walk?"

"What?" I had heard him, but I didn't know what else to say.

"You know, like you did with Alex."

I didn't realize anyone knew anything about the couple times Alex and I were together when Annie called lights out. "I don't know what you're talking about."

"C'mon, don't you wanna have fun? I'll make you forget all about him." His hand grabbed onto my thigh with a threatening tightness.

I turned to him with gritted teeth, "Don't ever speak like that to me again or I will rip your nuts off."

He recoiled and told me, "Take a chill pill."

I got up as Sam was walking back towards us. My hand grabbed her wrist and I pulled her into our room and told her what just happened.

"What a fucking creep!" She folded her arms over her chest. "Are you going to tell Alex?"

I shook my head. "What's he going to do about it?"

"Maybe you two can be more official and then guys will

stop hitting on you?"

I wanted that, but if Alex didn't then I didn't want to push it. "No, it's fine. I can handle him. He's no worse than Jake."

"At least Jake owns that he's a douche. I didn't think Mikey was going to be like this."

I shook my head, "Neither did I."

The aggressive flirting stopped after my threat towards Mikey and I decided I wouldn't tell Alex about it.

After the campers were picked up at the end of the week, all the counselors headed back to our campsites to clean. The clump we were in was dispersing as we all went our separate ways. Alex snuck up behind me and whispered a playful, "Hey."

Sam quickened her pace while Alex and I started to lag behind until it was just the two of us walking along the path. Our hands brushed and it emboldened me to quietly ask, "So do you want to hang tonight?"

"Uh, we can chill but you know-"

"Keep it on the down low." We got to the split in the path and stopped.

"It's not...it's not that I don't want to hang out with you." He ran his hand through his hair and it poofed up slightly. "It's just easier if no one suspects anything."

"I know."

He shuffled his feet. "It's just if Jessica finds out, I don't know what she'll do. She can go tell Kelly that we did something in front of campers and everyone will believe her."

I rolled my eyes. "No one would believe her."

"Everyone already thinks something is happening between us. If we gave them proof, if we corroborated what they already assumed, then..." He shook his head. "It's too risky. I can't, *we* can't get kicked out."

I was becoming standoffish, which I didn't mean to do,

but he just kept reiterating the same point and it was starting to piss me off. My arms crossed over my chest. "I get it."

Alex huffed, "Tonight doesn't have to be any different than what we've been doing."

"But it is different."

We stood there both feeling the weight of what I had just said. Alex and I couldn't pretend to be just friends because we weren't that anymore. We'd kissed enough now that all of our interactions going forward were different. Every time we touched the feelings that I had for him grew and that would only get worse if we had to keep spending the rest of summer only sneaking secret touches when we could be around each other.

Alex finally offered, "It doesn't have to be like that. I like the way things are."

When I took a step back from him, his eyes widened. He hadn't meant for it to hurt, but hearing him say things didn't have to change, that we could just go the rest of the summer not trying to get more from each other, that hurt. So I clipped back, "Fine. Then this," I motioned between the two of us. "Can stay the same."

"What does that mean?"

Out of frustration, I turned to walk away from him. He grabbed my hand and pulled me back towards him. Quickly, he looked around to make sure we were alone before he reached up to caress my cheek. "I do want to spend more time with you. Let's just see how tonight goes. Maybe we can sneak off together."

"We'll see."

He leaned in to kiss me but I twisted away. Keeping my lips away from his, I warned, "Someone might see us."

"No one is around."

His hand fell from my face to join his other one on my hips. I was expecting him to try to kiss me again, but he just froze there. The only movement was our chests barely touching while we breathed.

My hands went to his shoulders. I wanted to kiss him, but I didn't want to just concede like this. So I settled for a quick kiss on his cheek. "Then let's just see how tonight goes." I threw his words back at him.

Alex smirked as he nodded, "Fair enough." We let go of each other, and I instantly regretted not kissing him when I had the chance. He grabbed my hand before gently kissing it. "Until tonight."

Without ruining the moment and saying another word I turned and headed towards the lodge to help with cleaning. I snuck one last look back at Alex who was still standing there smiling at me.

16

After dinner, it didn't take long for the red cups to start appearing in people's hands but I was avoiding going out into the common area by hiding in my room with the others.

"So..." Hannah eagerly looked at me sitting next to Sam. "Are you and Alex-"

"No." I tried not to sound too mean when I said it. Hannah just wasn't someone I was comfortable sharing that information with.

She looked at Nicole and Aly. "I thought that you guys were like a thing?"

I shook my head.

Aly quickly changed the subject, "Do you want to join in on the short shorts then?"

"Huh?"

Hannah, Nicole, and Aly all giggled as they all stood up. Each of them had on a different color of cotton sport shorts. Aly started to roll the waistband up as she explained. "It's so hot tonight so we thought that doing this would help." She rolled her shorts up as high as they could go, covering about as much of her ass as a pair of underwear would. Hannah and Nicole had done the same.

"Maybe I'll join in. I need to check something before I go out."

"Don't take too long!"

They waved themselves out of the room and shut the door behind them.

I snuck my cell phone out and sent my check-in picture to my dad. Sarah had texted:

How is camp?

How is Alex?

I sent back: **Tell u l8r**

And there was nothing from Keith. I hadn't realized that I was worried about him contacting me again until he didn't. I was ready to feel upset or annoyed, but instead I felt peaceful. Stashing my phone in my bag, I sat back down on Sam's bed.

Without looking up from her book, she asked, "Why aren't you going out?"

I groaned, "Alex."

Her eyebrows shot up as she put her book down. "Tell."

"No, I annoy you guys enough with this."

"If it's bothering you then I want to be there for you."

As I started to open up, Aly came back into the room looking upset. When I saw her gray shorts I understood why. She was blinking away tears as she grabbed a new pair of sport shorts and a pad.

"I hate being a girl."

We both agreed with her.

"After I change, you guys want to come play never-have-I-ever?" Aly asked.

"I don't know. I wasn't ready to go out yet."

"Why?"

The words just erupted from me. "I really like Alex but he wants to keep just doing what we've been doing. I understand his reasons but he said he didn't want things to be different between us now and like how can they not be? I don't know how to just casually hang out with him now that we've kissed. I don't know how I'm supposed to act when we're all out there together. How flirty am I allowed to be? If I touch him will someone be suspicious? It's stressing me out."

"Oh no, no, no." Aly shook her head. "If he doesn't want things to change between you two, then you give me a reason to make him want to change it."

"What do you mean?"

"I mean, put on your shortest shorts and go flirt. With Alex and whoever else notices you. That's what single people do."

"But I just want to flirt with him."

"It's a summer fling, Hadley, not true love. You two will have to go your separate ways at the end of camp, so just have fun and use him until then."

I sighed, "I don't know."

"Just get out there and see how the night goes!" She let herself out of the room to change.

When she was gone I turned to Sam. "That's what Alex had said. 'We'll see how the night goes.' Like how does that help?"

She sat up and put her book down, "How do you want the night to go?"

"I..." I don't know why I was hesitating. I knew exactly what I wanted. "I want to make out with Alex."

"Then let's make him want to get you alone."

"How?"

"Aly's idea. Put on your shortest shorts." I quickly changed into my black sport shorts then rolled the waistband up three times. "And switch into that blink-182 shirt. That'll get his attention!"

"Oh, yeah, that's actually a good idea."

"I have those occasionally."

I found the shirt and changed into it before looking in the mirror hanging on the back of the door. Just to see what would happen, I rolled my shorts up one more time. They disappeared under the hem of my shirt so it looked like I wasn't wearing shorts at all. This would definitely get his attention.

"So what do I do now?"

"Play it cool." Sam got up from her bunk, "We'll go outside and see how long it takes him to come over to you."

"If you want to read-"

"I do, but the book isn't going anywhere."

"Thank you." I smiled and Sam rolled her eyes. We linked arms before heading out the door.

The common room was empty because everyone was

outside. Someone had left the sliding glass door wide open so the music that was playing would carry out into the night. Together we walked into the unfolding party scene.

Sam craned to look around, "Let's find Justin?"

I nodded to where I spotted him by a bonfire.

Aly, Nicole, and Hannah were giggling with Jackson, Nate, and Henry. Aly was practically in Henry's lap as the group of them played some drinking game with cards. Henry's hand was gently rubbing Aly's thigh and she looked so happy now despite how her night had started.

Alex was with Aaron and some other counselors, including Jessica. They were all laughing about something while Alex fiddled with a guitar.

As we made our way towards Justin, he jumped up and came running over to us. "Hot damn! Is this what took you forever to come out?"

Meekly, I shrugged, "It's hot out."

I quickly looked over and saw Alex staring at me, biting his bottom lip. He mumbled something to Aaron while passing the guitar to him.

"Earth to Hadley." Justin nudged me.

"Huh?"

He joked, "You were drooling." When my hand shot up to check my mouth, he started laughing. "Let's get drinks."

We walked over to the cooler full of 'jungle juice' arriving at the table the same time Alex did. After sharing hellos, Justin started to reach towards the stack of cups.

"Allow me." Alex grabbed a new cup and started filling it. "Aaron wants a rematch in poker, by the way."

"Tell him even if he wins, I'm not giving his chain back." Justin took the cup from Alex and started drinking to hide his blush.

"What?" Sam and I both asked.

He brought the cup back down. "I'm a really good poker player, and Aaron is a sore loser who doesn't know when to quit."

Alex clarified, "We all played last Saturday."

"He actually bet his chain?" I asked in disbelief. Aaron always had his chain on. He slept, swam, and showered with it on. It must have been some poker game if he had put that on the table.

"Yeah," Alex chuckled. "Because he is an idiot." It was Sam's turn to get a cup but she held a hand out to refuse it. He nodded and handed the cup to me.

"Justin, you can't keep it!" I smacked his arm.

"I'll give it back! Just not so easily."

Alex worked on filling another cup as he said, "Make him work for it. It's what he deserves for underestimating you."

Sam asked, "Since when have you been good at poker?"

"Since forever."

"Then let's go make some money." She grabbed Justin and started pulling him away. I quickly took a big gulp of 'jungle juice' as I watched them go.

Alex and I were alone in front of the cooler as he finished filling up his cup.

"You look..." He forgot to complete his sentence and his eyes scanned my body.

"Thanks." I grinned before taking a sip.

"Do you have shorts on?"

I lifted the bottom of the shirt enough to show the shorts underneath. "Yeah, why?"

"Just...curious." His eyes darkened.

I teased, "How's the night going?"

"Much better than I expected."

"Why's that?"

His words were slow and deliberate. "Because you're wearing *my* shirt."

I chuckled, "Your shirt? This is *my* shirt?"

The energy between us was charging. Alex took a step closer to me and lowered his voice, "Maybe we should go check my room and see if it's there or if you stole it during our laundry slot?"

"Aren't you worried we'll get caught?"

His voice was almost a growl. "I don't give a fuck about that right now. I just want to..." He went to reach for me but pulled his hand back. "I want to take that shirt off you."

My lips parted as my stomach tightened.

I nodded towards the lodge. "Your room?"

"Unless you have a better idea?"

After all the worrying about getting caught, this felt risky. If anyone noticed that we both were gone, it wouldn't be a far stretch to figure out where they would find us. But I wanted this so badly, I would risk getting caught. "I can't think of anything better right now."

"Ladies first." Alex gave me a crooked smile. I knew he wanted me to go inside and he would be close behind me after a few minutes passed. If we left at exactly the same time, we'd draw too much attention.

I walked back towards the inside of the lodge draining my drink as I went. Justin and Sam shot me a look but I motioned to let them know everything was good.

From what I could tell everyone was outside enjoying the warm, summer night. It was the perfect night for being outside despite the July heat. The air was swirling just enough to keep everyone cool. The breeze even floated in through the open sliding glass door. It rustled some of the discarded pizza boxes that were stacked next to a full trash can. When I went inside, the lodge looked empty.

I scurried into the boy's hallway, hoping that I was fast enough and no one outside was paying attention to where I went. As I approached his room, I found the door cracked but I didn't want to go inside without him.

Soon Alex's silhouette blocked the light coming into the hall. My body froze in anticipation as he stalked towards me. When he stopped in front of me, his hand grabbed mine as he pulled me in the room. I closed the door behind me and Alex reached around me to lock it. Once the lock clicked, he pinned me up against the door.

His mouth was greedy when our lips collided. My fingers

tangled in his hair as I tried to keep up with his kisses. His fingers were digging into my hips, trying to somehow pull us closer together.

He pulled away but it was to make a rough line of kisses down my neck. Our ragged breaths were the only sounds we were letting escape.

When his teeth gently bit down on my neck, I let out a soft moan. One of Alex's hands shot up to cover my mouth. His wide, dark eyes were burning with a plea to stay quiet. I nodded until he pulled his hand off my mouth.

My fingers still in his hair guided his lips back to mine. His tongue was circling mine as his fingertips lingered on the waistband of my shorts.

A loud knock on the door almost had me cry out.

'Ignore it.' He mouthed.

We both tried to be as quiet as possible.

"I know you're in there!" Jessica's shrill voice was on the other side of the door.

Alex shook his head but pulled me away from the door. "What do you want?"

She tried to open the door knob. "Why is the door locked?"

He put himself in front of me, trying to keep me hidden as he fumbled with the locked door before he whipped it open. "You know it gets locked if the door shuts too hard."

"We were looking for you to start a game of-" Jessica's gaze found me. Her voice rang out, "What the fuck?!"

She stormed into the room, her blonde pony tail bobbing with each stomp. I frantically looked into the hall to see if anyone else was with her. Everyone was still outside and no one else was around to witness whatever was about to go down.

Jessica was letting the spiteful words freely flow. "Are you fucking serious? You tell me you don't want to be with me so you can bang her instead?" She was pointing her finger accusingly at me but kept her eyes on him the whole time. "You lied to me! You hooked up with me when it was convenient for you and then dumped me so you could just get with the next girl you were paired up with!"

The whole time she was yelling, Alex kept saying, "Let me talk. Let me talk. Jessica let me fucking talk!"

She clamped her mouth shut long enough for him to start explaining. He wasn't loud enough to draw attention, but loud enough I could feel the annoyance in his words. "You and I are not together so it doesn't matter if I do anything with anyone else. And why do you think I'm hooking up with Hadley anyways? Where's your proof?"

I thought about hiding further in his room, yelling back at her, or just running away from this. Instead I stood there, the same way I just stood there when my ex and his step-brother yelled at me.

Her voice got louder. "I don't need proof, everyone fucking knows it! You two have been making stupid faces at each other since camp started!"

"That doesn't mean shit." He scoffed. "We're not hooking up."

"Then what are you two doing in a locked bedroom?"

Alex groaned, before walking around me. He rifled through his bag before pulling out a small bottle. "So I could give her this." He shoved it into my hands. "Here you go. It's the vodka I owe you." His words were tense and short, but his eyes were pleading with me to understand why he was pretending.

I shook the bottle in front of Jessica to prove what she saw was innocent.

Jessica wasn't buying it, but she didn't have any fuel for her fire after that. "So, you're not, you didn't-?"

"No." Alex said through gritted teeth.

She doubled-down. "But the door was locked."

"Hadley accidentally shut it when she came in here. It locked on its own."

She looked at me and then at Alex. His hair was just messed up enough that it could have been my fingers or his own that were responsible. Nothing else about our appearance could give us away.

"Sorry." She spat back but refused to yield.

Alex turned to me. "I'll catch up with you later."

Silently, I nodded and walked past Jessica, who smacked her lips behind me.

With each step away from Alex, I could feel anger starting to cloud my thoughts. This was twice now that Jessica has sought him out when he was with me. Why couldn't she just leave him alone?

Outside most people were huddled around the fire. Aly, Sam, and Justin saw me coming, and I must've looked wild because they all looked concerned. Sam got up and walked over to me. "You good?"

Justin asked, "What happened?"

But I shook my head. I opened my mouth to speak, but nothing came out. It was taking all of my willpower to not cry or scream out of frustration.

Aly tried to change the subject, "Do you need a drink?"

I shook my head and held up the bottle of vodka.

Aly greedily took it. Her words were slurring a little as she asked, "Where did you get that?"

Sam snatched it from her hand and handed it back to me. "Alex?"

I nodded.

Justin cautiously asked, "Do you want to go for a walk?"

I shook my head.

"You're freaking us out." He pleaded. "Just tell us what happened."

I couldn't. The words weren't forming correctly.

Something behind me caught Sam's eye and she grumbled, "Oh shit."

Justin tried to stop me from turning, but I was faster.

Alex and Jessica were walking outside giggling with each other. Her arms were wrapped around his waist as they walked.

The rage that had been shimmering beneath me started boiling over.

"Hadley..." Justin carefully called my name, in an attempt to snap me out of my anger fueled haze.

I watched as Alex and Jessica sat back down in their usual spots with the other counselors.

I started to march over to them, to him.

How could he flirt with me and make out with me then just drop me as soon as Jessica was around? We were supposed to make people think we're not together, but how could he go from making out with me one minute to giggling with Jessica the next? How was this at all okay?

Justin suddenly blocked my path.

I growled, "Move."

He calmly shook his head, "You don't want to do this."

"Yes, I do."

"If you confront him, it's over."

"What's over? We're not together."

"Exactly." He folded his arms.

There it was. I'd never done any kind of casual hook up before, and didn't know how to handle myself. It hit me that Alex and I weren't anything more than friends with benefits at this point. All this hurt was because I'm getting too attached to someone that clearly didn't want the same.

"I don't want to cry."

"Then don't. We can do whatever you want tonight."

I took a deep breath then hugged him. "I wanna drink." He looked down to the bottle of vodka in my hands. I didn't want to drink it. It was just an excuse to get me out of the room, it wasn't actually meant for me. But it was mine now and it would do the trick. I twisted the top off and lifted the bottle. "Bottom's up." I took the biggest swig that I could manage and choked it down. It burned my throat but I didn't gag.

When I went to pass the bottle to Justin, about a fourth of it was gone. "Shit," He looked at Sam. "Be ready on vomit patrol."

"My favorite." She groaned. Justin chuckled and took a sip.

When I finally dared a look over at Alex, he shook his head and mouthed, 'Sorry.'

I flicked him off.

His mouth dropped open.

I'm not sure what he did next because I turned my back on him as my friends led me to the table they had been sitting at. A few of the other counselors had joined us as Sam dealt out cards for poker.

In just a few hands, Justin and I had finished the bottle of vodka.

It was still early, and despite how drunk I already felt, I didn't want to stop. The warm feeling from the booze was making it easier to forget about Alex. I was laughing with my friends, having a good time, and I didn't want it to end.

I popped up from the table, taking a minute to steady myself.

"Where are you going?" Sam raised a concerned eyebrow.

"To get a drink."

"Let's go." Justin grabbed my hand.

"No, no, I'll go."

He scowled.

"I'll go straight there and back."

"Fine." He turned back to the poker game since he was winning too much money to walk away.

I managed to walk up to the cooler, but when I tried to pour myself a drink, there was nothing left.

Suddenly, Jake came over and wrapped an arm around me. "I've got my own stash of stuff if you still need a drink."

I shrugged his arm off me. "Nah, I'm good." But then it hit me, the best way to get back at Alex was to flirt with the guy he hated the most. So, I mustered up as much enthusiasm as I could, "Actually, I could use a drink."

Jake pulled out a plastic bottle of dark brown rum from his shorts. He twisted the cap off and I heard the plastic popping from being opened for the first time. When he handed it to me, I took a long sip. After the burning vodka, the rum went down easily.

"Shit." He breathed as I handed him the bottle back. His eyes scanned me, "You're looking good tonight, Hadley."

I tried not to feel grossed out as I smiled.

He took a sip, then offered the bottle back to me. I drank just a little bit this time before passing it back. My stomach was starting to hurt.

"You know, I thought you hated me."

"I do."

He laughed, not realizing that I wasn't being coy. "You know what they say about hate and love?"

"What?"

He held up his hand, leaving just his middle finger and ring finger up. "There's a fine line between them."

To stop myself from cackling, I just shook my head.

"It's true." Jake continued, "I've had the best sex with girls who hated me."

"I'm sure there's a *long* line of those."

"You want to cut to the front?" He closed the distance between us, daring to put a hand on my hip. When I didn't pull away, he started to lean in towards me.

As drunk as I was, I knew this was too much and it needed to end.

"No," I sighed and took a step back from Jake. "But I think Aly wants to join that line."

"I know. She'll have her turn."

I took one last drink and then handed the bottle back to him. "Thanks for the drink."

He grinned, "If you need to quench a different thirst, let me know."

I rolled my eyes, grabbed a beer from the backpack, and went back outside. As gross as that interaction was, it seemed to work. As I walked back to the table, people were whispering as they looked at me.

It was past midnight when we finally went inside. I had spent the night playing games with the other high school counselors, having a great time.

We were all getting ready for bed so I went back out to the bathroom. The halls were quiet as people were either going to sleep or had left the lodge to find somewhere sneaky to hook up.

Carefully, I shut the door behind me then looked up.

Alex was leaning against the wall across from me.

I snapped at him, "Are you lost?"

He straightened and took a step closer, "Please, let me explain."

"There is nothing to explain." I walked away from him and towards the girl's bathroom.

"Yes, there is." He was following me.

I stopped just outside the door, not wanting to risk being alone in there with him. I crossed my arms as I turned to face him. "Where's Jessica?"

"Does it matter?"

"Yeah, you guys are back together or whatever."

"Says who?"

"You!" I said louder than I intended. The booze from earlier was still coursing its way through me. Alex cautiously looked around to make sure no one else was coming.

When the coast was clear, he spoke. "I'm not with Jessica."

"You came out giggling with her and sat down with her and-"

With a straight face, he looked me in the eyes and said, "I didn't do anything with her."

"Well, you told her we hadn't done anything either, so how can I believe what you're saying?"

He shrugged, "You just have to trust me."

"Yeah, I'll just blindly trust you because your tongue has

been in my mouth."

"Do you trust Justin?"

My head tilted, "Justin? What does he have to do with this?"

Calmly, he stated, "His tongue has been in your mouth."

"Oh," I scoffed. "That doesn't count."

Alex shook his head in confusion, "How does that not count?"

I couldn't tell him Justin's secret. Instead I told him the truth that he could know. "Cause we're just friends."

"Okay." He mocked.

"No, I swear, Justin and I aren't like that."

"So then why did you guys-" Alex's face lit up with understanding and his body relaxed. "Was that to make me jealous?"

I smirked, "Only if it worked."

"Well, it did." He took a cautious step closer to me.

"Good." Even if we were starting to be playful with each other again, I wasn't ready to forgive him yet. "Did you do what you did with Jessica to make me jealous?"

He shook his head while he thought for a moment. "Not jealous, exactly. At first, I was butthurt that you ditched me for Aly and Jessica basically threw herself at me. I figured, if you left, then you weren't feeling whatever I was." He breathed out a sigh. "But after talking to Aaron, I knew I fucked up. I figured I would suck it up to make it through that week and then let her down easy on Saturday and I could try again with you. But Jessica wouldn't just take no for an answer. She even threatened to fight you so I was worried what she would do if she caught us."

"So then why did you spend all night with her?"

I watched as he lowered his head, took a deep breath, and then looked back up at me. "Tonight I told Jessica exactly what she wanted to hear and did exactly what she wanted so that she wouldn't go tell any of the Hamiltons that she found us in a locked room together. I can't get kicked out of here, Hadley. I have nowhere else to go."

"What do you mean? You can just go home. It'll suck but-"

His dark eyes looked almost black as he cut me off. "No, I don't have a home that I can go to. My mom moved back to Peru to help take care of my grandma and I am not going to my father's house. Until Tech opens their dorms back up, I have nowhere to go."

The sudden, overwhelming sadness that I felt when Alex confessed that to me, was like nothing I had never experienced. I had never known what he was going through, and I never would. My mind was scrambling for a way to help him, to fix whatever I could so he didn't have to have this burden on him anymore. All I could manage was a weak, "I'm sorry."

"It's my own shitty circumstances, don't be sorry."

"But I haven't made it easy on you."

"At least you get it now."

I nodded, "I'll do whatever you need. I won't jeopardize you staying here."

Alex put his hands on my hips. "There's one thing I need."

"What's that?"

He leaned in close and whispered into my ear, "No more flirting, making out, or hooking up with other people. You're mine for the summer."

My breath hitched, "You aren't going to do anything with anyone else either?"

His lips were right above mine. "I want you and only you."

I put my hands on his chest as his lips met mine. His kiss was tender and I was ready to melt into him. But before I did, I pulled away and asked, "So we're together?"

His face was sincere as he declared, "I'm all yours."

"Good." I pulled him back into the kiss. His hands slid around my body as he pulled me in tighter. I felt how sorry he was for how the night went with each kiss. They were soft, light, and I liked how gentle he was with me.

Laughter coming from down the hall had us both pull

away. Alex took a step back from me as we waited to see if anyone was coming. A door shutting somewhere in the lodge made me jump.

"We should get to bed." He suggested and I nodded in agreement. "I'll see you in the morning for laundry."

"I can't wait."

"Goodnight, Hadley."

"Goodnight, Alex." He gently kissed me on the forehead.

Relieved that things were back on track between us, I went back into the room, and silently got into my sleeping bag. My head was spinning but I wasn't sure if it was from the alcohol or how excited I was. I closed my eyes so that the morning would come faster.

17

Sam and I walked to the laundry room together so I could fill her in on what happened last night. "Alex came and apologized for how shitty the night was. He was just trying to keep Jessica happy so that she won't say anything about us being in his room together. I wish I would've just talked to him sooner. I feel like an ass for being mad at him."

"No, you both weren't communicating right and it's fixed now." She paused and then added. "It's fixed, right?"

"Oh, it's more than fixed. We decided not to do anything with anyone else for the rest of summer."

"Well done, Hadley."

When I tried to shrug, the hangover I had made my movements slow and awkward.

Sam opened the door and revealed Alex sitting on the couch with a book called *A Storm of Swords* spread in his hands.

He looked up at me, beaming as he greeted us. Sam and I quickly started our laundry before turning to talk to him.

"How's the reading going?" He motioned to the book Sam had tucked under her arm. It was Stephen King's *It*, the biggest book she brought to camp.

"Just starting it for the first time. I wanted to read through some of his other stuff first."

"Get ready for a wild ride."

"I'll let you know when I finish it and we can talk."

He enthusiastically nodded, "Cool."

Sam turned her washing machine on and then looked at me, "Switch it for me will you? I want to make a dent in this before the kids show up." I nodded that I would before taking a seat next to Alex on the couch.

"You guys have fun!" She called back to us as she walked out.

I looked over at Alex, worried he would be upset at what Sam had just said but he just gave me a crooked smile. "I figured your friends already knew. Aaron's known since the second I saw you."

Instinctively, I looked down as my face went warm with blush. I was trying to think of something to joke back when Matt walked in and silently started his wash. Alex pretended to read while I tried to relax into the couch so my face could go back to its normal color.

Once Matt was done, he turned to Alex. "Excited for *A Feast for Crows* next year?"

"Yeah man, that's why I'm rereading this one. I forgot half the shit that happened."

"You think they'll ever do a movie?"

"Maybe once all the books are written. There's supposed to be seven."

I tried to keep up with what they were saying, but I had never read the books they were talking about.

Jake shoved the laundry room door open, making Matt and I jump. As soon as Matt realized who it was, he scurried out of the room.

Alex set the book down and leaned forward, daring Jake to do something.

Jake's eyes flashed to me before he cooly said, "You owe me for the rum I gave you last night."

Alex's eyebrows shot up as he looked at me.

But I shook my head at Jake. "I don't owe you shit. You didn't ask for anything when you gave me the drink."

His lips curled, "Next time I'll be more explicit with what I want from you."

I could feel Alex tense up next to me but I kept looking at Jake, who had started putting his laundry in the wash.

"Say it." I dared him.

"What?" Jake spun around to look at me. His eyes turned

to sizing up Alex, who had crossed his arms over his chest and was scowling at him.

I repeated, slower this time. "Say what you want from me right now."

"Nah, I'm just fucking with you Hadley." He went back to fiddling with the washer.

No, he wasn't getting out of this that easily. After all the creepy shit he has done since I'd known him, I was going to call him on it. "No, I would love to hear it. Why won't you say it now?"

He started the washer and turned to face us. "I'll tell you next time we're alone."

Alex popped up off the couch.

Jake puffed his chest out.

With his hands in his pockets, Alex slowly approached. They were almost the same height. Jake was a little shorter and a bit stockier, but Alex clearly had the physical advantage over him. He got as close to Jake as possible without actually touching him and stated, almost too calmly, "I need to switch my laundry." Jake let out a huff and stood his ground. Through gritted teeth he continued, "And you need to get the fuck out of here."

I swallowed as my eyes darted between them, unsure what was going to happen next.

"I don't need to go anywhere." Jake smiled wildly in Alex's face. "I do whatever the fuck I want here. So you better watch your fucking mouth before I send you back to where you came from."

My jaw dropped.

Alex tilted his head, "You're gonna send me back to Florida?"

Jake's face twisted as he realized his insult didn't land right. He started to open his mouth again but I snapped, "Just fucking leave."

His attention was pulled towards me. The hostility that was tensing his body relaxed as he teased, "Ask me nicely."

"Please," My voice was dripping with sarcasm. "Please get far as fuck away from here."

"You officially owe me." He started to slowly back out of the laundry room. Right when he hit the door, he looked at Alex. "She won't always be here to save your ass."

"Don't need her to."

"We'll see." He slammed the door on the way out.

Alex's washing machine buzzed. He stormed over and started throwing his clothes into the dryer with such force they were thudding against the metal drum inside.

I went to sit back on the couch and waited for him to speak first. Once his dryer was going, he turned to me. "You took a drink from Jake?"

Carefully I replied, "I watched him open the bottle."

Alex sat next to me on the couch. We both adjusted so that we were facing each other and our knees were touching.

"Did you and him..." He refused to finish the sentence.

"Never! I would rather die than do anything with Jake."

"That's not how it looked last night."

Fuck. I had forgotten that I let Jake touch me when I was drunk. I needed to be honest now. "I was just flirting with him to make you mad. No matter how hard he tries, I would never do anything with him. Especially after last night."

"Good. If he touched you, I would murder him."

"Then you'd be in jail, and *I* wouldn't be able to touch *you*."

The scowl vanished from his face. His deep brown eyes glistened as he looked at me. We started leaning towards each other.

Alex's hand was slowly but eagerly sliding up my thigh. Each inch of my skin that his fingers touched was erupting with sensation. I was telling myself that his touch was good, that I wanted it, that I didn't need to feel scared, but I couldn't help it. My brain was throwing up warning signs and confusing my body.

I think he sensed my tension because his hand froze just

at the edge of my shorts. "I can hear your heart beating."

"I'm good." My reply was a barely audible whisper. I tried to keep myself still as I watched Alex cautiously move his fingertips under my shorts.

When he moved his hand to the inside of my thigh, my hips jerked away.

His hands went up and he tried a joke to ease the tension. "I'll keep my hands where you can see them."

"No, it's not-"

He shook his head. "We can just talk. I like just talking to you."

I forced myself to push past the haunting memories. "I don't wanna just talk." Sitting up, I swung my legs around to straddle him. Before he could argue with me, my mouth covered his with a greedy kiss.

My mind was screaming conflicting thoughts at me. I tried to just focus on how good kissing him felt. I pulled my lips away from his to kiss and nip at his neck. "Fuck." He breathed out as one hand grabbed the back of my neck while the other went up my shirt.

The bad thoughts had won the argument in my mind. Even though I wanted it, my body recoiled from his touch.

He took my face gently in his hand. "You good?"

I tried to nod.

"We don't have to make out every second we're alone together."

"Oh…" That's not what I was expecting him to say. I pushed myself off of him and sat back down.

Quickly, he recovered, "Not because I don't want you, but because I want to get to know you more."

"What do you want to know?"

He softly smiled at me as he brushed my hair behind my ear, "Everything."

It felt easy to talk to him, that kind of conversation that you weaved together, nothing was forced. Alex would ask me questions about things I liked and what my opinions were on things he liked. I found out his favorite food is lasagna, but only his mom's. He played lacrosse until a knee injury ruined that dream. He wants a ton more tattoos but he needs money first, so when he is an engineer he's going to get fully tatted.

Sam opening the door interrupted Alex explaining the book he was rereading to me. She smiled wide as she asked, "How was your morning?"

"Great." I replied, sharing a look with Alex.

He asked Sam, "How far did you get?"

"Almost 200 pages."

"Holy shit! You're fast!"

Sam shrugged and pulled her laundry out of the dryer. I got up to get mine and Alex grabbed his basket too. The three of us walked out together listening to Sam tell us about what she had read.

When we got back up to the lodge, Kelly was waiting outside. "Just who I was looking for!" Her tone was a little too light.

I looked at Alex with wide eyes but his face was stoic. When we got a little closer, Kelly said, "I need to see Alex and Hadley in my office. Go put your stuff down and then come meet me there."

"Be right behind you." Alex calmly replied before Kelly got back on her golf cart.

This was it. We were both going to get kicked out of camp now. I ruined everything for Alex and he was going to be homeless.

"Relax." He whispered once we crossed into the lodge. "Go put your laundry down and meet me by the door."

Sam grabbed my arm and pulled me with her. I was going through the motions of walking but nothing was registering with me.

When we got to our room, Sam took my laundry from me before grabbing my shoulders. "It's going to be fine." She stated like it was a known fact.

"You don't-"

"No, you're not going to freak out. It'll be fine. If it was really bad, Mr. Hamilton would be here."

I nodded even though I didn't believe what she was saying. Slowly, I walked back out to meet Alex and we left the lodge together.

We had a bit of a walk to get to Kelly's office. It is in the same small building that looks like a house right at the entrance to camp. All of the Hamiltons have an office there, and Kelly's was the second door on the right from what I remembered.

Alex took my hand in his once we were far enough away from the lodge. "Just let me do the talking."

"But what if she asks me questions?"

"You're smart and a quick thinker. You'll know what to say."

"If we get kick-"

"Don't say it." He flashed a crooked smile. "If you say it then it'll happen."

His hand squeezed mine as I sucked in a deep breath.

We walked the rest of the way to Kelly's office in silence. My mind was swirling with all the different lies I could tell or truths I could spin to get us out of this mess. Alex looked like he was just going for a walk. Nothing gave away he was anxious except he would run his fingers through his hair and shake his head every few steps.

As soon as the office building was in view, we dropped each other's hands. We walked in to find Mr. Hamilton on the phone to our left and Mrs. Hamilton organizing papers to our right. We politely waved at them when they looked up at us, both smiling before returning to what they were doing.

Kelly's door was open but Alex still knocked on it to get her attention. She looked over from her computer screen and motioned for us to sit. I shut the door behind us.

The office was big enough for a desk, her chair, and two chairs in front. On one wall there was a bookshelf filled with binders and framed pictures. The wall behind Kelly was a giant collage of different letters and pictures made by campers of the years. Once we were both sitting, she started. "I called you both in here because it was reported to me that you were found locked in a room together." She waited a beat before proceeding. "As you know, Camp Odyssey policy forbids fraternizing between counselors and the consequences for breaking this rule can include being removed from camp depending on how severely the rule was broken. So this is your chance to explain to me what happened."

Alex started, "I had bought something for Hadley when I went into town and brought her in my room to give it to her."

"What did you get her?"

"Goldfish. It's her favorite snack and she ran out." I just told him that this morning when we were talking.

"Explain the locked door?"

He leaned back in his chair. "She shut the door behind her not realizing that the lock was busted."

"Room 5?"

He nodded.

She grimaced, "I keep forgetting to make Lucas fix that."

"We just keep it cracked until we go to sleep so we don't lock ourselves out."

Kelly looked at me, "Nothing inappropriate happened?"

In the sincerest voice I could muster, I replied. "Nothing at all. It was a weird chain of events."

She scanned us both before visibly relaxing, "Good, because I don't want to kick you guys out. When I got told this information this morning I had to follow up on it because that's what we're supposed to do, but I knew you two wouldn't do anything like what was described to me. Especially you, Hadley."

Alex asked, "What was described to you?"

Kelly put her professional voice back on, "It's not camp appropriate."

The corner of his mouth lifted, "Got it."

"Be careful, and keep these item exchanges out of the rooms."

"Will do." I said and Alex nodded in agreement.

"See you guys at lunch." Kelly turned her attention back to her computer screen as we saw ourselves out.

Alex released a breath once we were back on the isolated part of the path back to the lodge. "Dodged that bullet."

"Good thing Kelly likes us."

"It was Jessica."

"Obvi."

"She's the fucking worst." A hand ran through his hair. "The irony of it is that no one said shit when I was in her room or she was in mine. No one said shit when any of her friends were in rooms with guys. But she went and ran her mouth to Kelly about us."

"She told anyone who would listen she would do this."

Alex looked over at me, "How many more weeks of camp are there?"

"Five including this one."

He had a devious smile on his face, "We'll just have to find somewhere else to hang out for the rest of summer."

18

At lunch, I filled my friends in on what happened in the meeting with Kelly. None of them were shocked and agreed Jessica was the culprit.

I wasn't listening to anything Mr. Hamilton was saying as he went through the groupings for the week. Everyone second I wasn't looking at my food, I was stealing glances at Alex. We would catch each other's gaze and smile before looking at something else only to be drawn back to each other a few minutes later.

When Mr. Hamilton said my name, it brought me back to what was happening around us. When he said Justin's name, I smiled at him.

He didn't look happy though.

I whispered, "What did I miss?"

He gulped, "We're with Jake and Jessica."

"Fuck." I breathed out and looked back up at Alex. His face slackened as Aaron finished whatever he was whispering to him.

I dared to look over where Jessica was sitting with other counselors, smiling maliciously at me from across the dining hall.

"Can I ask the Hamiltons to change it?"

Sam answered, "They don't do switches without reasonable cause. It's in our counselor contract that we work with whoever we're assigned to." I didn't have a reasonable cause that I could tell them without getting in trouble too.

Justin squeezed my hand. "We'll have each other."

"Along with the last people either of us want to be with."

"It's just a week." He was trying so hard to be positive.

Aly took over the conversation, "I can't believe I get Hannah, Henry and Aaron! It's like the perfect group!"

"Yeah," Sam groaned. "And I'm with no one that I know. How do these pairings even get decided?"

"Kelly once told me that they just kind of pick names as they go. They'll put people together again if they work well together. But for the most part, it's random."

"That's annoying." Sam replied.

Aly joked, "Only when it doesn't work for you."

Aaron and Alex sat down at the end of the table. "How is it that I keep having to deal with your ass?" Aaron teased pointing at Aly.

"The Hamiltons must think we work well together!"

"Maybe I should complain about you and then I won't have to carry your shit the rest of summer."

"Shut up. You love hanging out with me." Aly stuck out her tongue.

"You okay?" Alex quietly asked me.

"Nope, but I have Justin so I'll live."

His hand went to my thigh. It was risky, but I needed the contact. Feeling his fingers swirl on my skin was grounding me and keeping me from having a panic attack.

Alex smirked at Justin, "I owe you a bottle of whatever you want for helping her this week."

"No, no, no!" Aaron wagged his finger. "Justin doesn't get shit until I get my chain back."

"You can get your chain back when you get better at poker." Justin clapped back.

"C'mon Aly." Aaron stood up. "The best group of counselors needs to start preparing for their busy week."

Aly popped up from the table and they walked out arguing about how much shit she had stuffed in her bag.

Sam blew out a sigh as she stood. "I guess I'll go make some new friends."

Alex turned to me and stated, "You got this." His hand gave my thigh a squeeze before he stood up.

"I'll miss you." I dared to say.

"I'll miss you more." He quietly replied. Justin and him shared a nod before he left for his group.

"Ready to face the music?"

"Kill me now." I rolled my eyes but stood up. Justin and I linked arms as we walked out to meet up with Jessica and Jake, who were already at our assigned cabins, sitting around the firepit.

The grin on Jake's face was the opposite of the frown on Jessica's.

"Took you long enough." She spat.

"Sorry," Justin took the lead. "Won't happen again."

"It better not." Her gaze turned to me and she looked me up and down. "At least I can keep a close eye on you now. Don't want you violating any more camp rules."

"There is some weird tension here." Jake pointed to me and Jessica, grinning even wider. "Do you two not like each other?"

"Shut up, Jake." Justin and I said at the same time.

"Go pick your bunks." Jessica snapped. "We need to go get the campers."

We split to go to the boys and girls cabin. Jessica's stuff was already on the top bunk by the door, so I put mine on the bottom bunk. My plan was to avoid Jessica as much as I could. If I stick to Justin during the day then I only had to interact with her at night. It was just six nights.

I could handle six nights.

Silently, we went to get the kids. As soon as the first camper showed up, we all put on the fakest smiles and mustered up enthusiasm that was contagious to the kids.

As we were letting them run off some energy after dinner, Justin and I sat on a picnic table watching the kids run around. Jessica claimed she had something to handle, but she just wanted to go into the cabin and talk on her phone. When I went to go to the bathroom, I caught her but didn't say anything.

Justin got up to go to the bathroom, leaving me alone on

the picnic bench. I didn't mind it though. I just watched the kids run around playing freeze tag with each other.

Out of the corner of my eye, I saw Jake strolling over to me before parking himself in my line of vision.

"This must be like your worst fucking nightmare." He smiled but I refused to look at him.

"Leave me alone."

"Or what? You'll have Alex kick my ass?"

"No," I twisted my head to look at him. "I will."

A shit-eating grin spread across his face. "Anything to get you to touch me, Hadley."

"You're revolting."

"But I'll be here all week." He suggestively wiggled his eyebrows before turning to the kids. " Let's play tag! I'm it!" The kids all screamed and scattered as Jake started chasing them around.

Justin came back a minute later. He pointed to Jake, who was pretending to get tackled to the ground by some of the kids. "It's like Dr. Jekyll and Mr. Hyde."

"I wish the Hamiltons could see the Mr. Hyde part of him. They think he's such a great counselor."

"I mean he is. He's just a shitty person."

"How can someone be both?"

Justin shrugged.

Jessica made us late for breakfast the next morning. She took her sweet time getting ready while we all waited for her. When Jake threatened to leave her behind, because no one keeps him from getting food, she finally put some pep in her step. We barely made it there with enough time to get all the kids fed.

Archery was our forest activity for the week. I wanted to shoot off some arrows with the kids, but Jessica bullied me into helping her get arts and crafts set up.

"I don't mind going!" Justin tried to volunteer for me.

"Nah. I need you with me." Jake smirked, wrapping him in an awkward side hug. "You ladies have fun!"

Jessica and I silently walked up to the dining hall. Once she was sure it was just the two of us, she didn't waste any time. "I see Kelly didn't think what you and Alex did was worth kicking you out."

"That's because we didn't do anything. We're just friends."

"Like you and Justin are just friends?"

"What do you mean?"

"You seem to like making out with your guy friends, Hadley."

"I didn't make out with him."

Her blonde ponytail swished as she shook her head. "No, you kissed him during spin the bottle."

"That doesn't count. It was a game."

"And in the corner of the lodge. What game were the two of you playing then?"

Quickly, I shrugged and continued lying. "Chicken."

"Chicken?"

"You've never played chicken? It's where you lean in to kiss and the first person who turns away loses."

"That's not..." She frowned. "You and Justin are weird."

Her opinion didn't mean anything to me. I started putting out the red, yellow, and orange paper, scissors, and glue for the campfire craft we were having the kids do.

I was hoping Jessica would just stay quiet for the rest of the set up time, but she kept going. "So then Alex?"

Letting out a breath, I turned to face her again, "What about him?"

"I know you two were doing something in that room."

"No, you don't." It came out more threatening than I intended, but she didn't balk at me.

Her nostrils flared as she stated, "He's mine."

"That's not what I heard."

"That's what he told me on Saturday." She crossed her arms like she had won.

My breath hitched.

Alex said he told Jessica what she wanted to hear so that she wouldn't run and tell Kelly what happened. What had he said to her? It didn't matter anyways, Jessica had gone ahead and tattled to Kelly.

I adjusted my tone to sound nonchalant. "We're just friends. I don't care what or who he does." The lies tasted chalky on my tongue but I couldn't say what I wanted to.

She didn't seem like she believed me, but she stayed quiet.

During lunch, Jessica just happened to be up from the table throwing something away when Alex walked in with his group. She wrangled him into a conversation before he could even look at me. I'm not sure what they were talking about, but Alex kept looking at the ground while Jessica smiled.

Justin had gone to help the kids clean up, when I felt Jake sit down next to me but I refused to look at him.

He whispered, "This must suck for you."

"What must suck?"

His lips curled at the joke I had walked into.

"Jake…"

"That you have to watch Jess try so hard with Alex. And he is just pathetically trying to go along with it."

"No, it's whatever. We're just friends."

"That's not what I keep seeing in the laundry room."

I finally turned to face him. "You haven't seen anything."

"Want my advice?"

"No."

He continued anyway, "You need to get rid of Jess."

"Isn't she your friend?"

"No, she's a raging bitch. I only deal with her because she's friends with Becky and I enjoy Becky's company." His eyebrows wiggled suggestively.

A gag escaped before I could stop it. "But how do I get rid of Jess? By making out with you so she doesn't think Alex and I are up to anything?"

"As much as I love that suggestion, I was thinking more along the lines of getting her kicked out before she can get you kicked out."

I paused a beat, considering what he had said. Getting her kicked out would end all of this. But then I would be responsible for ruining her summer and her ability to come back here next year. Was it worth it? "How would I even do that?"

"I have a few ideas."

I looked back over where Jessica was still talking to Alex. She jokingly smacked his arm and he smiled to play along. He dared a glance over to me. When I smiled at him, he barely smiled back.

Jake continued, "It's what I would do if I were you."

"I don't think I would do anything you would do."

"That mouth of yours, Hadley." He shook a finger in my face before popping up from the table. "Alright!" He clapped, turning back into the counselor extraordinaire that the kids thought he was. "One more trash sweep before we head to the pool!"

Jake got the kids chanting, 'Pool! Pool! Pool!' as we marched out of the dining room. Justin met us outside and Jess obnoxiously called, "Bye Alex!" As she came to join us. She bumped her shoulder into mine before storming up to the front of the line where Jake was.

Justin asked, "You good?"

"Jake told me I should try to get her kicked out."

"Hadley..."

"It would solve a pretty big problem."

"You don't need that karma. She'll get herself handled soon."

"Not soon enough." I groaned as we walked to the cabins to get ready for the pool.

We made it halfway through the week without any more major incidents. Jessica relaxed on her attempts to talk to Alex at every single meal time we had, but I think it was because he would quickly wave at me before slipping into the dining hall line to avoid her.

At dinner towards the end of the week, one of his kids came up to me and handed me a piece of paper. "This is for you." He extended out the note.

I peeled it off his sticky hand and asked, "What's this for, buddy?"

"I don't know." He shrugged. "Mister Alex told me he'd let me have extra dessert if I delivered it."

"Oh," I blushed and hoped no one else heard him say that. "Thanks!"

"Okay!" The kid shrugged then skipped off and joined the rest of his campmates in line. When the kid reported back to Alex, they shared a soft high five. He caught my gaze, smirking before disappearing behind the wall that separates the food line from the dining hall.

Justin leaned in close, "What does it say?"

Under the table, I hurriedly unfolded the paper. I had never seen Alex's handwriting, but it was the typical quickly scrawled letters of a boy's script:

I miss you. I can't wait to kiss you on Saturday.

Justin read over my shoulders and teased, "Now that's cute."

I had to bite my lip to try to stop the smile from forming, so no one would catch wind of what was happening at our end of the table. I reread the line over and over again before finally tucking it into a pocket in my shorts.

When Alex appeared out of the line talking to the camper who had delivered the note, our eyes met and shared a quick, but sweet smile.

Jessica's glare was boring into the side of my face, but I refused to look in her direction.

Justin dared to ask, "What if you are just honest with her? Tell her that you and Alex are a thing now. Maybe she'll back off?"

"I doubt it. She hates me."

"No, she wants Alex and sees you as being the way. Same way you see her."

"But it's different. Alex actually likes me."

"But if the roles were reversed, wouldn't you want to know that the guy you're going after wasn't into you so you could just move on?"

"I guess…"

Instinctively, I found Alex sitting down. He was animatedly pretending to drive a car to the boys gathered around him. I'm not sure what story he was telling, but they were all enraptured as they ate their dinner.

Justin elbowed me, "Just something to think about. Maybe if you or Alex let her know there was no hope for her anymore, she'd relax."

"I doubt it."

Justin and I were watching the kids run around after dinner and before lights out. We had just finished leading them all through a big singalong of all the camp songs we could think of before letting them run wild. Jake had started a football game with some of the boys. Jessica was in her usual spot in the cabin talking on her phone.

"Justin," I asked, breaking the comfortable silence we were in. "The ex you told me about, was he your first?"

He smiled but his eyes were a little sad. "No, he wasn't."

"Who was?"

"Another kid in theater who was already out when I still wasn't. He helped me accept myself. Taught me a lot." He nudged my elbow to emphasize the last word.

"How was it being with someone new?"

"It was…" His eyes bounced as he searched for the word. "Different. In a good way, an exciting way. I wanted different, or I would have stayed with my ex."

I mulled his words over in my mind.

"Why did you ask?"

"Just thinking about Saturday."

"Not thinking about your ex, right?"

"No! I blocked his number actually."

"Good! You have more important things to focus on."

Jessica came out to get everyone to come into the cabins. The conversation I had with Justin prompted me to turn on my phone, even though I had blocked Keith, I suspected he would try to reach out to me in other ways.

Once my phone had signal, 5 text messages popped onto my screen. All from Sarah.

Hadley! Keith is crazy.
He harassed me at work
Also he got fired!
He gave me a letter 2 give 2 u
Call me!

The texts were from 2 days ago. Shit. I needed to call her.

I took a deep breath before looking at Jessica. "Hey, I wouldn't normally ask but I just got some emergency texts from back home. Can I go make a phone call?"

She sneered. "We're not supposed to have phones at camp."

"Then what have you been talking into every night?"

"Fine. Go." She groaned, "And be back before lights out."

I hurried outside calling Sarah on the way. She picked up before the second ring. "Hadley! It's about damn time!"

"I keep my phone off and away. You're lucky I even checked tonight. What the hell is happening?"

"Girl!" Sarah started before I heard her take a deep breath. "Keith was livid about the shit you and Alex pulled. Kept blowing up my phone with texts and shit. Then the whole time we were at work this past weekend, he was bothering me about you. I told Alan, who of course was the only manager all weekend, and he reprimanded Keith for it."

"What was Keith saying to you?"

"Wild ass shit. He didn't show on Sunday and Alan said he had enough of his bullshit and fired him when he came into work on Monday. Keith raged and broke some of the bottles in the bar on his way out."

"Holy shit."

"Then he came by my house and tried to apologize for what he did and gave me like a letter to somehow get it to you."

"Did you read it?"

"No."

"Open it and read it to me."

I heard paper rustle and rip. There was a long pause only interrupted by the crinkling of more paper. Finally Sarah breathed, "Hadley..."

"What?" My mind was already thinking of all the different ways Keith could have written this letter.

"It starts out kinda sweet, he like apologizes for the shit from January and then...he didn't think you would move on so fast...seeing you with another guy ruined him...he hopes you haven't slept with him yet so he can still be the only one and he wants to propose when you get home."

"I hate him."

"Me too." She laughed because that's all we really could do.

"I'm sorry you have to deal with this shit while I'm here at camp."

"Don't worry about me. Dylan already said he'd beat his ass if he came near me again."

"How're you and Dylan?"

"Good! We went to a nice Italian restaurant for our 6 month anniversary."

"You guys are too cute."

"Stop it!" Sarah joked into the phone.

I heard Jessica's obnoxious cough from behind me.

"I gotta go, but I love you. I'll try to call again soon."

"You better bitch. Love you."

I hung up and trudged back into the cabin.

19

"Maybe just have them sing a song?" Justin suggested, looking around at the kids all fidgeting in the circle we made them get into. We were trying to figure out what to perform for skit night.

Jake cut into our conversation. "Have them do that one where someone is a lightbulb and gets fired and then they all leave because they can't work in the dark."

"You think that'll work?" I looked at the kids who were now in less of a circle and more of a clump.

"If you make them do a song, we'll have to come up with a dance. This skit they can all pretend to be working in a mine."

"Who should be the lightbulb?"

Jake shrugged and then walked away. He had been like this all week, useful just long enough and then would just stop. Justin and I nodded at each other then sold the kids on the idea. We picked the lightbulb and the boss who fired them then ran through the skit a few times.

We had all gathered in the dining hall for skit night tonight because the clouds outside looked too ominous for Mr. Hamilton's liking. Everyone was crowded at the tables but we managed to fit inside. We heard a crackle of thunder as Mr. Hamilton called our group to the stage first.

The kids managed to pull it off and be understood over the murmur of voices that constantly went through the crowd. When the lightbulb was fired, the joke managed to get a good laugh out of the other campers. Then our kids ran off the stage and right back to our table when they were done.

I was sandwiched between Justin and Jake against the back wall of the dining hall, trying my best to avoid touching any part of Jake. He seemed to be intentionally taking up more space than he needed. I jutted an elbow into his side, "Make room."

"There's plenty of room."

"Whatever." I huffed and just crossed my arms over my chest.

I watched Jessica saunter over to where Alex was standing with his group. She made a face when Alex said something to her then pointed back over to where we were standing.

Alex just crossed his arms over his chest and shook his head when she tried to protest. Jessica stomped her way out of the dining hall.

"My offer still stands." Jake whispered just loud enough for me to hear. "I can get rid of her for you."

My gaze was still on the door that Jessica had walked out of. I turned my head to look at Alex, who was looking at me with a slight scowl on his face. It would be so much easier for me if she was gone, but Justin was right, I would be ruining her whole summer. It didn't seem worth it. "No, I don't need you to do that."

"This is what it would be like." He nodded his chin towards Alex. "You two could just stare at each other all day without worrying if Jessica was going to snitch on you. Once she is gone, no one else will give a shit."

"I said no, Jake."

"Let me know when you change your mind." He winked and then I watched him catch Alex's gaze. The scowl that was already there deepened as they both stared each other down. Jake just smiled back at him before propping his arm on my shoulder. "You're the perfect height for an arm rest."

Aggressively, I shrugged Jake's arm off me.

Justin pulled himself away from the wall, "Stop it."

"You're right." Jake turned to look at the stage. "We should be paying attention to skit night."

Justin huffed and switched places with me on the wall. Alex's eyes darted between Jake and me for the rest of skit night.

Jessica never came back, but she was there when we brought the kids back to the cabins after it was over.

  Once all the kids were gone the next day, Jessica and I ended up alone cleaning the cabin. I had been dreading this moment all week, knowing that Justin wouldn't be able to buffer any interactions between us. There was a lump in my throat as she turned to me. "I'll sweep."

  Instantly, I conceded to her. I wanted to argue with her but I also just wanted to be done.

  Jessica took 10 minutes just deciding which CD to put in the small boom box she had in the cabin. While she did that, I wiped down all the beds. With the music going, she spent more time singing off key to random pop songs than actually sweeping. I sped through cleaning the bathrooms. After a few songs played all the way through, I was finished and locked the cleaning supplies back into their cabinet under the sink.

  Jessica was still in the same spot that I had seen her standing in when I went into the bathroom.

  "Everything else is all set if you can just finish sweeping?" I asked, shouldering my duffle bag to leave the cabin.

  "On second thought," She moved the broom towards me. "I think since you've done such a good job so far, you should take over sweeping."

  "That's not fair." It slipped out before I could stop myself.

  She sneered at me. "The longer you take to clean the cabin, the longer it takes Kelly to check us off, and the longer it takes you to get back to your *friends*."

  My duffle bag fell to the floor with a thud. Taking the broom from her, I shook my head, wanting so badly to say something, but instead I stayed quiet.

  Jessica didn't say anything as she took her shit and left.

  At least I was alone. The repetitive motion of sweeping helped calm me back down. I should've expected her to pull something like this.

After I finally finished cleaning the whole cabin by myself, I ran into Alex and Aaron coming out of the lodge as I was walking in.

"I was wondering where you were." He stopped with about a foot of space between us while Aaron kept walking, quietly laughing to himself. "Justin said you were still cleaning."

"Yeah," Then tension in my body eased. "I had to do everything myself."

"Shit, I'm sorry."

I motioned to the keys in his hand, "Where are you going?"

"Into town, really quick."

"Can I come?"

His face uncomfortably fell.

"Nevermind." I mumbled and went to walk around him.

"No," He grabbed my arm. "I'd love to take you with, but I'm, I'm getting a surprise for you."

My heart skipped. "A surprise?"

"I'll show you after dinner."

"I have to wait that long to find out?"

"It'll be worth it." Alex took a quick look to double check no one was around. Once he was sure we were alone, he pulled me in tight for a quick kiss.

When we pulled away, I bit my lip before saying, "I can't wait."

Kelly and Lucas were bringing in the boxes of pizza as the boys slipped in, carefully holding a backpack that I assumed was full of booze.

As we all grabbed our pizza, we took our usual spot sitting at the end of the table with the other high school counselors. I was sandwiched between Sam and Justin, listening to Aly tell us the story of her camper that fell into the lake while canoeing.

Sam moving her chair got my attention and I looked to see why.

Alex was pulling up a chair next to me.

He smiled when he sat down, thanking Sam.

"What're you doing down here?" I asked him after glancing down the table at Jessica staring hard at the two of us.

He cooly responded, "I'm talking to my friends." Then he turned to Aly, "Aaron told me you tried to drown a kid."

"That's not what happened!" She huffed before glaring at Aaron and then launched back into her own version of the story as we ate. Alex moved his leg so that ours were touching under the table.

As dinner was winding down, he leaned over and whispered, "Remember the surprise I mentioned earlier?"

I nodded.

"Meet me by the front of the lodge at 9."

"Okay..." I watched him go into his room sneakily smiling the whole time.

People started to get up from the table and the drinks started coming out. As the drinks started flowing, the tension that had been filling the room disappeared.

All of us girls went to our room, like we normally did after dinner. But tonight, as soon as the door was shut, I squealed, "Aly!"

"What?" She matched my frantic energy.

"Alex said he had a surprise for me and to meet him at the front door."

"OMG!" She cried out. "He's taking you on a camp date. You need to change."

After an impromptu fashion show of all our clothes, we decided on a simple black tube top dress that Aly had brought. I had to wear a bra with it, there was no way my boobs would stay up without one, so I covered up my bra straps with my hair and put on my flip flops. I quickly did my make up and straightened my hair. The whole time Aly was blasting music and we were swapping date stories and advice with Hannah and Nicole.

"Gorgeous!" Aly cooed when we were all done. "What do you think the surprise is?"

"I think we're going to the lake. That's the only spot that's worth going to."

"That's got to be it. I wonder if anyone else will be out there?"

"I hope not."

I left my room at 9 on the dot and saw Alex waiting at the front door. His face lit up as I walked towards him, his eyes scanning my body up and down. "You look…amazing."

"Thanks, you look really nice too." He had on a navy blue American Eagle polo with his tan cargo shorts and flip flops, like he had just walked out of an ad.

"I put on my best shirt for the occasion." He popped his collar with his thumb.

"I see that."

"Ready?"

I took the arm he held out. That's when I noticed the blanket under his arm and the bottle of wine in his hand. "Where are we going?"

We walked out the door together. "I told you, it's a surprise."

The sound of the ground crunching under our shoes was soon replaced by the soft grass. "We're going to lay by the lake, aren't we?"

"Damn it, Hadley." He threw his head back and groaned, but it turned into a laugh. "You ruined it."

"Sorry! I just wanted to be right."

"Well, you are." We fell into a comfortable walking rhythm. Alex always slowed his pace down when we were walking next to each other.

It was easier to get to the lake from the front of the lodge. Normally, we would have to walk all the way around the woods to get to the clearing that is the front of the lake where the shed that holds all the life jackets and the stacks of canoes was. There was a path worn through the woods that separated the lodge from the lake and it leads to the opposite side of the lake. We walked that path with a quick, excited energy and found ourselves alone at the lake.

Alex put the blanket down and we laid together under the stars. After settling in, I whispered, "This is beautiful."

"I was out the other night taking a camper to the nurse and saw the stars. They reminded me of your freckles."

I giggled, "Cheesy."

"Cheesy but true. Aaron told me about this spot. He said it was the best way to be together and away from everyone else."

"This is perfect."

Alex screwed the top off the bottle of wine he brought. "I didn't bring cups. I figured it would be easier to drink from the bottle."

I took a slow sip when he passed me the bottle. It was rich and didn't burn like I was expecting. I'd only ever randomly had wine when people offered it, but never really enjoyed the taste of it. "What kind of wine is this?"

"Cabernet? Aaron helped me pick it out. I don't know anything about wine."

"Me either." I laughed before taking another sip then handed him the bottle.

"Shit, do you even like wine? I should've asked but I wanted it to be a surprise."

"I like *this* wine."

Alex relaxed and took a long drink from the bottle.

"Did you know Aaron before Tech?"

He shook his head, handing me the bottle. I took a sip while he answered, "No, we were randomly paired roommates. It just worked out."

"So you've lived in Florida your whole life?" He took the bottle back from me.

"Born and raised."

"What was it like growing up in Florida? Did you go to

the beach all the time?"

"I actually hate the beach." He ended his sentence with a drink.

My mouth fell open. "What?!"

"Yeah," He laughed and handed the bottle back to me. "I hate sand. I don't mind the ocean, but that's fun for like a little bit and then what else is there to do?"

"Play games? Tan? Read?" I took another sip to avoid listing off more things.

"Nah, the beach gets boring. Plus we live like an hour away from the beach so it's not convenient, ya know?"

"So what did you do for fun?"

"Go to theme parks."

"That's awesome!"

He took another long sip before continuing, "But even that gets old after a while."

"I think if I could ride roller coasters every day of my life I wouldn't get bored."

"Come down to Florida and I'll put that to the test."

"You want me to come to Florida?"

"I'm not in charge of who comes into the state." We both laughed but I wanted to ask him if he thought that this, whatever this was between us, could become something more than just a summer fling. I formed the question in my head, but I didn't ask it.

I didn't want to hear the wrong answer.

Alex handed me back the bottle and asked, "What was it like growing up in Virginia?"

"Not as cool as Florida."

"C'mon," He nudged my arm. "There's gotta be something cool about it."

I drank while I thought. The wine was starting to warm my cheeks. "I mean the museums are cool."

"I do love a good museum."

"Well then you'll have to come visit me so I can take you to D. C."

"I will." He stated. I took another sip to hide the blush spreading across my face that we both knew wasn't from the wine.

The bottle was almost empty when I handed it back to Alex. He finished what was left before putting the bottle on the ground. The sound of crickets chirping was filling the silence between us as I looked around the lake. With the moon and stars there was just enough light to see the shed and canoes on the other side. No one else was out here as far as I could tell. With the wine working its way through me, I leaned in close to Alex. "Well, we're all alone out here."

He leaned in closer, "And there's no bathroom for me to push you into."

"No laundry room for people to walk in on us." Our noses were touching.

My eyes closed as he whispered, "I don't know what to do then."

"I do." I grabbed his shirt and pulled him into a kiss.

This kiss felt different. Up until this moment, there was always that layer of fear that someone would catch us, but now we were totally alone.

His body started to push into me and I lowered myself down onto the blanket. His mouth was eagerly moving mine. He took my bottom lip between his teeth to suck it just hard enough to get a moan out of me. Our lips came back together and his tongue wound into my mouth. While our mouths were busy, his hand was gripping my thigh.

Alex's fingers found the end of the dress and began to push it up. Slowly he slid up my thigh, then my stomach as goosebumps erupted everywhere his touch had been. As his fingers grazed the hem of my thong, my body shuttered and a harsh tingle of dread ran up my spine.

Before I could stop the word, I cried out, "No!"

Alex recoiled from me as panicked eyes looked me up and down trying to see what was wrong. "Are you okay?"

"I'm so sorry," Hot tears began to pool in my eyes.

"Don't be sorry, did I-?"

"No!" I cut him off. "No it's not you, it's me. I just-" As I hesitated the tears started to fall.

"Hadley," Alex brushed a few tears from my cheeks. "What's wrong?"

"It's nothing you did." My cries swelled up my throat making it harder to speak. How could I explain what had happened? Would Alex still even want to be with me if he knew?

His touch was like a light, illuminating the dark corner that was hiding the memory of what happened to me. As I grew excited and eager to experience the feeling of being with him, I couldn't help but feel like my body was tainted, and it was fucking everything up.

I started to say, "I should explain-"

Alex vehemently shook his head, "You don't have to explain anything to me."

Did he know? Was he able to guess what I was going to say without me having to say it?

He saw the confusion on my face. To help ease my panic, he took my hands in his. "I'll be here to listen if you want, but you don't owe me any explanation. I'll gladly just kiss you, hug you, even just hold your hand if that's all you want to do. We could lay here and just look at the stars and keep talking if you want. I just want to be around you."

I simply mouthed 'thank you' before hanging my head low.

Alex gently lifted my chin up. "I told you, I'm yours for the summer."

"And I'm yours." I smiled before wiping my face. A deep breath filled my body to help calm me. As I laid back down on the blanket as Alex followed right next to me. His hand found mine and he gave it a squeeze before he started rubbing his thumb up and down. This little touch meant everything to me.

I wasn't fucking this up. Alex, even without knowing everything, still wanted to be here with me. He wouldn't make me do anything that I'm not ready for. He wouldn't make me feel bad that I couldn't give him more of my body. He was completely understanding.

I looked over at him and saw he was just staring up at the stars, smiling. The sweet smile was still on his face as he turned to look at me. "Now that I'm looking at both, I think your freckles are better than the stars."

My smile deepened as I curled up into him.

20

It was getting harder to keep my eyes open as I laid wrapped around Alex. The combination of the wine we drank, the darkness of the night sky, the gentle warm breeze, and the sounds of the crickets were all making it hard to stay awake. Alex was playing with my hair when he asked, "Do you want to head back?"

I nodded, slowly popping up. Alex followed by gathering up the blanket and the empty wine bottle. We walked silently back up to the lodge where the party was still going. Instead of trying to avoid people so no one was suspicious, Alex grabbed my hand and led me through the small crowd. I immediately heard our names thrown around in careless whispers.

Alex and I were officially, publicly, unapologetically together.

We took seats on the log that Aaron and Justin were sitting at. Both of them looked surprised that we were being so bold now.

Aaron recovered quicker than Justin and simply gave Alex a pat on the back. "Want us to start the game over?"

"Sure!" He answered, "What're you playing?"

"Ride the bus."

"We need drinks."

Justin shot up from the bench. "Hadley and I will go!"

"Great idea!" I said hopping up, linking arms with Justin.

"I'm guessing your date went well then?" He asked once we were out of ear shot.

"Yeah, it did." I smiled thinking back on the time Alex and I had just spent by the lake.

"Did you guys...you know?"

I shook my head and I filled Justin in on what happened while he filled four plastic cups before walking back to the log we were sitting on. Alex doled out the cards and the drinks as we guessed correctly or incorrectly at the card on the top of the deck. He kept giving me hints as to what card it was, so I kept winning and giving out drinks to Justin and Aaron.

When we finished the game I excused myself to go to the bathroom. I had been on such a high all night, I hadn't even thought about Jessica.

Until I was face-to-face with her in the bathroom.

"You." She snarled at me as I was coming out of the stall. She had put herself right in front of the door, blocking my only way out.

Now that Alex and I had been so public, there was no denying anything. I tried to stay calm as I washed my hands. "What?"

"You and Alex are together." She took a big step towards me.

Was she about to fight me? I'd never been in a fight before, but could probably hold my own against her. "And?"

"I look like a fucking idiot because of you two."

"You look like an idiot because of yourself."

Her nostrils flared, "I am going to fucking ruin your summer. You are getting kicked out first thing in the morning."

"How?"

She scoffed, "Like I'd tell you my plan. I'm going to make sure Mr. Hamilton drags you out of here before you get a chance to do laundry."

Could she really do that? Kelly hadn't believed her last week, but maybe this week she would? We already had one complaint filed against us. "Alex and I will both get kicked out."

"No, I'm going to make sure it's just you."

I couldn't fathom how she could do that. Plant drugs in my duffle bag? Frame me for something? Knock me out and put me in a boy's bed? Whatever she was planning, she seemed confident that it would work.

"Enjoy your last night with him, Hadley, because you'll never see him again." She stomped out of the bathroom.

A numbness was starting to spread in my body. I had to stop her. Maybe I could have Alex talk to her?

I hurried out of the bathroom, bumping right into someone.

It was Jake.

"Watch it." He sounded bitter.

Jake could help me. As much as I didn't want his help, he had offered it to me. I just needed to get past my disdain for him and accept it. "Is that offer still good?"

He shifted back into his normal douchey demeanor. "Which offer?"

"The one to get Jessica kicked out."

"Oh, that one?" He leaned against the wall, forcing me to take a step closer to him. His head jerked to a room down the hall. "They're going on about you in that room. I just got kicked out so Jess could finalize her diabolical plan with Becky."

"So you'll help me then?"

"It'll cost you."

"I'll buy you whatever you want."

"I don't want you to buy me anything." The grin on his face was making my stomach turn.

Even though I was afraid of the answer, I asked, "What do you want?"

"Your panties."

The churning in my stomach stopped because it had dropped. I managed to breathe out, "No."

He shrugged, "Then I can't help you."

I scrambled to reason with him. "But this benefits both of us. Jessica will stop cockblocking you if she's gone."

"She really isn't as big of a problem for me. Eventually, Becky will ditch her and we'll go do what we do. I can hold out until then. *You* don't have the luxury of time anymore. From what I hear, Jess is going to make sure Mr. Hamilton gets you in the morning. I can make sure that doesn't happen."

Jake made it sound like he had a surefire plan. I didn't know if Alex had sway over Jessica anymore. He had tried to convince her not to say anything to the Hamiltons last week and it didn't work. If she went through with whatever she had planned, there's nothing anyone could do to stop her. Jake was the best choice and as disgusting as his price was, it was a small one to pay in order to get rid of Jessica and save the rest of the summer.

"Tick tock, Hadley."

"One condition?"

A grin erupted on his face. "Let me have it."

"No one else finds out about this, especially Alex."

He whined, "But fucking with him would be so much fun."

"No. He doesn't need to know. No one does."

"This will be our dirty little secret then."

I took a deep breath. "Let me go get-"

He held out a hand to stop me from walking away, "No, I want the ones you have on now."

My whole body slumped. I should've known he would make this as uncomfortable for me as possible.

"Just slide them off and hand them over." His hand turned over so his palm was out and ready to accept my offering.

Before the disgusting embarrassment could fully spread through my body, I carefully shimmied my pink thong down and took it off. As fast as I could, I put it in Jake's outstretched hand. His fingers curled around the fabric and he quickly put it in his pocket.

I tried to sound threatening as I said, "If she isn't gone in the morning, I'll tell Kelly you stole my underwear."

"She'll be gone by morning." He winked and patted his pocket. "You need to go along with whatever I say for the rest of the night."

What had I just gotten myself into? "What's the plan?"

"We're going skinny dipping. You need to make sure Alex is going to come. She won't come unless she thinks he'll get to see her naked." He patted his pocket as he walked outside.

Skinny dipping? *That* was his brilliant plan. I didn't think I would've come up with that, but I thought he would have something a little more creative or diabolical than that.

Quickly, I went to my room to put on new underwear and change before I went to convince Alex to go skinny dipping with me.

Sam was lying on her bed reading, barely looking up from her book as she asked, "How was the date?"

I was still flustered from my interaction with Jake, so I tried to look calm as I answered. "It was great! Alex is super sweet. I'm gonna change into comfy clothes and go back out."

She nodded then went back to reading. As fast as I could, I put on underwear and sleep shorts, then took off my dress and threw on an oversized t-shirt. As I went towards the door, I thought about telling Sam what I just did. The weight of my hasty decision was sitting on my chest. But I had to get Jessica kicked out before she could kick me out. There was no way around it. Sam might see it that way, but I couldn't risk her talking me out of it. Especially after what I had to give Jake for his help. I couldn't tell Sam or anyone else what I had done.

I said goodbye to Sam before leaving the room, passing a few people coming back into the lodge as I went out. Alex, Aaron, and Justin seemed to be seriously talking about something.

When I was right behind them, Alex said, "I'll ask Hadley, but I doubt she'll want to."

"Doubt I'll want to do what?"

"There you are!" Justin threw his hands up. "You changed?

"I wanted to be comfy." I shrugged. "What are you going to ask me?"

Justin continued, "Jake is trying to get people to go skinny dipping. Aaron and I are down. Alex said it was up to you."

"I'll go!"

Alex's eyes widened. "You want to go skinny dipping?"

"Yeah, I'm down."

He ran his fingers through his hair before shrugging. "Okay."

We started following the herd of people heading to the pool. Jessica and Becky were walking at the front of the group with Jake, passing around a vodka bottle.

Alex took my hand in his. More people were walking past us as we all made our way to the pool. Aaron and Justin charged ahead of us, deep in conversation about musicals.

"Hadley!" Aly's voice squeaked as she caught up to us. She was walking with Hannah and Henry but stopped to give my arm a squeeze. "I should've known your ass would be coming!"

I mustered up some enthusiasm. "This'll be fun!"

"We're gonna see everyone naked!" She giggled before turning back to Henry.

Alex had purposely slowed our walking so we were at the very back of the crowd. "Do you really want to do this?"

I felt like I was answering a different question as I replied, "I think so."

"Have you ever done this before?"

"No, you?"

He nodded, "A few times."

"In a pool?"

"Pool and ocean."

"So fish have seen you naked?"

He breathed out a laugh, "I guess."

Laughter and splashing interrupted us. Jake had stripped all the way down and done a cannonball into the pool. Jessica was finishing off the contents of the vodka bottle before she started to strip. Becky was already in the water. More and more people were taking big drinks of whatever they had brought with them, then ditching their clothes and jumping in the pool.

Aly kept on her bra and underwear as she jumped into the pool holding Hannah's hand.

I watched Aaron and Justin smile at each other before getting naked and jumping into the pool together.

Alex and I walked through the gates. A few people were still lingering outside the water or in different stages of undressing but most people were in the water now.

"Alex!" Jessica called from the water. Her words slurred together as she yelled, "Come in! The water feels great!"

Alex took his shirt off in one swift motion. He calmly said, "Last chance, Hadley."

I looked at the pool filling up with drunk naked bodies, trying not to linger on anyone too long. Was I okay showing everyone all of me?

Jake's eyes caught my gaze. Discreetly, he gave me a thumbs up.

This was as far as we needed to go. Now that Jessica was in the pool, Jake could take over doing whatever he planned. We weren't needed here anymore.

I turned to look at Alex, who had started to undo his belt but I put my hand out to stop him. "I changed my mind."

He was visibly relieved before buckling his belt back together. "Then let's go back."

We turned to leave.

"Alex!" Jessica called out.

I heard Jake say, "Jess, you know what you need? Another drink! Jackson! Get her another drink!"

Alex kept his shirt off and slung it over his shoulder. His hand was in mine as we retraced our steps back to the lodge.

Once we couldn't hear the noises from the people in the pool, he confessed, "I'm glad you changed your mind."

"I could tell."

"I didn't want anyone else to see you."

I admitted, "I didn't want anyone else to see you either."

He squeezed my hand and we walked in comfortable silence.

Almost everyone had gone down to the pool to go skinny dipping, and those that had stayed behind must've gone to their rooms because no one was outside as Alex and I approached the lodge.

He pulled me back to the log we had been sitting on before. His arm wrapped around me. I leaned into his chest as we both looked at the fire.

His breath tickled my ear, "You good?"

I nodded before he softly kissed the top of my head. I pulled myself as tight as I could next to him. His skin was warmer than the fire in front of us.

"Do you like absorb heat? I've never felt anyone as warm as you."

His hand started rubbing my arm. "I might feel warmer to you because you're always cold."

"Really?" I lifted my head up to look at his face.

"You are but it feels good and helps cool me down."

My head went back onto his shoulder. Sitting next to the fire with him was relaxing, but it wasn't enough to take my mind off the deal I had made with Jake. I wanted to keep having moments like this: just the two of us, completely comfortable with each other. This was why I made that deal. Alex would understand that if I told him, right?

I couldn't risk it yet. I would tell him about the deal tomorrow once it was confirmed that she was gone. But I would leave out the price I had to pay.

A huge yawn escaped my mouth and Alex laughed. "Let's get you to bed."

He walked me to my room but lingered outside the door. His lips softly touched mine before he whispered, "Sweet dreams."

"Sweet dreams, Alex." I gave him another quick peck.

He started to walk backwards away from me, holding my gaze the whole time. I was smiling watching him smoothly move one foot behind the other until his back hit the door on the other side of the lodge, he finally turned and went into his room. I sauntered into my room and threw myself in bed, squeezing my pillow like it was Alex.

21

The next morning during laundry, Alex and I filled Sam in on the skinny dipping from the night before. Everyone who had gone to the pool got back late last night and lots of people were struggling to get up this morning. Matt was leaving as we all went into the laundry room, each of us taking a washer and loading our stuff.

"I miss so much by hiding in the room." Sam chuckled as she finished setting her laundry. "Justin and Aaron made it back okay?"

"Yeah," Alex answered. "I checked on them this morning. They're just really hungover. Apparently, Jake kept telling everyone to take shots. Aaron said they went through a few bottles while down at the pool."

"Explains why Aly and Hannah were still passed out this morning." I shared a look with Sam.

"Today is going to be rough." She shook her head. "And it's CIT week."

"CIT week?" Alex asked.

"The week the Hamiltons let kids going into their senior year of high school be counselors-in-training or CITs." I explained, "They get to practice and hopefully come back next year to be actual counselors. Sam, Aly, Justin, and I did it last summer. The CITs do a lot of the cleaning and grunt work so we get a bit of a break."

"We're gonna need all the help we can get." Alex joked as we took our usual spots on the couch while Sam excused herself to go read. "CIT week is when you met Aaron, right?"

"Yeah, we got really close that week."

"You know, he told me all about you before we came

here."

"What did he say?"

Alex rested his hand on my thigh and started drawing circles with his thumb. "That you were chill, had an awesome taste in music, and liked a lot of the things that Aaron and I did. He saw you like a little sister because you kept asking him for boyfriend advice that week. He wasn't sure if you were still with that shitty boyfriend but if you were single, he thought we'd be perfect together."

My face was turning red but not from embarrassment. It felt more like a weird mix of happiness and pride. I wasn't used to feeling this so I deflected. "Aaron didn't know if I was going to be at camp. I hadn't talked to him since last summer."

"Nah," Alex leaned closer. "He knew you'd be here."

Our eyes locked and I adjusted myself so I was right next to him. The hand on my thigh glided up my body until it wound into my hair. I sucked in a breath as he pulled me into a kiss. While his lips were gently kissing mine, my hands went to his shirt, pulling him in closer.

I had just slid my tongue across his bottom lip when the door slammed open.

Alex held onto me but we pulled our faces away from each other.

"You guys celebrating the good news?" Jake chuckled before he started loading his clothes into the last empty washer.

Alex tightened his hold on me, "What are you talking about?"

"Jessica and Jackson got kicked out this morning."

We both called out, "What?" It was just supposed to be Jessica. How did Jackson get kicked out too?

"Yeah, they were passed out naked by the pool when Mr. Hamilton did his rounds at 7 this morning."

Alex finally let me go. I sunk into my spot on the couch while he crossed his arms. His tone was accusatory as he asked, "You left them passed out at the pool?"

"I'm not in charge of them. They got too drunk. I just

made sure they were far enough away from the edge of the pool so they wouldn't roll in. What did you want me to do? Carry their asses back here?"

"You could've tried to wake them up."

"I did and when they didn't wake up I made sure they wouldn't drown."

Jackson must've been trying to get with Jessica. That's why he was still with her at the pool. He had said before that he would love the chance to hook up with her. But I hadn't meant for anyone else to get in trouble when I asked for Jake's help. That wasn't supposed to happen.

Alex kept going at Jake. "Still, you should've done something. It was your idea to go skinny dipping."

"I thought you two would be happy about this." Jake looked at me and patted the pocket of his shorts. That's when I noticed they were the same shorts from last night.

Alex went to say something but I stopped him. "It's not his fault they got too drunk to function. He said he tried to help. That's all there is to it." When I dared to look into his dark eyes, there was a swirl of concerned shock in them. He opened his mouth to start to say something, but then shook his head and decided not to.

Jake grinned and finished his laundry, "Thank you for defending me, Hadley." I watched him slide his hand into his pocket as he started to walk out. "You two have fun."

Once the door was shut, Alex turned to face me. I couldn't look up at him so I just kept looking at the floor.

His voice was rough as he asked, "Why did you defend Jake?"

I needed to be honest with him. I could tell by his tone and body language he already suspected something was off. Before he assumed something worse than what actually happened, I had to let him know what I did. My eyes stayed on down while I confessed, "What happened to Jessica and Jackson isn't his fault. It's mine."

"Your fault?"

I nodded. "All week Jake offered to help me deal with her but I told him no. Then last night, Jessica threatened me in the bathroom. She said she had some plan to get me kicked out first thing in the morning. When I left the bathroom, I ran into Jake so I panicked and asked him for help. He agreed and the whole skinny dipping thing was to get her in trouble and thrown out before she could do that same thing to me."

Finally, I looked at him but he was staring at the floor now. His whole body was rigid, except his hands that were flexing in and out of fists.

Tears were starting to sting my eyes. "I couldn't let her win. I didn't want her to be able to even try whatever she was going to do."

He refused to look at me. "You should've told me when she said that shit to you last night. I would've stopped her."

"You tried to stop her last week but she still snitched to Kelly. You wouldn't have been able to stop her. Jake said could and he did."

"What did he want in exchange for helping you?"

I had to lie now. "Nothing. He said it was mutually beneficial to get Jessica out of here. She kept cockblocking him."

His jaw was clenched so tight, I could see the muscle straining.

"I'm sorry."

A few minutes passed, then he hung his head and then finally turned to look at me.

"Are you mad at me?" I cautiously asked, ready for the answer to be yes.

His dark eyes darted around my face. He took a deep breath, relaxed his body a little bit, and then said, "I'm frustrated. You should've told me about this sooner. I hate that you trusted Jake instead of me to help you take care of this. We could've figured it out together."

Those words made me feel even worse. Tears started to run down my cheeks while I focused on trying to not have a full blown panic attack. I started to curl into myself on the couch, desperate to make myself as small as I felt. Alex took another deep breath before pulling me into him. He gently kissed the top of my head then slowly started rubbing my back. His voice was soft as he whispered, "I'm not mad at you. I get why you did what you did. I just wish you didn't have to do it."

All I could manage was a nod. My crying was slowing down. After a few more minutes and some deep breaths of my own, I was calm again.

We stayed curled up with each other until our washers beeped and we got up to switch our laundry. Sam came into the laundry room with a hungover Justin to discuss the now widespread news that Jessica and Jackson got kicked out.

Justin launched into his story, "Jackson was hardcore trying to get with Jessica. Jake kept having him get her drinks, I guess to help set them up to do something that night. They did fool around a bit in the pool from what I could see. It was hard to see everything in the dark. The pool lights shut off around midnight and the whole vibe went from silly to steamy. Aaron and I left at that point with Aly and some of the other counselors that didn't want to be a part of whatever was going to happen in the pool."

Alex and I shared a knowing look.

Justin rubbed his eyes. "People were hammered last night. Aaron was the drunkest I've ever seen him. He had a hard time walking back up to the lodge. I wasn't much better than him."

"Why did everyone get so drunk?" I asked.

"Jake kept pushing everyone to do shots. It happened so fast, too fast for anyone to realize how drunk we were until it was too late. I'm surprised more people weren't passed out by the pool this morning."

I wanted to tell them what I had done but I wasn't sure they would understand. Justin was against the idea when I had told him earlier in the week. He would probably react the same way or worse if I told him how I worked with Jake to get Jessica kicked out with Jackson as collateral damage. No, this was something that they didn't need to know.

The murmur in the dining hall was quieter this afternoon. It was a mix of exhaustion and anticipation because the CITs would be arriving any minute. Some counselors looked more recovered than others. Aaron just looked like he hadn't gotten much sleep and Aly still had her sunglasses on inside.

We had just sat down with our trays of food when the Hamiltons walked in with about a dozen high schoolers behind them. Some had smiles on while others looked intimidated. Mrs. Hamilton led them through the line to get food before they all sat down at an empty table.

It was obvious that all the conversations around the dining hall had changed to discuss them.

"They look like babies." Aly said before turning to Aaron. "Did we look that little last year?"

"Oh yeah." He laughed but then winced.

"Hard to believe we're only a year older than them." Justin commented.

Once the final CIT was at the table, Mr. Hamilton clapped his hands. "Let's give a warm welcome to our counselors-in-training this week!" He started to applaud and the rest of us did the best we could. "This is always a special week here at Camp Odyssey. You all get to help shape and influence what will hopefully be next year's camp counselors. I know that all of you will do an excellent job guiding and teaching them everything they need to know!" He paused and shifted his stance and his tone. "We, unfortunately, had to let some counselors go this morning. It shouldn't have too much impact on the way we're running things this week. We'll continue to combine the teen group together at the lodge. The CITs will help fill in any gaps as well. I just want to emphasize that Camp Odyssey is about having good, *clean* fun. I know it's exciting being away from home with people you are close to, but this is still a camp for children. I expect all of you to act appropriately at all times, even if myself or the campers aren't around."

Everyone started to look nervously at each other.

Alex moved his leg closer to mine.

"Now that we've cleared that up. Let's discuss who is paired together this week. This time, when I call your name, stand up so that the CITs can see who they are with. CITs, you all stand up too."

Mr. Hamilton started reading out the names. People were popping up and down and waving to each other as their name was called. Justin and Aly were called together for the youngest group. Sam and Alex were together for the 10-11 year old group. Then Aaron and I were called together for the 12-13 year old group along with Nick and Ashley, who I hadn't worked with yet this summer. Our CITs were a short, blonde boy named Connor and a perky redhead named Megan.

Aaron gave me a high five when our names were called.

When we sat back down, I turned to whisper to Alex, "If I can't be with you, Aaron is the next best thing." He brushed his hand against my leg.

"Now," Mr. Hamilton waited until we were all focused back on him to continue. "The expectation is that the CITs do the same work as a counselor, but not all the work. You are all still in charge and responsible for the campers. They are learning from you, not doing everything while you kick back and relax. Once you are finished eating, get together with your group and head over to your assigned cabins. Make sure the CITs feel ready before the campers arrive." Mr. Hamilton turned to face the CITs. "You are all going to do great. Come see me or Mrs. Hamilton if you need anything." With that he walked out of the dining hall.

"That's the same speech from last year." Sam noted before eating the last bite of mac and cheese.

"It's the same one every year." Aaron quipped. "You ready, Hadley?"

"Yeah," I turned to Alex. "Miss you this week."

He squeezed my thigh before letting go. "I'll miss you too."

Aaron pretended to gag as I stood up. Alex rolled his eyes before turning to Sam. Justin and Aly were already up and on their way to their group.

"We've got some catching up to do this week." Aaron nudged me with his elbow.

22

I felt like I had hit my stride as a counselor now that the CITs were here. Megan seemed to hang on my every word, but that had a lot to do with Ashley not being very helpful. Despite what Mr. Hamilton said about not making the CITs do everything, Ashley kept getting annoyed when we asked her to help out. Her reasoning was always, "It would only be the two of us normally, so why can't just the two of you do it now?" Megan and I stopped asking for her help after the fifth time she'd said that.

With Megan attached at my hip, it's been hard to talk to Aaron. I finally managed to get some alone time with him when Megan and Connor started a big game of Red Rover with the kids.

Aaron motioned to where Megan was laughing in line with the campers. "She reminds me of you."

"Really? Was I this clingy?"

"Yes and no. All day long you were so into doing all the camp things, but as soon as we got back to the cabins, you were all about your boyfriend."

I shook my head, "What a waste that turned out to be."

Aaron paused for a beat and then said, "He fucked up."

"He did." I started to fiddle with the friendship bracelets on my wrist. There were five now, one for each week of camp, with a sixth one soon to be completed.

He spun the bracelet I had made him around his wrist. "I find it helps to talk to people you trust about it."

"Did Alex tell you…" I let my question trail off.

"No, Justin did that night you had your panic attack. He said it was about something your ex did. That's all."

I could trust Aaron enough to tell him a very abridged

version of my trauma. "Something bad happened to me in a bathroom. That's why I freaked out."

"He'll understand, you know that, right?"

Quietly, I admitted, "I don't want him to think differently of me."

"He won't." His watch beeped, so he stood and shouted, "Alright, it's time to get ready for bed." He turned back to me, "Just think about it. Telling him what happened could help." Aaron gave me a smile and a soft pat on the back before heading to his cabin.

As I walked to mine with Megan and the girls, I mulled over Aaron's words. I should just tell Alex. He would be understanding of it and it would help explain why I kept freaking out every time we touched. But how could I bring it up? It's not something you just naturally weave into a conversation.

While lying in bed, I kept thinking of different ways to tell Alex and what his reaction would be. I just needed to be open and vulnerable with him.

After talking about him with Aaron, I missed Alex too much. I usually saw him for a quick moment when we were leaving the dining hall while he was bringing his kids in. All we had time for was a wave. Saturday was too far away and I needed more than a wave to get me through. During arts and crafts that morning, I thought of a simple plan and wrote a quick note that said:

I miss you. I can't wait to have you all to myself.

Ashley called for everyone to start cleaning up and taking their dirty dishes to get washed. Just as the last camper got up from the table, I *accidentally* spilled my cup of fruit punch all over the table.

"Sorry!" I squealed, as I looked over at Ashley just as she started to groan. "I'll clean up and I'll catch up with you guys back at the cabins."

Ashley huffed away as I grabbed paper towels to start cleaning up. It really wasn't that big of a spill, but it gave me the little extra time I needed to wait for Alex.

I didn't even have to search him out. As I was putting the soiled paper towels in the trash can, he came up behind me. "Everything okay, Hadley?"

"Yeah!" I jumped a little at his voice. My hands fumbled to pull out the note that I had tucked into my shorts before holding it out for him. "Here."

He did his best to hide a smile as he took the note from me and stashed it in his pocket. I left the dining hall and quickly caught up with my campers, still buzzing from being so close to Alex after a few days without him.

At the end of the week, the campers went home and everyone seemed to be more relaxed as we went through our usual routine. Cabin clean up was a breeze and dinner was full of laughter. This felt so normal now.

After dinner, Alex grabbed us both drinks before we sat down in his usual spot with Aaron. Justin and Sam joined us after Aly ran off to go play a drinking game with some of the other counselors.

Alex and Aaron took turns passing a guitar back and forth playing songs for us to guess. The person who guessed right got to give out a drink, and if anyone guessed wrong they had to drink. I knew almost every song they played, but Justin was quicker to yell out the song name.

Aaron had just finished playing a song when Aly came over to us. "Who wants to play truth or dare?"

Sam popped up from the log, "That's my cue to call it a night."

I looked at Alex who subtly shook his head at me. Smiling, I told Aly, "We're good."

"I figured you two wouldn't want to play." She rolled her eyes and walked off with Justin and Aaron.

Alex leaned in to whisper, "We can play our own game of truth or dare." He stood up grabbing the blanket that was on the ground.

"Did you have that all night?" I took his extended hand.

"Yeah, I was waiting for the right moment to sneak you away." With a crooked smile, he squeezed my hand as we started walking towards the lake.

We set up in the same spot as last time, cuddling next to each other. He didn't move any closer or try to touch me beyond the hand he had wrapped around my shoulder. There was an uneasy feeling building between us and I knew it was my fault. Aaron was right. I needed to just tell him what happened, but how could I bring it up?

"You still want to play truth or dare?" I asked.

"Sure," He smirked. "Truth or dare?"

"Truth."

Alex asked, "Which one of your siblings is your favorite?"

"A tie between Emmy and Mikey. John was but now he's too moody. Unless he needs a ride somewhere, he just ignores me."

"I've always wondered what it's like to have siblings. My cousins are the closest thing I have, but I know it's not the same. Sounds fun though."

"It can be." I shook away the thoughts of my siblings that were changing my mood. "Truth or dare?"

Alex answered, "Truth."

"Tell me a secret."

He twirled one of my curls around his finger while he thought. "When I was five, I broke my grandma's fancy vase my grandpa had bought her in Italy. I knocked it over while I was pretending to be Raphael from *Teenage Mutant Ninja Turtles* but blamed it on my cousin. He got his ass beat because of me but I never owned up to it. To this day my grandma still thinks it was him. She reminds us of it every time we visit her in Peru."

"So no one knows the truth?"

"Nope," He chuckled, "And if word gets out I'll know you

snitched."

I giggled, "I would never."

"You better not." His smile softened. "Truth or dare?"

"Truth."

He cleared his throat before asking, "What's something you want me to know?"

Here it was, the perfect chance to let Alex in. We both looked into each other's eyes, anticipation filling the space between our bodies. "I want you to know what happened to me."

He shook his head, "I didn't mean you had to share that, Hadley."

"No, I need to, I just, I need to finally tell you what happened."

He nodded, keeping his eyes locked on me. But I couldn't meet his gaze while I trudged through my trauma, so I looked down at the blanket and started pulling at the fraying strings. Taking a deep breath to settle myself, I started. "It was back in January. My parents had finally bought me a car, so my ex and I made a plan for me to sneak out, drive over to his house, and hang out. I accidentally fell asleep, then woke up panicking at like 4 in the morning, and was rushing to get out of the house so I could drive back home before my parents woke up. I had to use the bathroom real quick and when I opened the door to leave, his step-brother was waiting. He shoved me back in and-" The knot in my throat was suddenly too hard to speak through, so I took a minute just to cry.

Alex started rubbing small circles into my back.

I steadied my breathing before continuing, "He shoved me back into the bathroom and locked the door. He had me pushed up against the bathroom sink. I was frozen but felt his hands grope and touch all over me. He kept telling me he had been wanting to do this for months and my ex didn't need to find out. It took me a moment to realize what he meant then I tried to push him off of me. He wrestled me to the ground and got on top of me. He even managed to get my pants off and..." My voice trailed off as I realized I couldn't say the ending to that sentence out loud.

Alex's hand was rubbing up and down my back now. I tried to focus on matching my breaths to the pattern of his touch. "I didn't know what to do. If I screamed then I might wake up his parents, but he wouldn't listen to all the ways I was saying no. I kept fighting him, and when he was adjusting himself on top of me, I managed to get out from under him. As I went for the door, he grabbed my hips and pulled me on top of his half-naked body. That's when my ex opened the door. He looked down and saw me with my pants down on top of his step-brother and just assumed the worst."

I shivered at the memory of my ex's face going from half asleep to full of rage. Alex took his hand off my back and started to look at the lake. "He pulled me out of the bathroom by my hair. His step-brother kept saying that I came onto him and it was all my idea. I was kicking and struggling, so my ex snatched me up and carried me to the basement door I had used to sneak in. He whipped the door open and literally dumped me onto his back lawn. I'll never forget how he looked at me and said, 'I always knew you were a fucking whore.' Then he slammed the door in my face."

The tears kept flowing as I groaned. "My pants were still around my ankles so I pulled them up and moved as fast as I could away from his house. My shoes were still in his house so I walked barefoot out of his yard and down the street where my car was parked. Thankfully, I had my keys in my pants' pocket so I could drive. But I was barely able to make it home because it was so hard to see the road while crying."

I dared to look over at Alex, whose whole body was tense. His gaze was on the water, his arms hugged his legs, with wrists crossed, and his knuckles were turning white from being held in tight fists. I knew this would be upsetting for him to hear. I put my hand on his arm to feel the warmth of his skin on mine. He looked down at my hand then back up at me. "Did anything ever happen to those pieces of shit?"

My head felt light as I shook it. "No, I couldn't even tell

my parents what happened because then I had to admit I snuck out. So I just went into my room and cried until I fell asleep. In the morning I just pretended like nothing was wrong."

Alex waited a beat, flexed his fingers out of the fists they were in, then asked, "Your parents had to know you were upset?"

"I think they did. They kept checking up on me so eventually I told them that I broke up with my ex. They never liked him and they were so happy that I was completely done with him that they took me out to dinner to celebrate." I had to laugh at the absurd ending to this traumatic story.

His hands ran through his hair, "That is fucked up." I could tell he wanted to say more, but didn't. "I'm sorry you had to go through it alone."

I shrugged while wiping away tears. "I had my best friend, Sarah, and she helped me through a lot of it. I really thought I was over this but I haven't done anything with anyone since so I'm, I don't know, I'm broken."

"You're not broken." He paused then squeezed my hand, "Your ex is the broken one. I know it's easy to blame yourself when shitty things happen but some people are just shitty and that isn't your fault."

My gaze went to the ground. "But it's still affecting me, us. I was never like this before, it's like he ruined me."

He gently lifted my chin with his finger until I was looking into his eyes, "I didn't know you before, but the you in front of me right now isn't ruined. You're a survivor, Hadley. This shouldn't have ever happened to you, but you survived it. Do you even realize how strong you are?"

"I'm not-"

"Don't you dare say you're not strong."

I swallowed my words.

"You are." His hand moved so his thumb could stroke my cheek. "You are, Hadley."

His words swelled in my heart. Tears welled in my eyes, but they were different this time. I felt relieved that Alex knew everything and he understood me better because of it. With a shaky voice, I whispered, "Thank you."

My whole body felt like jelly so I leaned into him for support. He laid us down onto the blanket, then kissed the top of my head. I snuck my hand up his shirt, placing it right over his heart. I could feel it beating a little faster because of my touch.

My heart started thumping as I confessed, "I want to give you more."

His hand gently landed above my heart, "We can work up to more."

I nodded, closing my eyes and snuggling into the crook of Alex's arm.

The sound of birds chirping in the trees woke me up. When I opened my eyes, the world was sideways and bobbing up and down. I panicked before realizing that Alex's chest was moving my head.

Then I started panicking for real.

I sprang up, "Oh my god!"

Alex starled awake, "¿Qué pasó?"

"We slept out here all night!"

He looked around and chuckled, "I guess so..."

"What time is it? We have to get back!" I started to get up but he gently pulled me back down.

"Relax. It's only 5 am, we have plenty of time." I started to stand up again but Alex kept pulling me back to him. "You can't walk into the lodge like this. Just breathe." I mimicked how he was slowly breathing. "Good. We'll quietly sneak back in, get in our bunks, and no one will ever know."

Now calm, I stood up. Alex followed and folded up the blanket into a bundle that he stowed under his arm. His hand slid into mine as we started walking back.

"I can't believe we fell asleep like that."

He squeezed my hand, "That was the best sleep I've had

in a long time."

The sunlight was just starting to give the world color so it would be hard for Alex to see the blush eruptings into my cheeks.

When we got to the lodge, Alex slid the door open and we silently tip-toed inside. He gave me a quick kiss on the lips before going to his room. I decided to stop by the bathroom before I went to mine.

In the bathroom, I heard muffled sobs coming from one of the stalls. I tentatively asked, "Hello?"

A voice I couldn't quite place called back, "Who is that?"

"It's Hadley, who is this?"

"Rachel." There was a pause and then she added, "Are you alone?"

"Yeah...are you okay?"

I heard her stand up and unlock the handicap stall at the end. "Come in."

When I walked in I saw her hunched on the toilet seat but she wasn't using it. Based on the jumbled pile of toilet paper on the floor, she had been crying for a while. "What happened?"

She shook her head.

Something was very wrong. "What can I do?"

"I don't know. I didn't want to wake anyone up."

"I can go get Kelly, if you want? She usually knows what to do."

Rachel nodded and grabbed some more toilet paper as her sobs picked up again.

"I'll be right back. I have to go get the radio."

She just nodded.

Quickly but quietly, I went searching for the radio. It was charging on the mantel above the fireplace in the lodge. I quickly set it to 5, Kelly's channel, before pushing the button to talk. The crackling of the radio turning on was loud enough to echo in the empty common area. "Hey Kelly?" Was all I could think to say. I didn't hear anything for a solid minute.

I thought about calling again when I heard a groggy voice

from the other end, "This is Kelly."

"There is a situation at the lodge."

She seemed more alert, "Who is this?"

"Hadley..."

I heard a door open from somewhere down the hall and Kelly quickly emerged wearing a t-shirt that was two sizes too big for her. "What is it?"

"It's Rachel. She's in the bathroom."

Kelly stormed over there. I wasn't sure if I should follow her in or I should just go to bed.

Cautiously, I poked my head into the bathroom and heard Rachel sobbing and Kelly reassuring her, "You're okay. You're safe"

"No," Rachel protested. "I'm not safe here."

"Why not?"

"I don't want to talk about it."

"Anything you tell me will stay between us."

"I just want to go home. Just get me home."

"If you tell me what happened I can help you."

"No, you can't. Just help me get home."

"Okay, let me start getting everything ready. Do you want to start packing now or do you want to wait until everyone goes to breakfast?"

"I wanna wait."

"Well, you can't wait in here so let's get you into another room."

Rachel nodded and started to get off the toilet. Quickly, I pulled my head back out then snuck into my room. As I shut the door, I heard Kelly's voice again but couldn't make out what they were saying.

23

I managed to sneak into my bunk and get a few hours of sleep before Aly woke me up. "We were worried sick about you when you didn't come to bed! I asked Aaron and he said Alex wasn't in his bed either."

Meekly, I responded. "Sorry, we fell asleep by the lake."

She smacked my arm. "Well, be careful next time. Or let one of us know. You probably could've just gone to Alex's bed now that Jessica is gone."

"That's where Aly was last night. She was in Henry's bed." Sam gave her an accusatory look.

I cried out, "Aly!"

"What?!" She protested with fake outrage.

"Did you guys…?"

"No." Her voice was hard. "I told you, I want my first time to be romantic, not on some camp bed or in the woods. I want to be in love with the guy I lose it to."

"So you don't love Henry?"

She pretended to gag. "No, I like him, and I *really* like making out with him, but there's no point in anything beyond that when camp ends and we'll go our separate ways."

"I get that."

"What are you and Alex doing?"

"I don't know." Which was true, we hadn't talked about it. I knew what I wanted, but that didn't mean it would work out that way.

"What do you mean you don't know?"

"We're still figuring it out."

"You guys only have a few more weeks."

I groaned, "Don't remind me!"

Sam and I grabbed our laundry and left Aly in the room. Alex was already in the laundry room when we arrived.

While we started our laundry, I filled them in on what I saw in the bathroom this morning. "I'm not sure what happened to Rachel, but I think it's safe to say she left camp." I plopped down on the couch next to Alex.

Sam sighed, taking the chair next to us. "We'll find out when Mr. Hamilton reads the names off at lunch."

"Did you guys know her? I hadn't worked with her yet."

Alex said, "All I know about Rachel is the little bits from when I worked with her at the beginning of the summer. She's nice and plays softball."

"Was she hooking up with anyone?"

"I don't know anything about who she was hooking up with or anything. I thought she was one of those waiting-until-marriage girls so she wasn't hooking up with anyone. No one really tried anything with her either. Why do you ask?"

"I think someone did something to her." I quietly confessed.

Sam and Alex shared a look then turned to me. He cautiously asked, "Why do you think that?"

"When I saw her this morning, I knew what she was feeling." I recognized that look in her eyes. She wanted to be out of her own skin and far away from here. It was the same way I had felt six months ago.

Alex took my hand in his. "You should tell Kelly what you think."

"And say what? I think something like what happened to me also happened to Rachel? I have no proof and no idea who it could have been. Plus, I think she already has an idea of what happened based on what she was saying to her, even if she was refusing to tell Kelly anything."

Sam hopped up. "Let me go see what Justin and Aly know. Word should've gotten around by now."

We waved her out and then I turned to face Alex, whose eyebrows were furrowed with concern. "You okay?"

I nodded as he started stroking my hand with his thumb. His touch was comforting and now that he knew the extent of what I had gone through, it felt good to be able to talk to him about it. "Just sucks because someone is going to get away with something awful because Rachel can't say what happened to her. It's hard admitting shit like this."

"I know."

"What do you mean?"

"I know what it's like to have something shitty happen and not be able to talk about it. My-"

Matt came through the door, stopping Alex. He gave us both a quick smile, dropped off his clothes, and left.

Alone again, I turned to Alex to see if he was going to pick the conversation back up. He ran his fingers through his hair before stating. "My father abused my mom and me." I couldn't stop my eyes from going wide, but Alex squeezed my hand and I blinked to adjust them back. "I'm not trying to overshadow what happened to you, I just want you to know that I get it."

I cautiously asked, "You and your mom?"

"Mostly my mom." He shrugged. "But I wasn't spared from his drunken bullshit. He did awful things to us for years and was really good at bruising us in places that weren't obvious. I thought it was just how fathers are. Until I got old enough to realize that it wasn't. Then a few years after that I realized that I was bigger than him and I could fight back. So I did. I beat the absolute shit out of him then left with my mom."

"How old were you?"

He swallowed. "14."

"Alex..." I squeezed his hand because I didn't know what to say. No words felt right.

"I got my mom away from him and into a better spot in life, so it all worked out." He smiled but it didn't reach his eyes.

I let go of his hand and wound my arms around his neck, pulling him into the tightest hug possible. He rested his head in the nape of my neck, putting his arms around me. We just held each other until the washing machines beeped.

He pulled himself away from me just enough to look up at me. "We should switch that."

"We should."

But neither of us moved to get up. Holding him just felt right, safe. While neither of us knew exactly what the other had gone through, we both had been deeply hurt by people who supposedly loved us. We'd both been vulnerable with each other and it was making this connection we had deeper.

"Okay, I didn't get-" We whipped around to see Sam walking in but stopping when she saw us. "Really?"

We all shared a laugh as Alex and I detangled ourselves.

I started getting up to switch my clothes. "What did you find out?"

We all maneuvered around each other as we made the switch from washer to dryer. "Nothing really. Rachel didn't tell any of her friends what happened. They just woke up and she wasn't in her bed. Apparently she had stayed up late flirting with some of the other counselors but was fine when everyone else went to bed. When they came back from breakfast, all her stuff was gone."

"Damn." Alex said starting his dryer.

"She didn't tell anyone?"

"Nope." Sam shook her head. "I even went by the clinic again, pretending to need a bandaid for someone. Rachel wasn't signed into the clinic. So whatever happened to her wasn't enough to warrant medical attention."

I said, "Someone knows what happened."

"Yeah," Alex replied, "But we'll never get that person to fess up to it."

At lunch Mr. Hamilton addressed us all, "I want to thank all of you for being so flexible. We'll manage as we always do when unexpected changes in staff happen. We'll have Kelly step in to make sure our groups can still run smoothly this week. Just make sure you all are keeping a diligent eye on everybody and everything. We're going to do our best to make sure all our campers and staff feel safe and have the best time, but it's a team effort to make the whole operation work."

I squirmed in my seat.

Alex moved his hand so he was rubbing my thigh.

Mr. Hamilton read off the groups, Kelly being added to the teen group. When Mr. Hamilton called out my name with Aly, Alex, and Justin, I had to look around to make sure I heard it right.

Aly was grinning so hard I thought her teeth would crack.

Justin whispered, "Thank god. I needed a break from other people."

"This is perfect." Alex whispered in my ear.

"Literally perfect."

Once Mr. and Mrs. Hamilton left, everyone started to gossip about why Rachel had left. We all did so carefully, because Kelly seemed to whip her head towards anyone that said Rachel's name. No one knew anything though. She hadn't told anyone what happened to her.

When we were done with lunch, Aaron and Sam trudged off to their groups, while Aly, Justin, Alex, and I grabbed our stuff and made our way to our cabins.

"Hadley, you can take the top bunk!" Aly was too excited as Alex plopped her giant duffle bag onto the bottom bunk. "And thank you for your help, Alex!"

"It was no trouble." Alex said, moving his arms to shake the tightness out of his muscles.

I threw my duffle up onto the top bunk then followed him out of the cabin. He smirked, stopping by the fire pit. "Go get ready."

"I just need to change my shirt."

He gave me a quick peck. "I need *you* to make sure Aly is ready on time."

I rolled my eyes and went back to the girl's cabin, where Aly was in the bathroom making sure her hair was still pin-straight. "You two make me want to barf, you're so cute."

"Thanks, I think." I chuckled and changed into my shirt.

24

That first night the kids had organized themselves into boy and girl teams to play a very intense game of flashlight tag. Alex captained the boy's team and I was in charge of the girl's.

"You all can hide first." Alex flipped the flashlight in his hand. The boys all tried to copy him, most of them dropping their flashlights on the ground. Justin laughed behind them.

"You're on." I turned to face the girls.

"Eyes closed boys!" Alex said behind me.

We walked a few feets away from them to strategize. "Okay, you guys need to find good hiding spots. You can't leave this area." I pointed to the thin layer of trees that separated our cabins from the others. "No going into other campsites or the boy's cabin. Everything else is fair game. Get creative and if you can climb trees, do it."

"One!" Alex's voice boomed.

"Run!" Aly shrieked and the girls scattered. The sound of giggles was drowning out Alex's loud counting. I watched almost all the girls going straight for the trees. A few went into the cabin, and one even tried to hide under the picnic table.

"Nine!" Alex was almost done counting. I ran around to the backside of the boy's cabin and sunk myself into the shadows.

"Ten!"

A chorus of 'found you' and 'stop' started to fill our campsite as the boys spread out to search. I didn't dare peek around the corner of the cabin to see where anyone was. I was hoping my unconventional hiding spot would keep me safe long enough to win.

"There's a bunch of girls in here!" Justin yelled from what

sounded like the girl's cabin. Muffled giggles and taunts were mixing together then it faded into whispers.

A stick crunched behind me and I turned my head just enough to see who it was.

Alex was standing on the other side of the cabin, pointing his flashlight into the woods.

"We're just missing Hadley!" Justin called out.

My breaths were silent but I could hear my heart pounding.

The light from the flashlight started moving closer and closer to me.

I sunk myself as deep into the shadows as I could. My body was flat against the cabin's wooden wall when the light caught my shoes.

"Gotcha."

The light moved up my body but before it got to my face, he flicked it off. As my eyes adjusted, I could barely make out Alex's silhouette stalking closer to me.

He pinned my body against the wall with his hips. Without saying anything, he kissed me.

I pushed him away, "There are campers around."

He smirked, "They're all sitting by the bonfire with Aly and Justin. You were the last one to be found."

I grabbed his shirt and pulled him back to me. We shared one more desperate kiss before he pulled away. "Found her!"

The boys cheered as we rounded the corner of the cabin together and saw all them high fiving each other.

I snatched the flashlight from Alex's hand. "Your turn."

"Boys, hand over the flashlights." They groaned but handed them over to the girls, who all looked ready to hunt them down even faster.

Justin gave Aly his flashlight. I nodded at her. "You count, you're louder. Girls, eyes shut!"

She shouted, "One!" The boys pushed each other out of the way to get to the woods. I laughed before shutting my eyes.

Alex's body was right next to mine. I recognized the

smell of his Old Spice deodorant. He whispered, "You'll never find me."

"Five!" Aly screamed.

I whispered back, "I will if you don't hide."

His chuckle hit my ear and reverberated through my body. I could sense him move away to hide. Aly finished counting and we were quiet as they spread out looking for the boys.

The girls almost immediately found the ones who hadn't really done that good of a job hiding. Aly stayed by the firepit to watch them while the rest of us kept looking.

They spread out into the woods and I checked all around both of the cabins.

Alex was going to be hard to find.

I looked up in the trees and we found a few boys hiding up there. Then I took a few girls with me to check inside the boys cabin.

Justin did a quick count. "All the boys are here. Just missing Alex."

"Wait here." I groaned, returning to check the cabins again. I slowly made my way around them, swinging my flashlight all around to see if I caught a glimpse of his burgundy camp shirt.

I was turning the corner behind the boys cabin, when he grabbed my shoulders. "Alex!" I quietly chided him as his arms wrapped around my waist.

He nuzzled into my neck, "Told you that you wouldn't find me."

"I found him!" I shouted and pushed myself away from him. "You win."

He looked so proud of himself that I couldn't help but smile. We walked back to the bonfire where the campers were all cheering for him. I asked, "How did you do that?"

"I just kept moving around." He shrugged as his watch beeped. "That's 9:30."

"Time for bed!" Aly shouted then led the girls into our

cabin.

"I'm going to call lights out." I told Alex. He nodded before walking to the boy's cabin.

The girls were going on about the game we had just played while they changed into their pajamas and took turns in the bathroom. When the clock in the cabin hit 10, I went outside to double check that everyone was inside the cabin and the fire was out.

Alex was standing by the now put out bonfire, kicking a little more dirt over it. He looked up at me as I walked closer.

I bit my lip before admitting, "We need to be careful this week."

He nodded, "I know. I just can't help it…"

"Same, but we only have a few weeks left. We can keep our hands to ourselves until Saturday." I laughed at my attempt at a joke but he didn't.

Alex's dark eyes looked at my mouth, "It's not our hands that I'm worried about."

My stomach tightened at his words. "The campers can't see anything. Justin and Aly can cover us for a lot of things but if the campers see and we get in trouble…"

He shook his head and ran his fingers through his hair. "I'll do better. I just can't think right when you're around me, but I'll control myself."

I had to look away as heat was spreading through my body and I started to blush.

His hand reached out and grabbed mine. "Goodnight, Hadley."

"Goodnight, Alex." He let my hand go before we walked back to our cabins.

At high ropes the next day a couple of the girls were whispering as we were all getting our harnesses on. I kept hearing them say Alex's name but couldn't understand what exactly they were saying. As we went through the high ropes course, they kept pointing at him and fanning their faces.

"Remember being that little and having a crush on an older guy?" Aly nudged my elbow while we were waiting on the final platform together.

"Oh yeah, I had a huge crush on Brad when we were 12."

"I remember Brad! He was def crush worthy! I wonder what he's doing now..."

"He was 7 years older than us."

"So?"

I rolled my eyes. Aly took her turn ziplining down and I followed her.

Once everyone was back on the ground, we took off the harnesses and helmets before making our way to lunch. Alex and I were walking next to each other when one of the girls came up to him. "Mister Alex, do you have a girlfriend?"

Alex smiled, "Yeah, sorry ladies, my heart is already taken." He looked up and winked at me.

They all groaned in disappointment before mumbling insults at this girlfriend who was ruining their image of Alex. According to them, Alex's girlfriend is a fat, dumb butt head. Little did they know I could hear it all.

"Miss Hadley?" The same girl looked at me. "Do you have a boyfriend?"

"I do."

"What is it like having a boyfriend?"

"Well, it's pretty cool cause you have someone who you can always talk to."

"Have you kissed your boyfriend?"

I crossed my arms. "I'm not going to answer that."

"She has!" The girl giggled and looked at her friends. They all started making kissing faces at me. Alex joined in before he doubled over laughing.

"Stop it!" I playfully smacked his arm. "It's not that funny."

He pulled himself together before we went to the dining room for lunch.

We let the kids run flashlight tag the next couple nights while the counselors just sat around the bonfire and talked. On the low, I told Justin and Aly that it was too tempting for Alex and I to be alone in the dark. Thursday night we were all sitting around the bonfire, Alex and I sitting right up next to each other and facing Aly and Justin.

Aly's face soured as she stared into the bonfire. "You guys, we only have two weeks left after this."

"Don't even!" I groaned at her. "I don't want to think about camp ending."

"I do." Justin smirked. We all shot him a look and he shrugged. "I have people back home that I am looking forward to seeing."

Alex started to ask, "But you and Aaron…"

"Are having a lot of fun. But we both know what this is."

He nodded his head at the answer.

"That's like what Henry and I are doing." Aly replied. "I want to go into freshman year totally free so I can date around and not settle."

"Is it settling if it's the right person?" Justin asked.

"I just want to know I've seen all there is to see." She winked.

"Just be careful." Alex leaned in closer to her. "The grass isn't always greener."

"You're the only one of us who has been to college." Aly nodded at him. "You're telling me you didn't make the most of freshman year?"

"No I did." I tensed at his words. Of course he had been with other girls at Tech, but I didn't want to hear about it. He gently placed a hand on my thigh. "Aaron and I did some damage. But that shit gets old after a while. Justin's right about settling down when it's the right person."

Alex's watch beeped and saved us from continuing the conversation. We all ushered the kids into the cabins but thinking about going home and then going off to school had me rattled. Aly didn't mean to stir up anything by saying what she did, but it didn't change the fact that it did. I was now worried about going home, potentially seeing my ex, then figuring out whatever was going to happen with Alex and I.

I grabbed my phone out of my duffle bag and turned it on. Aly was just coming out of the bathroom when the phone finished loading my texts. I only had one from my dad: **Call me.**

Fuck.

"You good?" She asked next to me.

"I need to call my dad."

Aly sucked in a breath but nodded. I left the cabin and quickly called my dad's cell phone. He answered it in one ring.

"I texted you on Monday." He sounded annoyed, but without being able to actually see his face it was hard to know for sure.

In a whispered yell, I said, "I'm sorry! Normally I have my phone off until I text you on Saturday!"

"Doesn't matter." Shit he was pissed. "I need you to explain to me why I caught Keith sneaking into your room to leave you a letter on Monday night."

My stomach dropped. Keith used to sneak in and out of my room through my window all the time. He must've thought he could get away with it, even without me there to cover up the sounds of him climbing up the side of the house. "I don't know, Dad. I'm not home."

"I read the letter he left you."

I tried to keep my voice calm. "And?"

"Apparently you have a new boyfriend?"

"I don't have-" From the corner of my eye, I saw Alex waving at me. "A boyfriend."

"Keith's letter says differently."

Alex was walking over to me now, looking both confused and concerned. I needed to get off the phone. "Dad, Keith is delusional and thinks I'll get back together with him. He wrote a bunch of bullshit in a letter he gave to Sarah to give me. He must've tried to drop off another letter like that thinking I would get it whenever I got home. Otherwise, I have no idea why he would be in my room. That's actually terrifying because my window should be locked."

"Oh, it's locked now."

I looked at Alex, who was waiting there with his hands in his hoodie pocket for me to finish. "I'm sorry, Dad."

He took a deep breath. "I was just really worried about you, Hadley. The letter freaked your mom and me out."

"I'm fine."

"I still better get a proof of life picture on Saturday."

"You will but I have to go."

"Love you, kiddo."

"Love you too, Dad."

I hung up and looked at Alex. "Did you get all that or do I need to explain it?"

He shook his head, "If I ever meet this ex of yours…"

"I think you'll have to get in line behind my dad."

Alex breathed out a laugh. "You good?"

"Yeah, just shitty that all this is happening while I'm here."

"I think it's better that all this happens while you're here." He wrapped me in a quick hug before I called lights out.

The torrential rain started during dinner, so the Hamiltons made the decision to just keep everyone inside and get skit night started. Alex, Aly, Justin, and I huddled with our kids to discuss what to do. We could only use what was in the dining room and there was barely any space to really practice anything.

"What's something we haven't done yet?" I asked Justin, who shrugged in response.

Aly suggested. "We could just have them sing a song?"

The kids all booed at her idea. Alex chuckled and then tried, "Have Nate tell one of his scary stories and the kids act it out."

"Yes!" Nate cheered from the floor where the kids were all huddled.

I asked, "What scary stories?"

"He tells these awesome stories while everyone is getting ready for bed."

"Better than nothing!" I motioned for Nate to stand up. He talked all the kids through the different parts to reenact the story of the Bunny Man Bridge.

Nate narrated the story while the kids acted it out. When it came time for the Bunny Man to actually kill someone, the kids made their death scene so wild and animated that everyone just laughed.

When our kids were done, everyone cheered. Their skit was so different from any of the other skits we've seen all summer and I was so proud of them. I squeezed Alex's hand as the kids were sitting back down. "That was a great idea."

"I have those sometimes."

We watched the rest of the skits but none of them earned the same applause that ours had. At the end of the night, Mr. Hamilton stood up and said, "I think it goes without saying that the Bunny Man Skit wins tonight!" Justin pulled Nate up and had him go accept the skit night trophy.

The kids all ran around into the pouring rain with the trophy. We counselors all scrambled after them, laughing as they took turns sliding in the muddy path on our way back to the cabins. They rolled around in the mud, passing the trophy back and forth, and cheering themselves on. The rain kept pouring down, getting some of the mud off them only for it to be replaced by new mud when they slipped back onto the ground.

Aly, Justin, Alex and I just laughed as we watched. The rain soaked through our clothes but no one wanted to end the celebration. Eventually, enough of the kids were tired enough that we marched them back into the cabins and they all washed off before going to bed.

25

After staying up way too late the night before, we all struggled in the morning. Nate hauled the skit night trophy with him to breakfast and we even let him keep it to show it to his parents at pick up. Only then did he part with it, after giving it one last hug.

Alex and I returned the skit night trophy to Mr. Hamilton before heading back to the cabins to finish cleaning with Justin and Aly. We sped through the checklist and then went to the lodge to meet up with everyone.

Dinner was spent catching up with Sam and Aaron, then Jake and Lucas made their 'jungle juice' and set it out for people to drink from. Kelly didn't leave the lodge like she had been before. Instead she parked herself right by the 'jungle juice' cooler. Only Jake and Lucas went near it after that.

Aaron brought out his bottle of rum for us to pass around. We played a few rounds of Thumper until the whole bottle was gone.

Alex leaned over and whispered, "Wait for me at the front of the lodge."

I nodded as he excused us both, "We're going to find somewhere more quiet."

"I could use some quiet too." Sam laughed, getting up to go read.

"I need another drink!" Aly popped up. "Justin and Aaron, come with me."

They groaned but followed her.

I got up with them, moving to the door while Alex headed to his room. I waited for just a few minutes for him at the front of the lodge. He had the blanket tucked under his arm and took my hand without saying anything.

We carefully opened then closed the door behind us. Once we were a few feet away from the lodge, Alex admitted, "I just didn't want Kelly to catch on to what we were doing."

"She seems like she's ready to get people in trouble tonight."

"Let's make sure we don't get caught then." His hand squeezed mine.

When we got to our usual spot, Alex spread the blanket out and we sat down on it. I looked up at the stars then over at him. His hand slid up my cheek as he pulled me in for a kiss. Our lips moved together in a familiar rhythm, but I wanted more.

My tongue skated across his bottom lip, an invitation he eagerly accepted. His tongue found mine, and as he expertly manipulated it, I let out a soft moan. His hand wound into my hair, deepening the kiss, until I had to lay myself down on the blanket. Alex followed me and made a trail of kisses down my neck back up to my lips.

With a soft peck, he pulled away just enough so we could look into each other's eyes. His words were a coarse whisper. "I have been dying to kiss you all week."

"Then don't stop."

He adjusted himself so he was laying on his side, his head hovering above mine, and his hand resting on my stomach. Softly, he instructed, "Wrap your hand around my wrist."

I tilted my head in confusion.

"Trust me." He reassured. "Grab my wrist."

My fingers couldn't connect as I wrapped them around his wrist, gently squeezing to let him know I was ready.

Alex's voice was confidently calm, "You're in total control here, Hadley. Move my hand where you want me to touch you."

His breathing was even as I tested how maneuverable his hand was by dragging it up and down my stomach. Alex had relaxed his hand just enough that I could control where it went without it being totally limp. Nothing would be a surprise this way. I would know exactly where his hands were going instead of it shocking my system. I would get to decide where he would touch me.

I wanted him to touch me everywhere.

But I needed to work myself up to that so I used Alex's hand to slowly push my shirt up until my bra was exposed. That familiar pulse of panic was starting to make my heart race. When his hand landed on my chest, just above my heart, I paused to let his warm touch sink into my skin while my heartbeat steadied.

I wanted this.

More than anything I wanted him to touch me.

Once I felt ready, I slid his hand down onto my breast. My heartbeat started to pick up again. I could hear it pumping in my ears over the sounds of our breaths. I took a deep breath to help steady my heart before nodding up at him. He gently squeezed, his eyes darting around my face to track my reactions. One gentle knead led to another, and soon Alex didn't need to wonder if I was enjoying his touch. My breathy moans were confirmation.

With my free hand, I tugged on his shirt to bring his lips back to mine. Our lips worked together, the pace increasing as his hand worked me.

My heartbeat was increasing again, but not from panic. I wanted more of Alex's warm touch on my skin. My hand moved his and encouraged it to slip under the fabric of my bra. His thumb skated across my nipple and a soft moan escaped my lips between kisses.

"You like that?" His deep voice filled my ear.

"Yes." I moaned as he dragged his thumb lightly over the hardened bud.

I squeezed his wrist to let him know that I wanted to move it. He relaxed his hand so I could slide it over to my other breast and under my bra. The pad of his thumb stroked my nipple back and forth while his lips and tongue kept my mouth occupied.

My core was tightening with a need to be touched. My fingers gently squeezed Alex's wrist again. He smiled against my lips and his thumb came to a stop. Slowly, I trailed his fingers between my breasts, down my stomach, and stopped him right at the rolled up waistband of my shorts.

Alex pulled back just enough to lock eyes with me. His dark brown eyes were almost black but there was a sparkle in them that rivaled the stars in the sky. The tips of his curling fingers lightly brushed my exposed skin.

My breath hitched, and he held his own. We were both waiting to see if I would recoil.

I didn't.

He carefully gripped the waistband, pulling it down slightly while scanning my face for a reaction. The hand I had on his wrist slid up his arm. His breathing was ragged but the rest of his body was frozen over mine.

In a barely audible whisper, I told him, "I want more."

A faint smile was on Alex's face as he nodded. He leaned back down to kiss me as his hand slid under my shorts and thong. A shiver ran up my spine as he slowly, purposefully moved his hand until his middle finger barely skimmed my bundle of nerves. That light touch sent ripples of pleasure through my body. A moan forced my lips away from his.

Once he knew where it was, Alex's finger started to work me in lazy circles. Our eyes were locked on each other's but as his finger picked up its pace, my eyes started to close instinctively.

"Keep your eyes on me, Hadley." His voice was level as he whispered. "Stay in this moment with me. Focus on this right here." He emphasized the last word with a flick of his finger that forced my eyes wide open and my core to pulse. "I want the only thing you think about right now to be how good my touch feels."

I nodded and kept my eyes on Alex's dark gaze, thinking only about his hands on my body. My hands were squeezing his muscular arms as more moans built up and left my mouth. It was getting harder to keep my eyes open.

He must have noticed, because he told me, "Look up at

the stars."

My gaze focused above his head. Thousands of stars were shining down from the sky. The full moon was beautiful in its place, but the stars were sparkling all around us. Different sizes of brilliant white light were freckling the deep blue sky. Their beauty was the only thing that filled my gaze.

While the beauty of the night sky was distracting me, Alex slipped a finger down into my core and his thumb took over working the apex. "Fuck," He hissed out, "You're so wet already."

My breath hitched in my throat.

"Now close your eyes." He instructed in a coarse voice. I shut my eyes and only saw darkness. "Picture all those stars you just saw." The white lights that had just been twinkling above me came to life behind my closed eyes. Alex started curling the fingers inside me. A delirious sensation radiated through me as I arched my back.

Alex's lips started on my neck, giving me time to adjust to all the sensations happening to my body at once. Light kisses made a path down to my exposed nipple. He took the bud between his teeth and started to flick it with his tongue. The twinkling stars in my mind burned brighter. My fingers went into his hair as I softly called his name.

This feeling running through me was the most intense pleasure I had ever felt. My body never reacted this way to another's touch like this. The thought of that jolted my thoughts to the last person I wanted to be thinking about at this moment. I shook my head, desperately trying to force the image of that person out of my mind.

Alex's voice snuck into my ear and back into my mind, "Don't let the stars disappear, Hadley. Look back up at them."

My eyes shot open and took a second to adjust the stars into focus. They were still shining radiantly above us, illuminating our bodies. Alex's movements had slowed down, but his fingers kept enough pressure on me to bring my mind back to this moment.

I looked over to Alex's face, wearing the slightest grin of

pleasure and his eyes were coals ready to be ignited. He started to speed up his movements, "Stay in this moment with me."

My fingers in his hair pulled his mouth back to mine to help ground me in this moment. Our lips crashed together. He greedily swirled his tongue into my mouth. The only thing I could manage to say was his name in between quiet moans. I couldn't think of anything else to say. Words weren't forming right and a sentence would have been impossible.

"Look at me." His voice was rough when he asked, "Does my touch make you feel good?"

My core pulsed around his finger. "Yes."

He flashed me a crooked smile. "I can make you feel even better." I bit my lip as he commanded, "Picture the stars."

My eyes shut again. The thousands of bright stars were back in my mind's vision. Nothing else. My breath stuttered as Alex slipped another finger inside me. The two fingers curled in rhythm with his swirling thumb. Alex's mouth went to my other nipple, tugging it with his teeth this time. My back arched off the blanket and I barely contained the loud gasp at the sensation. He hummed in satisfaction that he'd gotten my body to do that. I could feel him smirking against my skin before he tugged my nipple again.

My hips started to unabashedly grind against his hand. The friction between our bodies was sending too much heat throughout me. The stars were blazing brighter as I felt my toes start to curl.

"I'm-fuck, I'm so close."

As his fingers kept working m, Alex pulled back to whisper in my ear, "Are you going to come for me?"

I nodded in time with my body writhing under his hands.

He growled, "I want to feel you come on my fingers. It's going to feel so fucking good."

The stars were all colliding and combining into one giant white light. The tightness in my core was about to snap. Alex's lips glided down my neck then his teeth gently bit down.

I cried out as blinding white light took over my vision and I crumbled around Alex's fingers. Waves of pleasure spread out through my entire body. I held on tight to his arms until the white light finally ebbed out of my vision.

When I was finally able to breathe evenly, I opened my eyes to look at him. All I could think to say was, "Fuck."

Alex smirked as he languidly slid his hand back out of my shorts. His fingers went into his mouth then he slowly pulled them back out, tasting me. I could feel his arousal against my thigh and expected him to want to finish what we had started.

Instead, he rolled his body away from mine and laid down on his back. He threw his hands behind his head and looked up at the stars with a satisfied grin.

I dared to ask, "What's next?"

Alex turned his gaze to focus on mine. "I don't want to push you too far too soon."

"Very considerate of you." I joked, sitting up on my heels. "But how far am I allowed to push you?"

"Like I said," The coals in his dark eyes sparked into flames. "You're in control here, Hadley."

I bit my lip then swung my leg over him. With our hips lined up, I could feel all of him barely contained by his gym shorts.

My fingers started to lift his shirt up. "Take this off."

Alex sat up just enough to pull it off over this head. He returned his hands to their spot behind his head. I ran my fingers down his bare chest, his skin puckering in goosebumps as I did. He moaned my name but didn't try to touch me.

I sat back and whipped off my shirt and bra.

Alex's dark eyes went wide as they took me in, "You're fucking perfect."

Even in the moonlight, it was obvious how much I blushed at his words. They meant so much more than he realized. I smiled down at him, "Gimme your hands."

Alex pulled his hands out from under his head and put them in mine. I adjusted my grip so my hands were holding his wrists and then brought them up to grip my bare breasts.

As he began to knead them in his hands, I leaned down to kiss him. His skin was so much warmer than the cool summer air surrounding us. Every inch of our bodies that was touching tingled with heat.

I started to move against Alex's hips. "Fuck." He groaned out as he threw his head back and started slowly grinding back into me. I watched as his fingers adjusted their grip until both of my nipples were between his thumb and pointer finger, and he began to roll the stiff bud between them. My soft mewl turned into a moan as he moved his fingers faster.

"Hadley," His deep voice forced my eyes back open. I didn't even realize I closed them.

When his eyes snapped to look at me, he choked out, "Tell me what to do."

Confidently, I pulled myself off of him. Lying down on my back, I slid my shorts and thong off so I was completely naked.

Alex sat up, his burning gaze scanning my body. "Hadley..."

My hand went to his chest. "I want you in control now."

His hand started on my thigh, skimmed my hips and waist, and grazed my breasts before he settled it above my heart. Strong, confident beats were pounding in my chest. Alex paused for a moment, then stated, "You're still in control. You tell me to stop any time and I will."

"I know."

Quickly, he took a condom out of his gym shorts pocket before removing the rest of his clothes.

I giggled to fill the silence, "I thought you weren't going to push me too far?"

He flashed a smile, "I wanted to be prepared for the best case scenario." He used his teeth to rip open the wrapper then rolled the condom on and settled his body between my legs.

Alex leaned down so our bodies were flushed with each other's and gently kissed me. The sweet, slow kisses built into something needier as he started to work himself into me. It took my body a moment to adjust to his fullness after half a year of nothing inside me. My mind shot a picture of the last person who had been where Alex now was to the forefront of my thoughts. I shuttered at his image and pulled away from Alex to look up at the stars.

He whispered in my ear, "Just like that, Hadley. It's just you and me in this moment right here. I want you to focus on feeling me."

Inch by inch, Alex slid into me while I looked up at the dazzling stars. I moaned his name and closed my eyes once he was completely inside me. The stars were twinkling as the pleasure radiated in my body. "Fuck." Alex growled, sucking in a breath. He started to carefully thrust in and out of me.

Our breathing became shallow as Alex's thrusts quickened. I moved my hips to meet his pace, allowing him to hit a spot inside me that causes the stars to flash.

"Alex!" I softly cried out as he grabbed one of my legs and pulled it up so it was flush against his chest. At this angle, he could keep hitting that same spot with each thrust.

"You feel better than anything, Hadley."

I moaned in agreement.

"I've been thinking about this all summer, imagining what you would feel like." His thrusts were harder now, making the stars in my mind twinkle. "I thought about what it would feel like when you came for me over and over again." His hips were snapping into mine. "You feel better than I imagined."

His words were making the stars burn so bright, too bright. One of his hands moved from my hip to the top of my core so his finger could rub those fantastic circles into me. My toes were starting to curl again and my grip on his arms tightened. The stars in my mind started to melt together as the tension built.

Alex leaned in closer. I could feel his breath tickle my ear as he asked, "Are you gonna come again for me?"

"Yes!" I cried out as his thrusts rapidly hit the same

sensitive spot in a rhythm that was making the stars twirl and crash together. The white light blinded my vision again as I crumbled hard around Alex. He kept working himself in and out of me, going too fast for my hips to keep up with. He slammed into me one more time before he found his release.

Our ragged breaths filled the space between us. A thin layer of sweat was coating both our bodies. Alex pulled out of me before lowering himself onto the blanket. Once I had recovered my breathing, I sat up and looked at the lake.

The moon and stars' reflections were glittering along the calm surface of the lake. The dark water looked like it would be perfect for washing the sticky sweat off our bodies. I looked at Alex who was looking up at the sky with hooded eyes.

Popping up off the blanket, I put my hands out. Alex shot up, his face crinkled with confusion. I nodded my head to the lake behind me. He stood up and took my hand, letting me lead him into the lake.

The water was cool now that the sun wasn't out to warm it, but it was refreshing as we waded into the lake. The sand and soil squished beneath my toes as we walked further in. Once the water was up to our hips we stopped. We didn't say anything as we gently splashed each other, replacing the hot sweat with cool water. I started to shiver so Alex wrapped me up in his arms.

"I think this is the most quiet you've been all summer." He laughed and kissed the top of my head.

I breathed out a laugh through my chattering teeth.

His arm went down and under my legs, scooping me up against him. He held me tight and carried me out of the lake and back to the blanket. Once we were both lying down, he pulled my back into his chest and threw the part of the blanket we weren't lying on over our bodies.

Closing my eyes, I relaxed into the warmth of Alex's body.

I started feeling something trickling down my face. It took me a minute to realize that it was rain drops gently falling all over me.

"Alex!" I hoarsely whispered. The stars had disappeared behind clouds and it was nearly impossible to see anything.

He bolted up, "¿Que?"

"It's starting to rain."

He held his hand up, "It is."

I stood up with my own hand out. "It's like sprinkling now so let's get inside before it pours."

He nodded before hopping up. Quickly, we threw our clothes back on. Then he bundled up the blanket and tucked it under his arms. "I don't even remember falling asleep."

"Me either. What time is it?"

He looked at his watch. "It's about to be 2 am."

Our hands wound together as we started walking. The sky was dark. Clouds were covering the stars and moon. We carefully made our way back to the glowing light coming from the lodge windows. We quietly slipped into the lodge, the rain getting heavier the closer we got to the door.

Right as Alex shut the door, the downpour began. The sound of rain hitting the ground was so soothing. I felt like I could fall asleep right there listening to it.

Alex slipped his arm around my waist and pulled me closer. "Thanks for saving us from that."

"Wish we could spend more time together though."

"There's always next week." He lifted my chin up to kiss me.

I wanted to just lay down on the nearby couch with him but I knew it made more sense for us to go back into our rooms.

My eyes felt so heavy as I mumbled, "Goodnight Alex."

"Goodnight Hadley," He kissed my forehead and we went our separate ways. I went into the bathroom, worried I would find someone there, but luckily it was empty. As I finished up and was heading back to my room, I heard Kelly whisper, "Shit, I had no idea you guys were even gone."

Alex's voice replied, "Sorry, we didn't mean to fall asleep outside."

"Just don't let it happen again."

Soft footsteps pattered away and the lodge was quiet again. As curious as I was about that conversation, I needed to get to bed. My head felt foggy so I didn't even bother changing before crawling into my bunk.

26

Sam and I walked to the laundry room together the next morning. "You came back late." She nudged my arm.

"It was a pretty *eventful* night."

Sam's jaw dropped. "Did you and Alex...?"

I nodded, biting back a grin.

She smiled, "I'm so happy for you."

Alex was already in the laundry room when Sam pushed the door open so she didn't say anything else about it to me, but she sounded extra happy as she greeted him.

"Morning," He smirked and I felt my whole body go red. It wasn't embarrassing that she knew, it was more having to be in the room with him right after telling her.

We quickly started our wash then I took the seat on the couch right next to Alex. Sam smiled, "Don't get caught in here."

"We won't!" I groaned as she walked out.

"I didn't even tell Aaron yet." He lightly laughed.

"She asked me why I came back to the room so late."

Alex grabbed my legs then laid them across his lap. He started gently stroking a line up and down them.

His touch almost distracted me from what I needed to ask, "Who were you talking to last night?"

"Kelly came out when she heard our voices. She had no idea we weren't in the lodge."

"Shit, was she pissed?"

"She didn't seem happy but she didn't say anything else to me."

"Fuck, we can't fall asleep out there again."

"We won't." He whispered as he leaned in for a kiss.

Our lips were just about to touch when Matt came in.

We pulled away from each other, but he kept my legs in his lap.

"Jake's right behind me." It was a warning but Alex just gripped my legs tighter.

Matt was moving as fast as he could to get his laundry in the washer when Jake slammed the door open. He looked as if he had gotten the best sleep of his life with how perky he was walking into the room. He was silently smiling as he dumped his clothes into the washer and started them. Matt scurried out and Jake turned to us.

"So," One of his eyebrows rose, "What is she like, Alex?"

Alex's body went rigid. He glared at Jake but didn't say anything.

"Any chance you'd let me watch?"

I yelled, "Get the fuck out!"

"I love it when you yell at me." He winked and turned to Alex. "Is she loud? In my imagination she is."

Alex shoved my legs off of him and stood up. I grabbed his arm to try to pull him back to the couch. He wouldn't budge, but he also didn't take a step closer to Jake.

Instead, Jake took a step closer to him. "Just two more weeks, man. Two more weeks and then…" His pointed finger tapped Alex square in the chest. Alex's hands were clenched in fists so tight, I could see them shake.

"Get. The. Fuck. Out." I snapped at Jake.

"Say please." His hand patted his pocket as he looked at me. It wasn't the same pair as before, but I knew what he was referring to.

Through gritted teeth, I clipped out, "Please."

"That's my girl." He looked back at Alex. "You're lucky I like her so much."

Before either of us could say or do anything else, Jake left.

I tugged on Alex's arm again. He looked down at me with rage still swimming in his eyes, but he sat back down on the couch. He took a few deep breaths before grabbing my legs and putting them back on his lap. After another beat, he looked at me and said, "You need to stop giving into him."

My mouth dropped open. "I'm not. I'm standing up for myself."

Alex shook his head. "That's not what he thinks. He loves saying shit to you to get a reaction out of you. You make it too easy for him."

"So this is my fault?" I tried to pull my legs away from him, but he stopped me.

He sighed, "It's not your fault at all. He is a gross piece of shit that for whatever reason loves fucking with you. So stop giving him ammo. Just ignore him."

"I can't ignore the shit he says."

"Please." His fingers started stroking my leg again. "Because I don't know if I can wait two more weeks to kick his ass."

"Fine, I'll ignore him." I huffed. "Maybe we should get out of here then? I don't want to see him when he comes back to switch his stuff."

Alex nodded. "Let's go."

We went and hid in Alex's room, just cuddling and talking until we had to switch our laundry. We managed to avoid Jake until lunch.

Mr. Hamilton started calling out the groups for the week. "Our 8 and 9 year old group will be Zac, Kelly, Jake, and Hadley."

My whole body slumped in my chair.

Alex's hand snatched mine under the table. He started gently rubbing circles with his thumb.

Mr. Hamilton read out the rest of the names, but I didn't hear anything after I realized what my week was about to look like.

When it was time to meet up with our groups, Alex and I lingered at the table. Sam must've sensed something was off and shooed everyone away from the table for us.

Alex quickly whispered, "Just ignore him. Tell Kelly if he says anything awful."

"I will."

"You got this." He squeezed my hand and started to pull me up from the table.

We split up to go to our cabins. Kelly had already picked the bottom bunk when I arrived. She was finishing setting up her bed, only pausing to say hi to me as I walked in. I just threw my duffle bag onto the top bunk. My plan was to use getting set up for the week as an excuse to avoid Jake later.

Kelly clapped her hands together when she was done. "Hadley, before we go get the campers, I wanted to ask you something."

Had she figured out what Alex and I did at the lake? I tried to act natural when I responded, "What's up?"

"Can you let me know if Jake says or does anything *odd* to you."

I breathed out a laugh. "Outside of his normal Jake stuff?"

"Yes, let me know if he does anything particularly weird."

"Will do."

Most of the week, I did a pretty good job of avoiding or ignoring Jake. Kelly kept having to leave to go handle things in her office while we let the kids run around after dinner. Zac was doing a good job of buffering us with his dark, sarcastic humor that seemed to confuse Jake.

But he couldn't be around all the time.

So when Zac got up to go to the bathroom Thursday night, Jake came over to where I was sitting on the picnic table. He leaned in close, nudging my arm with his elbow. "Why have you been ignoring me all week?"

I didn't say anything.

"Icing me out won't work. I know how to push your

buttons."

My eyes stayed on the kids running around.

"Does Alex say sexy shit in Spanish to you while he's fucking you? Does that turn you on? That explains why you never wanted me-"

"Shut up." I snapped at him.

He grinned.

I lost.

"C'mon, Hadley." He nudged me again. "I know you've got more in you."

"Stop."

"Stop? No, this is the game we've been playing all summer. I say disgusting things to you and you yell at me for it. I love watching you squirm and you make it so easy."

"I never wanted to play this game with you. None of this has been fun for me, Jake. Just stop, please."

He looked down at his feet. For a second, I thought he would apologize or show some kind of remorse, instead he said, "And if I don't want to stop?"

I looked him straight in the eye, "I will tell Kelly all the vile, disgusting things you've said to me. I'll tell her I saw you steal my underwear, and that you tried to touch me."

Jake laughed, "Go ahead and tell her. Lucas knows the truth about your underwear and how I got them. He knows you let me touch you when you were drunk. He knows exactly what kind of girl you are."

Anger was making it hard to think straight. "Kelly already suspects you of something. She asked me to tell her if you did anything weird to me. I'm sure she'd *love* to hear about this conversation."

He confidently said, "Then tell her and see what happens or should I say doesn't happen."

A comeback was starting to form in my mind, but I had nothing to say that actually mattered. My head hung in defeat. My only threat meant nothing to him. There was nothing I could do to stop Jake.

He leaned over me and sinisterly whispered, "I've only got two more weeks to fuck with you, Hadley, and I'm going to enjoy every minute of it."

I swallowed back tears. He wasn't going to get the satisfaction of seeing me cry.

"You guys good?" Zac's voice startled me. I jumped up as Jake leaned away from me.

"Just tired." I said running straight into the cabin as Kelly came back to help us get the kids in for the night.

I spent the rest of the week feeling numb and barely listening to anything the campers or the other counselors said to me.

27

The second Kelly and I were done cleaning after the campers left, I grabbed my stuff and went to the lodge. We were one of the first groups to be done, so I went to my usual room and threw my stuff onto my bunk. I waited until I heard Alex's voice before I walked out.

He was with Aaron, turning to go to their room, when he saw me at the entrance to the girl's hallway. Without saying anything, he handed Aaron his bag and came over to hug me.

"I'm gonna kill him."

A hollow laugh escaped me as my arms wrapped around him. "You don't even know what he did. "

Alex pulled himself away just enough to look at me. "Doesn't matter. I know it upset you. Did you tell Kelly what he did?"

"I threatened to tell Kelly everything and he just laughed at me. Nothing I say matters when Lucas will just go to bat for him."

His head dropped. "I'll kill both of them then."

"Please do."

His arms tightened around me. "Want to come to town with us? We're going to pick up some stuff for tonight."

I didn't want to go anywhere or really do anything now. I could feel myself slipping back into the dark place that I had crawled out of a few months ago. Going into town seemed so draining, and I already felt empty.

He kissed the top of my head. "I don't have to go if you want me to stay with you."

"Do you mind?"

"Of course not. Aaron is a big boy. He can go buy booze

alone."

"Thank you."

Alex lifted my chin to look at him. "What'll cheer you up?"

"Normally, watching *10 Things I Hate About You* but seeing as that can't happen here…"

"You can recite that poem she does and I'll pretend I'm the guy."

"No," I laughed at his eagerness. "But I appreciate the offer. Just you being here is helping."

By the time Sam, Justin, and Aly got to the lodge, I was in a much better mood. Alex and I cuddled and talked in my bunk. We only came out because Kelly and Lucas had arrived with the pizzas for dinner.

We took our spots at the table and everyone eased into talking about their weeks. I didn't say much, though. I had told Alex what Jake had said and I didn't feel like repeating it again, especially with Aly around. She, like so many others, still saw Jake as this awesome counselor and generous guy who provided them with free booze.

The cooler of 'jungle juice' made its appearance once dinner was over and that signaled for everyone to start partying. With Kelly out of the lodge, Jake and Lucas got a beer pong tournament going.

Alex and I left as the first game started.

We spread the blanket out in our spot and cuddled into each other. For a while, we just laid there in a comfortable silence.

"You're really quiet tonight." He gently stroked my hand.

"I'm fine."

Alex gave me a look like he didn't believe me.

"Really." I smiled. "I didn't have a lot to say to everyone

else. I just wanted to be alone with you."

He smiled back at me. "I always want to be alone with you."

I finally dared to ask, "What do you want to do after we leave? I mean, is this just a camp thing or is this-"

"Let's not worry about that just yet. We've still got all of next week and then we can figure out what we want to do."

"Oh, okay." I was upset by his dismissiveness of it.

"But," He lifted my face so our eyes met. "I want to keep seeing you for as long as I can."

I'm sure his hand could feel the warmth of my blush as he stroked my cheek. To avoid him seeing how red I was, I pulled him into a deep kiss. It just spiraled from there. Something about discussing the finality of camp made me want to soak in as much of Alex as I could.

He made quick work of getting me out of my clothes. I tried to take his shirt and pants off, but my hands were too eager and Alex ended up stripping himself down.

His naked body slid down mine, leaving a trail of kisses and nips on my skin as he went. I spread my legs out, expecting him to sit up and slip into me. His soft lips met the inside of my thigh, sending a shiver up my spine. Another kiss soon followed, along with another shiver. I propped up on my elbows to look at him as his kisses moved closer and closer to my core.

I sucked in a breath when his lips gently pressed the bundle of nerves there. "Alex..." My voice was full of hesitation.

His eyes shot up to look at me. "Just close your eyes and picture the stars, Hadley."

"It's not that..."

His mouth was hovering just above me and I could feel his breath tickling my sensitive skin. Alex's brow flexed asking me to clarify.

"I've never, I mean no one has ever..." I jerked my chin towards him. "No one has ever done this to me."

"Good." He started with a crooked smile. "I'll be the only one you think of now." His tongue darted out to lick me and my back arched in response. "Hold on to my hair."

Shaky fingers slipped into the soft waves of his dark hair just before he dipped his head down. His lips wrapped around me as the tip of his tongue began to move. My eyes closed and the stars took their places in my mind's vision.

Alex's tongue expertly worked me in a pattern of long licks, tight circles, and swift flicks. With each movement, I felt the pressure building up inside me. My fingers gripping his hair started to pull in time with my hips moving. He hummed against me as he slid a finger into my core. "Alex!" I moaned out, and I could feel his lips curl into a smile before he picked up his pace.

Another finger slid inside and I started to grind hard against him. More content humming was vibrating through me. I moaned out his name, pulling hard on his hair.

He pulled away long enough to breath out, "I fucking love the way you say my name." His mouth was back on me as I called out his name again. Over and over, I softly called out to him, and each time his name left my lips, he sped up the way he was twirling his tongue and fingers.

The pleasure inside my core was about to explode. The stars were all one giant white light that blinded me while I called out his name one more time then crumbled around his fingers while his mouth worked me until I was completely undone.

I laid flat against the blanket as Alex pulled himself back from me. He dragged the back of his hand across his mouth, holding my gaze as he did. When he was finished, a crooked smile curled his lip and he let his hands land on my knees. His chest was heaving as he steadied his breathing.

Alex's toned arm reached down to the blanket and I saw the moonlight reflect off the condom wrapper. "Wait." I put my hand on his arm to stop him.

"You okay?" He leaned closer to me, scanning my body for signs that something was wrong.

I smiled to let him know I was more than okay. "Lie down."

He sucked his bottom lip and then followed my

command. I let him adjust before I positioned myself on top of him. I started a trail of kisses that went down his neck, chest, then stomach. His abs clenched under my lips as I went lower and lower.

With one quick movement, I took as much of him in my mouth as I could. "Fuck Hadley," He groaned out.

His words spurred me on and I began bobbing my head. He filled my mouth as my tongue licked him up and down. Hearing him moan in pleasure lit a fire inside me. My pace increased and I found a rhythm that was making all of his muscles clench.

"Hadley," His voice was rough. I kept him in my mouth but looked up at him. His eyes were dark as he choked out. "If you don't stop, I'm not gonna to last much longer."

With a satisfied smirk, I let him go. I sat back on his thighs so he could put the condom on. He nodded when he was ready and I sank myself down onto him.

I threw my head back as all of him slid into me.

"Fuck. Yes." His hands grabbed onto my hips as I started grinding back and forth.

The faster I moved, the tighter he made his grip. I kept rocking myself against him, angling my body so that my apex was rubbing against him. The sensation of everything at once was building upon itself.

I didn't need the stars now. One look down at Alex with his head back, eyes hooded, and mouth parted had me coming undone. Watching him react to how I made him feel had me crumbling again, even harder than before.

He hissed my name when I started to slow down. Instead of saying anything else, his hands on my hips took over and kept me moving against him in a rhythm I couldn't have kept up with.

"You feel so fucking good." His voice was gravelly as he moved his hips into mine. I held onto his arms to steady myself. "So. Fucking. Good."

He sped up, harder and faster, until finally he found his

release.

The rocking of his hips slowed until it stopped. He gently tapped my leg as a signal to get off. I carefully moved my one leg over him and laid down right beside him. He was still finding his breath but his hand shot out and grabbed mine, drawing gentle lines with his thumb on my sweaty skin.

"Wanna go for a swim?" He asked, recovering quicker than me.

"Gimme a minute." I said with my eyes still closed.

I was still replaying over and over again what had just happened.

I needed to keep this feeling in my life.

I needed to keep Alex in my life.

Alex's fingers were running across my hips, making me shiver. "We won't make it to the lake if you keep that up." I teased but those fingers kept sliding back and forth.

"We can put that off-"

The sound of a golf cart turning on spooked us both. Alex threw enough of the blanket over us to cover our bodies up. We silently waited to see if the golf cart was heading this way.

It stopped at the top of the slope that led to the lake. A flashlight beam shot out and quickly scanned around, barely missing where we were tucked into the blanket.

"See, no one is out here." I recognized Lucas's voice. "I told you that you were just being paranoid."

It was Kelly's voice that responded. "No, lots of counselors are missing from the lodge right now."

"You're just looking for trouble. Stop it."

"You never listen to me-"

"Because you're being a bitch."

"No, I'm right about it this time and I'm going to prove it." The golf cart motor whirred to life again then the sound started to fade away.

Then the only sounds I could hear were the crickets chirping and our hearts beating loudly.

I swallowed. "We should head back."

Alex nodded and handed me my clothes. We quickly got dressed and Alex grabbed the blanket. Our hands found each other and we started walking back towards the lodge, using the trees to cover us. It would take longer to get back, but we wouldn't be as exposed if Kelly and Lucas came back around on their golf cart.

28

"What do you think they're looking for?" I whispered to Alex, as we snuck in and out of the trees. It was hard to see where we were walking, even with the stars and moon above us.

He shrugged. "Could be anyone. She could be looking for us. We're not up at the lodge right now."

"Shit. Do you think we'll get in trouble?"

"Nah," He shook his head. "If she asks us where we were, I'll say we were getting something from my car."

I breathed out a sigh and squeezed his hand.

The faintest moaning was coming from the woods to my right. It wasn't an animal. It sounded like a person, but I couldn't figure out what it was. "Did you hear that?"

Alex looked around confused, "Hear what?"

"It sounded like someone moaning like they were hurt or something."

"I don't-" It was louder this time and followed by an angry shushing sound. "Hold on." Alex pulled me behind him and started walking towards the noise.

A few steps further into the woods, we could see someone or maybe two people lying on the ground, but I couldn't tell who it was.

Once we were a little closer I could see Jake's blonde hair sticking out against the tree bark. "Oh shit!" I whispered as I watched Jake move his hips into someone underneath him.

"Let's just go." Alex tried to tug my hand.

"No." I pulled him back. "He enjoys fucking with me so much, let's see how he likes it."

"Hadley…" He warned me but I didn't listen. I had caught Jake in a very compromising position and it was the perfect opportunity to give him a taste of the creepiness he so easily dished out to me. I dropped Alex's hand and took a few steps closer. I wasn't even sure what I was going to say.

Jake was pumping his hips awkwardly. I was trying to figure out how someone so obsessed with sex could be terrible at it. The insult formed in my mind as I took another step closer.

I said, just loud enough for him to hear, "You know-"

Jake shot up, frantically pulling his gym shorts back over himself. "Hadley, what the fuck are you doing here?" He rushed towards me, shoving me away from the tree in an attempt to shield me from who he was with.

But I still saw who was lying there.

It was Aly.

"Oh my god!" I screamed. "What did you do to her?"

"Shut up!" Jake hissed as he shoved me again.

Alex whirled past me and charged at Jake, slamming him into a tree. He used one arm to pin him against the tree then started slamming his fist into Jake's face.

I ran over to Aly and saw her eyes were barely opened. She kept moving her mouth like she was trying to talk but no words were coming out, just moans. Her shorts and underwear were around her ankles and her shirt had been pushed up. "Aly?!" I cried out, trying my best to adjust her clothes so she was covered again. She tried to lift her head up, but she barely made it a few inches off the ground before she gave up.

"Alex!" I looked up to see him still holding Jake against the tree. "Something is really wrong with her!"

In the brief second Alex took his focus from Jake to look at me, Jake swung his fist hard into Alex's rib cage. He doubled over, holding his side while Jake started throwing punches at his exposed side and face.

Alex dropped his shoulder and tackled Jake to the ground. They scrambled and rolled around in the dirt. Alex was on top of him at first, his fists colliding with Jake's face. Then Jake managed to get a strong kick into Alex's already hurt ribs, making him recoil. Jake took the advantage and got Alex onto his back.

"Stop!" I kept screaming at them. "Just fucking stop it! We need to get Aly help!"

"She'll be fine!" Jake shouted back. Alex socked him in the nose while he was distracted. Jake rolled off holding his nose as blood started to stream through his fingers. Alex shoved him down then put his legs on top of Jake's arms, holding him in place. Jake was struggling underneath Alex, trying to hit him despite his arms being useless now.

The sound of the golf cart engine pulled my attention away. Kelly and Lucas's eyes both widened as they came closer to the woods. Kelly shut off the golf cart before running over to where Aly and I were.

I watched Lucas sprint over to Alex and shove him off of Jake. "What the fuck, man?"

When Alex stood up, Lucas shoved his chest to try to get him away from Jake.

Kelly was shouting into the radio. "Mom, Dad, you need to get to the lodge now and call 911!"

Alex cocked his fist back and landed a loud punch on the side of Lucas's head.

Lucas crumbled to the ground.

Kelly screamed as she watched her brother fall.

Alex went back over to Jake, who was starting to stand up. He kicked him back to the ground then got back on top of him.

His jaw was clenched and he was grunting each time his fists found their mark, beating Jake's head from side to side.

Over and over Kelly was shouting, "Alex! Stop!"

"He's gonna kill him." I whispered.

Kelly looked at me like she believed me. "Stop him."

"Alex!" I shouted but he didn't do anything to indicate he heard me.

Aaron's voice rang out behind me. "Alex! Stop it, man!" He ran over and grabbed one of his arms. Justin was right behind him, grabbing the other arm. Together they pulled him off of

Jake.

Alex frantically looked around, his dark eyes unable to focus. Aaron grabbed his shoulders. "You got him, man. You can stop now. You got him."

He nodded and Aaron let him go. Blood was starting to trickle down from a cut by his eye that was already looking swollen. He put a blood covered hand on his ribs and winced.

Jake's face was a bloody mess, but his chest was still moving up and down as he wheezed. Lucas looked like he had just fallen asleep on the ground.

I couldn't hear what Aaron was saying to Alex, who was staring at the ground and shaking his head. Justin walked over to where Kelly and I were still kneeling by Aly.

"Jake was on top of her." I told Kelly, taking my eyes off Alex. "She can't get up. I don't know what he did to her."

"What the fuck?" I heard Sam's voice behind me.

Kelly ordered, "Sam, go back to the lodge."

Sam just shook her head and knelt down next to Justin.

Mr. and Mrs. Hamilton arrived on a golf cart a moment later. Mrs. Hamilton gasped before running over to Lucas. She lifted his head up, crying out his name.

Mr. Hamilton knelt down by Jake's head. He reached out to his blood covered neck to find a pulse and calmly asked, "Kelly, who did this?"

Kelly's gaze flickered towards Alex.

Compared to how uninjured the rest of us were, it was obvious that he had been part of the fight. Alex winced as he crossed his arms but stayed silent.

"He was defending Aly from Jake!" I yelled before looking at Kelly.

Kelly nodded. "Lucas tried to get in the way and was knocked out."

Lucas started to regain consciousness then. His eyes rapidly blinked, "Mom?"

"Oh thank God!" Mrs. Hamilton squeezed his head.

"Careful, honey, careful." Mr. Hamilton left Jake to help

his son sit upright. He looked Lucas up and down before standing up. "I'm going to go meet the emergency responders at the front of the camp." He scanned us all with the most serious look I had seen from him. Everyone looked down at the ground while he left. Except Lucas, who was swatting away his mom's hands.

Aaron and Alex slowly walked over to us. Kelly tensed but she didn't move to go be with her mom and brother. She just kept holding Aly's hand.

Aaron knelt down behind Justin while Alex did the same behind me.

I turned around just enough to see him.

His face looked even more swollen up close and he had a busted lip.

I reached out my hand to gently cup his face. My thumb wiped away some of the blood from the cut by his eye as he gave my palm a soft kiss.

We were all quiet as the sirens from the ambulance grew louder the closer they came. No one dared to speak.

A cluster of voices were getting louder and coming from the direction of the lodge. Everyone stood back up, unsure of what to do. Kelly turned to face the group of counselors who had dared to see what all the noise was about.

Her voice boomed. "Every back inside the lodge! This does not concern you!"

I heard a few groans, but everyone who had come out turned and walked back. Some of them were already loudly telling each other about what they had been able to see.

We could see the lights from where the emergency vehicles had parked in front of the lodge. Mr. Hamilton was leading them through the woods, carrying giant bags full of medical supplies and two gurneys.

The emergency responders quickly attended to Aly, Jake, and Mrs. Hamilton insisted on Lucas being looked at.

"You need to get looked at too." An older woman pointed at Alex.

"No, I'm fine. I've had worse."

The woman put her hands on her hips. "Not up for debate."

Alex looked at me and sighed before walking around to meet up with the EMT.

Once the medical team gave the all clear, the officers moved in to interview us. Separate officers took each of us and walked far enough away that we couldn't hear each other's answers.

The officer who talked to me was a nice but pushy lady. "Hey, Hadley? That's your name, right? I need you to focus." She snapped her fingers in front of my face to get my attention. I hadn't realized I was watching as the cut on Alex's face was stitched up.

She nodded at him. "He's going to be fine." Then she pointed to Jake and Aly who were now on the gurneys. "We need to know what happened to your other friends."

"Jake isn't my friend. Aly is."

"Okay, then what happened with your friend, Aly?" The EMTs easily lifted Aly's gurney up to quickly carry her out of the woods.

I made eye contact with the officer. "Aly was attacked."

"You saw her get attacked?"

"Well no, but look at her."

The officer put her hands up. "Start from the beginning."

I recapped exactly what I saw Jake doing to her.

"Who was with you?"

My shaky hand pointed at Alex who was talking to a male officer. His bandaged hands were holding an ice pack on his ribs and another one on his eye. I couldn't hear what they were saying but Alex kept shaking his head.

"You said he got the other male off of the female. How did he manage to do that?"

"I didn't see. I was too focused on Aly."

"So you have no idea how that one ended up looking like that?" She pointed over at Jake lying unconscious on his gurney.

The sheet that covered him had blood seeping onto it.

I shook my head, "No, I was too distracted comforting my friend who had just been raped to notice what happened. Maybe he tripped and fell on a rock?"

"That's all we need from you."

"What will happen to Aly?"

"They'll determine that at the hospital." She turned and walked over to the car where the officer and Alex were still talking.

The two officers said something to each other before the officer who had talked to me took a big step back. The other officer spun Alex around and quickly put him in handcuffs.

"What?!" I shouted starting to walk over to him but Mr. Hamilton intercepted me.

His voice was trying so hard to sound calm as he stated, "They are just taking him for questioning."

I was in disbelief. "You don't handcuff someone you're questioning!"

"Hadley, you need to go back to the lodge."

"No!" I shouted so they would hear. "He didn't do anything!"

"That's not true. Look at Jake."

"LOOK AT ALY!" I screamed back at him.

Mr. Hamilton didn't say anything but he didn't move out of my way. I looked over at Alex's face as the cops shoved him to start walking towards their cars.

He mouthed. 'See you later.' There was the flash of a reassuring smirk before he turned to focus on where he was walking.

Mr. Hamilton sighed. "Kelly, make sure your mother and brother get home safely, then you go spend the night at the lodge. The four of you need to go straight back to the lodge and not speak a word of this to anyone. It's an open investigation and I don't want any of you to get in trouble."

Aaron nodded on our behalf.

29

We didn't go back into the lodge. Aaron led us to the lake instead. "Hadley, you start."

I told them all about how Alex and I found Jake with Aly. It was still so fresh in my mind, especially how messed up Aly was. I told him how Kelly and Lucas had shown up then Alex knocked Lucas out cold. Those were the missing pieces of the story, up until Justin and Aaron pulled Alex off of Jake. I turned to them, "Wait, how were you guys able to hear us?"

"We were already in the woods." Aaron winked.

Justin smirked despite the blush on his cheeks. "We heard you scream and started running."

"Sam, did you hear me screaming from the lodge?"

She shook her head. "I was already out looking for you guys. Kelly had come through the lodge and checked all the rooms, making a list of the people who were missing. I was down here by the lake looking for you when I heard you scream. I'm just not as fast as these two." She motioned to Aaron and Justin.

Aaron asked, "What did you guys tell the cops?"

She replied, "Only what I saw, which was nothing."

Justin and I nodded in agreement but he added, "He really fucked Jake up though."

"And the piece of shit deserves it." I replied.

Aaron chimed in, "Oh, he certainly does. And the cops will figure that out and Alex will be let go."

"You sure?" I asked because I wasn't.

Aaron nodded.

Sam looked at her watch. "Let's get back before Kelly does."

We walked silently back to the lodge, Aaron and Justin

holding hands.

Almost everyone was in the common room of the lodge waiting for us. Aaron shouted over all of them asking questions at once, "We can't talk about it so don't ask!"

Sam and I split up from them to go crawl into our bunks. After a few minutes of silence, she asked, "You good?"

"No, but I'll live."

"Okay." I heard Sam roll around in her sleeping bag. I tried to move and get comfortable, but no matter what I did, I couldn't relax.

Every time I shut my eyes, I saw Aly lying on the ground. I didn't sleep.

When the sun started coming up, I got out of bed and went to see if Alex was there.

Aaron answered the door, "He's not back yet. But don't worry. These things can take a minute."

Reluctantly, I went back to my room. Sam was up and pulling on her shoes to walk to breakfast.

At breakfast, we didn't say much to each other, not with everyone's eyes constantly flickering on and off of us. Even though we didn't say anything, rumors were starting to fly about what happened last night from the little bit people had witnessed when the emergency responders had arrived.

People kept saying it was lucky that we were there to stop Jake. No one questioned what Alex and I were doing together by the lake, but I think that's because everyone had figured it out already.

Every time someone said something or smiled my way, I just felt shittier. We didn't save Aly or stop Jake. I should have done something about him sooner. If I had told Kelly what he did to me last week, he might have been kicked out and then Aly wouldn't have had to go through what she went through. Alex told me to tell Kelly and I didn't think it would make a difference, but maybe it would've?

Mrs. Hamilton brought all us girls separately into the dining hall to talk. Everyone was staring at me and I just kept my head down.

"Ladies, I want to, well, I suppose thank you all for all the amazing work you have done here at Camp Odyssey. In light of the incident last night, we will be shutting down the camp and contacting your parents to come pick those of you who were dropped off. If they cannot come today, arrangements can be made so that you can spend the night. If you drove yourself, you are free to leave once you are ready. It is not...not an easy decision, but we need to handle what happened and it has become too much of a liability to have campers here. I hope you all understand."

We were all mumbling and shaking our heads.

My hand shot up.

Mrs. Hamilton was surprised, "Yes?"

"Do you know what happened to Alex or Aly?"

"It is an ongoing investigation and we can't discuss it."

"He's a hero!" I heard someone say and others started to agree.

Mrs. Hamilton's mouth crinkled into and finished out the meeting by saying, "The investigation is ongoing so make sure you aren't discussing the case with anyone, even among yourselves. Again, thank you all for your hard work this summer. We'll make sure you are all paid before you leave and let you know what the future holds for Camp Odyssey." She nodded and we all took the hint that it was time to get up and leave.

All the girls avoided Sam and I as we walked back to our rooms to get our stuff packed up. We noticed that someone had come and gathered all of Aly's things while we were in the meeting with Mrs. Hamilton.

I felt heavy as I packed up my things to leave, stuffing all my dirty clothes into my duffle bag. I should be doing laundry with Alex right now. That realization brought tears to my eyes. Sam heard me sniffling and wrapped her arms around me.

"You hate hugs." I said as the tears started to flow.

"Yeah, well, you look like you need one."

When I squeezed her back, I heard a soft sniffle from her. We both just held each other and cried until we felt spent. Then we finished packing and headed to the dining hall to wait for our parents.

As we were walking there, I saw Aaron loading up his truck.

Sam nodded at him, "I'll catch up with you inside."

"You sure?"

She walked backwards so she could reply, "Yeah, you two need a moment."

Aaron was throwing his last bag into the bed of his truck. When he turned around and saw me, he frowned.

I sighed, "This whole thing is such shit."

"At least we're getting paid to go home early."

"I guess. But have you heard from Alex?"

He shook his head. "Nothing yet, but that could mean anything."

"Really?"

"If he is still in jail, he won't be for long. Once they figure out why Alex did that to Jake, he'll be right out."

"I hope so. I'm really worried about him."

Aaron shrugged, "Nothing he hasn't dealt with before."

"What?"

His body went rigid, "I thought he told you about his dad."

"He said he beat the shit out of him and isn't welcome at his house anymore."

Aaron folded his arms across his chest. "Then that's all there is to it."

"Aaron. Tell me."

"Look, he's got a clean record. You need one to work at the camp. But," he begrudgingly admitted, "Technically he's been arrested and gone to jail before. He was a minor when all that shit went down with his dad so his record is sealed."

"Shit." Why didn't Alex just tell me this? He didn't need to hide it from me.

He sighed, "I'm sorry, Hadley."

My shoulders dropped, "I don't have any way to get ahold of him now."

"Give me your number and I'll give it to him as soon as I hear anything from him."

I quickly punched my number into his phone and called myself so he would have it saved. "Thanks Aaron."

"For what it's worth, it was a great summer."

"It was." We shared a quick hug. I turned around to see Justin behind me, with his hands in his pockets. "See you inside." I said to him before leaving the two of them alone.

More and more people were getting picked up or leaving. The counselors that didn't drive themselves to camp were all gathered in the dining hall. I found Sam sitting alone and reading her book and slumped down next to her.

Justin came in soon after to join us. "Heard anything from Aly?"

I took out my phone and sent her a quick text. Aly would normally respond to a text message right away, but this situation is anything but normal.

Sam suggested, "Call her." I pressed the green phone button. Ringing filled my ear.

"Hello Hadley." Aly's mom's voice came through the speaker.

I had my phone in between the three of us so we could all hear. "Hi Mrs. Green. How is Aly?"

"She's good. We should be released from the hospital later today."

"That's good!"

"I'll have Aly text or call you when she is feeling up to it. She's doing good, all things considered."

"Of course. I'll wait for Aly. Give her my love."

"I will. And, Hadley, thank you for being there and saving my little girl."

I felt an awkward wave of embarrassment in front of Sam and Justin. I didn't save Aly. Alex and I hadn't stopped anything from happening to her. All we did was *discover* the horrible thing that had happened to her. But I just said, "Anything for Aly."

"Bye Hadley."

"Bye Mrs. Green."

"Well," Sam sighed. "At least she's okay physically."

"That's something." We settled into a tense silence. Campers should've been arriving today. We should all be getting ready and setting up for that, instead of awkwardly sitting here.

"I saw something that I shouldn't have." Sam confessed, breaking the unsettling quiet.

"What?" Justin and I said at the same time.

Her voice was so low, we had to lean in closer. "Some papers fell out of a folder Kelly was holding and I helped her pick them up. It was a copy of a police report. Jake confessed to doing things to not just Aly, but also Rachel and Kylie."

"That fucking creep. I knew it."

Justin agreed, "Alex should've killed him."

Kelly called my name to let me know that my parents had arrived.

"I'm really gonna miss you guys." The tears I had been holding back came bursting through as I hugged them simultaneously. "I'll text you as soon as I'm home."

"Miss you already." Justin smiled and gave me one more squeeze.

"Alright, too much emotion for me." Sam joked before sitting back down.

I grabbed my duffle bag and followed Kelly outside. When it was just the two of us, she whispered, "I'm sorry, Hadley. I paired him with you so much because Lucas said you guys got along. If I had known exactly what I was doing, I wouldn't have."

I shrugged, "You couldn't do anything to stop him anyway. He told me so."

Her eyes grew wide, "Did he do something to you too?"

"Not like that. What he did to me was different, but he didn't touch me. When I threatened to tell you, he just said he'd use Lucas to cover him."

She sighed. "Lucas is another factor in all of this. But that's nothing you need to worry about. Take care of yourself."

"Thanks, you too." I smiled at her before turning to walk to my parent's SUV.

30

Normally, when my parents picked me up at the end of camp, all of my siblings would be in the car. We would stop to get Burger King off of exit 7 and then I spend the whole time going over what happened at camp and trying to fill them in on everything.

This time, when I got in the car, I only saw my parents.

I cautiously asked, "Where is everyone?"

"Your aunt is watching them. We need to talk to you about this." My mom informed me as she drove down the dirt road leaving camp. Her voice softened as she asked, "Hadley, what happened?"

How much did they know? I wasn't about to admit to anything unnecessary so I just said, "Camp closed early…"

"Yes," My dad started. "We got the call this morning to come pick you up because there was an incident. All Mrs. Hamilton could tell me was that you were safe but the camp needed to close down for the investigation to proceed. What are they investigating?"

"A counselor was doing things to some of the girl counselors." It felt more than awkward trying to find the words to explain what Jake had done to my parents.

My dad turned around in the passenger seat to look at me. "Why didn't you call me? That's literally why you had a phone, in case of an emergency, and this seems like an actual emergency."

"I don't know," I shrugged. "It all happened so fast, and then the cops showed up, and the camp handled things, so I just figured I'd talk to you about it when you picked me up."

"You talked to the cops?"

I looked out the window at the trees rolling by. "We had to talk to them because we found Jake hurting Aly."

My dad kept asking questions so my mom could focus on driving, "Who is Jake?"

"The piece of shit who was doing terrible things all summer. He hurt Aly, and he did horrible stuff to a few other girls."

"Did he...?"

"He didn't touch me."

My dad let out a small sigh of relief. "You said we, who is we?"

Shit. I was hoping to avoid this, but they were going to find out eventually. "I was with Alex."

"Who is Alex?"

I shot back, "He's just a boy from camp."

"That doesn't sound like he's just a boy from camp." My mom tried to look at me from the rear view mirror but I looked away.

I rolled my eyes. "That's besides the point."

"Hadley..." My mom continued. "We can tell when you're avoiding talking about something, and I know you think you're grown because you'll be in college in a few weeks, but you're still our little girl. We need real answers from you."

I groaned, "Alex made sure nothing bad happened to me so I'm fine."

"You saw something terrible happen to a friend." My dad stated. "That's what has us worried."

The image of Aly lying on the ground flashed in my mind. I shook it away. "I'm not going to get all depressed again if that's what you're worried about. I am fine. Sad, but fine."

My parents sat with that information for a minute then finally my mom asked, "How is Aly?"

"Her mom told us she will be released from the hospital. I'm waiting for her to feel better and text me back."

My mom sighed, "Well, I'm sorry that happened to your friend."

My dad continued, "What happened to this Jake character?"

"He was arrested but we don't have any update on him."

"And what about Alex?"

"I'm waiting for him to text me." Was all I would admit.

"I still wish you would've called us, but I'm glad you weren't hurt." My dad gave me a smile in the rearview mirror. "We missed you at home."

"I missed you guys too."

The rest of the drive home was more uncomfortable than wearing a harness. My parents kept trying to make small talk and ask about other aspects of the summer but all I could think about was Alex. I hadn't heard anything from Aaron. It had only been a few hours since he'd left but still, I just wanted to know if Alex was alright.

When we skipped the exit for Burger King, I sunk into my chair and closed my eyes. Eventually, I dozed off.

We pulled up in front of my aunt's house. Emmy and Mikey were outside holding a giant poster they made saying, 'Welcome Home Hadley!' It was covered in stickers and all the letters were a different color. I gave them both a big hug to thank them. Even John hugged me, but told me I smelled bad.

My siblings all climbed into the car and my aunt waved us off. We drove the 15 minutes home, Emmy and Mikey asking me tons of questions about camp. It was chaotic, happy energy but I was glad to be caught up in their joy after everything that had happened.

As soon as I was home, I went upstairs and dropped my stuff off while my dad took my duffle bag to the laundry room. I needed to decompress alone.

Camp was over.

I forced myself into the shower. The hot water blasted my body and I let it wash away all the tears I was crying. There were so many reasons to be crying, so I let myself feel them all. My dream of being a camp counselor was over. Jake had tainted this whole summer with what he did. It went beyond the creepy shit she would say to me. He hurt and scarred those other girls. Aly will never be the same again. I didn't know if I'd ever see or hear from Alex.

I never even got to say goodbye to him.

When the water started to go cold, I pulled myself out of the shower. For a moment, I started to look for my duffle bag, then remembered where I was and turned to my dresser. I put on the comfiest things I could find before heading downstairs.

"I ordered pizza." My mom motioned to the boxes on the kitchen counter.

I grabbed a few slices and then took my usual seat at the dinner table. When I bit into it, the unfamiliar taste overwhelmed me. For the last two months, I've had the pizza the Hamiltons ordered us from a local restaurant. The pizza my family always orders tasted so different from what I had gotten used to at camp.

My mom coughed to get my attention. "Your father and I were supposed to be going out of town tomorrow. Emmy and Mikey were going to stay with your aunt and John was going to stay at his friend's house. If you're up to it, we can just have everyone stay here? Your dad and I aren't opposed to canceling, we just wanted to check in with you."

"Just 3 kids will be no problem."

My mom gave me a skeptical look.

"Really. It'll be fine."

"Okay." She gave my hand a squeeze. "I'll get groceries for you guys tonight and leave some money. We're only gone for three nights."

"Can Sarah sleepover?"

"Of course." She smiled.

When I got back upstairs I had texts from Aly, Justin, Sam, and my best friend Sarah.

I opened Aly's text first. It read: **Call me.**

So I did.

Within a few rings, she picked up. "Hadley."

"Aly! How're you?"

"I'm out of the hospital now." It was her voice, even raspy it sounded like her. But the energy that Aly's words had before was gone.

"How're you feeling?"

"Numb."

My voice cracked, "I get it."

"You do get it. You're the only one I know who gets it."

I swallowed back some tears. "I'm so sorry."

"You know, the fucked up thing, is that I went into the woods with him willingly."

"Aly, don't-"

"No, I need to tell someone that gets it. No one gets it. Not my parents, not my friends here, and definitely not the therapist my parents dragged me to today. I know you'll understand."

"I will. I do." Silent tears started to fall, anticipating what Aly was about to tell me.

I heard her sigh. "Jake finally asked me to go somewhere alone with him while I was getting a drink. I was so surprised and happy that I didn't go back to the game we were all playing around the bonfire. I literally left Henry so I could go makeout with Jake." She made a sound somewhere between a sob and a laugh. "We went to the woods and he was nice, Hadley, almost too nice. He started trying to do more than kiss but I told him I wasn't into that. He seemed so cool with it, he told me he respected that I had boundaries and was fine just hanging out alone with me. He pulled out a water bottle of some drink he mixed. I think I drank most of it by myself while we were talking and kissing but I don't remember anything until I heard you scream. I don't remember much, but I remember you screaming."

"Fuck." I breathed out.

"I know it was Alex that stopped him. My uncle is working to get the charges Jake tried to press against him dropped. I saw what Alex did to him. He deserved worse."

"He did."

Aly paused and then asked, "How did you...get over it?"

I froze up before slowly saying, "It took a long time."

"I don't have time, Hadley. I go to school in two weeks. How the hell am I supposed to move into a dorm when I can't even leave my house without panicking that someone is going to touch me? How am I supposed to go to classes? How am I supposed to go to parties? It's not fair! It's not fucking fair! He ruined everything!"

I just let Aly scream everything out into the phone. When all I could hear was her breathing, I started. "Aly, you are strong. Stronger than I am. It sucks and it's not fair at all that this happened to you, but you will be okay."

Through sobs I heard her say, "I don't even remember what he did to me, but I know...I know."

"Then it doesn't count. Nothing he did counts. He violated you. He doesn't get to be anything to you. He's just a piece of shit that is going to rot in jail for what he did. You get to go live your life and I promise you it will get better. This part is awful right now, but it will get better. I'll be here for you whenever and wherever. I'll drive down to your dorm and stay with you anytime you need me if that's what it takes. You'll get through this, Aly."

She sniffed. "I hope so."

"You will."

"I love you, Hadley."

"I love you too, Aly."

We both said goodbye and hung up. Aly's story rattled me so much that I had to lie down in my bed and shut my eyes.

I woke up to the feeling of my phone vibrating in my hand. My eyes shot open and it took me a second to remember that I was in my room at home, not at camp. A moment later I realized that I passed out in bed last night after talking with Aly.

Sarah was calling my phone.

"Hello?" I croaked out.

She practically yelled, "You're home?"

"How did you know?"

"Your brother was bitching to my brother that you were home and it ruined some party they were going to throw with their friends at your house while your parents were away."

"That little shit."

"Both of them are little shits. But I'm more mad that you didn't call me first! I shouldn't have to find out you're home through my little brother."

"Sorry, it's been…a lot."

"I'm coming over."

"Sounds good."

I looked out my window and saw Sarah crossing her lawn into ours. Then I heard her yell hello to my parents before she ran up to my room. As soon as the door was shut, she asked, "Why are you back so early?"

"Oh Sarah…" I shook my head as we settled into our usual spots on my bed.

She squealed, "Spill!"

"Do you want the good, the bad, or the ugly?"

"Start with the good."

"It all started when I saw this guy Alex. Literally since the second we saw each other we started flirting. He kept finding little ways to touch me and flirt with me every time we saw each other. And when we finally kissed, it was everything. But there was this bitchy girl, Jessica, who was literally determined to get me kicked out of camp so she could get with Alex. So I got her kicked out instead."

"Ruthless."

I shrugged, "I didn't want to leave Alex."

"Why?"

"Because he…he like made my summer. He likes the same music that I do, the same books, and movies. He laughed at my jokes, told me how smart I was, and I just wanted to spend every second with him. He was so sweet with me and helped me get past all that lingering shit from what happened in January. He literally made me see stars."

"He was that good?"

"Better than anything."

Sarah smirked, "When do I get to meet him?"

"So that's the bad part."

"What happened?"

I sighed, "I told you about that creepy counselor Jake, the one that untied my bathing suit last year."

Her eyes went wide, "Yeah…"

"Well he was worse this year. He literally made it his mission to say shit to antagonize me all summer. He would say these pervy things in front of Alex, knowing that he couldn't do anything about it until camp was over."

"Why was this Jake guy even there?"

"He's best friends with the camp director's son. When I threatened to report what he was saying to me, he used that fun fact to stop me." I shook my head. "But the shit he said to me was nothing compared to what else he was doing."

"What did he do?"

"He sexually assaulted girls. We think he did it to at least three girls. You remember my camp friend, Aly?" She nodded her head. "He violated her on Saturday night. Alex and I caught him and tried to stop him but…" I trailed off as a warm tear slid down my cheek.

"Oh my god." Sarah's hand shot out to mine. "Is Aly okay?"

"As okay as you can be."

"Are you okay?"

"Nothing actually happened to me."

"You were traumatized by Jake too."

"Well, he's in jail now."

"Good." She squeezed my hand. "And what about Alex?"

"I don't know." I wiped away a tear.

"What do you mean you don't know?"

I whispered, "He also got arrested."

"What?!"

"Not like that! He beat the shit out of Jake and they had to take him in. At least, that's what I was told. That fight was a long time coming, though. Jake deserved what he got."

"So Alex is still in jail?"

"I don't know…"

Sarah shook her head, "Well can't you text him?"

"No," I looked down, embarrassed as I admitted, "I never got his number."

"You hooked up with him all summer but didn't get his number?"

"We were going to talk about what we were going to do at the end of camp during the last week, but we never had the last week of camp so we never had the talk."

I started crying from all the frustration I was feeling. I thought I had gotten everything out yesterday, but rehashing it all for Sarah just made my heart sting again. I failed. I failed to help Aly. I failed to keep Alex. I failed at being a counselor all summer.

I just failed.

Sarah leaned over to hug me, trying to calm me down. "Maybe you guys will find each other! Maybe you can ask someone at camp for his number or something?"

"I don't know. I could text Justin." I still hadn't opened his text from last night.

"Do it!"

I wiped away the tears and pulled away from Sarah. Leaning forward, I grabbed my phone off my nightstand then put myself back in my spot on the bed. When I flipped open my phone, I went to Justin's text. It said: **Miss u. Aaron said 2 b patient ;)**

I read it outloud to Sarah.

"That's sketch." She took my phone to read it for herself. "Aaron like the counselor from last year?"

"Yeah, we all got closer this summer."

"Text him then!"

"I don't have Aaron's number, he has mine. He is supposed to give my number to Alex."

"Get Aaron's number from Justin."

I typed out my reply to Justin: **Miss u 2. Aaron's #?**

While we waited, I looked at Sam's message. It said: **Here if u need me. Luv u.**

I texted Sam back: **Luv u 2. Call u l8r.**

Then Justin texted back. It was just one word: **patience.**

I frowned and Sarah scoffed. "Fuck patience."

"I don't have any other choice." I went to the pictures in my phone and showed the two Alex had taken of us to Sarah.

"I get why you're so sad. He's hot."

"He's hot but it was deeper than that." I stared down at the grainy picture of us smiling next to each other then scrolled to the one where he kissed my cheek. I'd have to drag Aaron's number out of Justin. I couldn't just let this be the end.

"You'll find him, girl."

I let out a long sigh then turned to her. "Enough about me. How was your summer?"

"You want the good, the bad, or the ugly?"

"Hit me with the bad."

"Keith's crazy ass bothered me until Dylan actually chased him away from my car with a bat. He would not stop."

I groaned, "I'm sorry you had to deal with this shit."

She waved a hand, "Dylan did a pretty good job of letting him know what would happen if he came around again."

"How are you two?"

"Amazing! Mom said he can come with us on the Labor

Day trip! Dad isn't thrilled but Mom already said it was cool, so he'll deal!"

"That's so exciting!"

Sarah continued on about all the fun things her and Dylan did this summer and I compared it all to what Alex and I did. My mind could not stop thinking about him.

I should've asked for his number or given him mine or done something to make sure I could keep talking to him. There was no reason to rush all of that before and I didn't know I would suddenly be taken away from him.

And now I didn't know if I would ever get it back.

31

After a little bit of sleep, the morning felt slow. My parents left for their getaway, double and triple checking that I was going to be fine without them for a few days.

"Just go," I shooed them out the door. "I need some quality time with my siblings."

My mom gave the twins one more kiss before my dad dragged her to the car.

"You better call if anything happens!" My dad called out the window as they drove away.

We all stood on the front door, waving good-bye until the SUV was out of sight.

"I'll be in the basement." John immediately walked away.

Mikey turned to Emmy, "Sonic?"

She nodded back, "Sonic."

"Can I play?"

Mikey grimaced, "It's only two players."

"Cool," I nodded. "I guess just come get me if you need me."

They ran off in a flurry, talking over each other about beating the level they were stuck on.

Slowly, I went back up to my room.

I had already tried texting Justin, Sam, and Aly trying to get ahold of Aaron, but it didn't help. They either couldn't or wouldn't give me his number.

I kept looking at the only pictures I had of Alex, trying to burn his face into my mind. It had only been three days since I had last seen him, but I felt achy without him. It didn't help that the last time I had seen him, he was being escorted away by cops. The whole situation felt surreal.

The summer started with the simple goal of getting over my ex and putting myself first. Alex helped me do that. He bolstered me to be able to stand up to Kieth and made sure he wouldn't bother me again.

Without that weight bringing me down, I found myself again. The haunting shadow that had been hovering over me for months was gone. Going forward, I could be this new version of myself that Alex let me see was possible.

I would see him again.

I had to.

But my phone was the only possible way I could connect with him now.

I sent another annoying text to Justin and got a flippant answer back.

The doorbell ringing brought me out of my thoughts.

"John, get the door!" I shouted.

I heard his feet stomping their way to the door and him talking to someone. The other voice was muffled so I wasn't sure who it was.

"Hadley!" My brother screamed from downstairs. "Someone is at the door for you!"

"Who is it?"

"He says he's your boyfriend!"

"What the hell?" I shouted back, springing off my bed. My heart was pounding with anticipation. I was wound up enough that I was ready to get Keith out of my house no matter what. He would pull something like this. He must've been stalking me to see when I got home from camp and waited until my parents were gone to show up.

At the top of the stairs, I scowled at the person in the door frame.

It took a moment for my eyes to adjust to the glare of the sun, but I saw dark, wavy hair then tan skin, and finally I caught his deep brown eyes staring up at me.

"Hey Hadley," Alex said with a crooked smile. "Nice shirt." He softly nodded at my blink-182 shirt. All the tension I had just been feeling melted away. My heart was still pounding, but for a different reason now.

I managed to breathe out, "You too."

"Gross." John groaned before walking away.

I ran down the stairs and jumped into him, wrapping my arms around his neck. "I thought I was never going to see you again."

He tightened his arms around my body, leaving no space between us before whispering in my ear, "I wasn't gonna to let that happen."

Alex was here.

He was in my home and in my arms.

I pulled away to look back up at him. The bruise around his eye was deep purple, but the stitches were gone, replaced by a thin scab. His split lip was almost healed, just a tiny cut left. I carefully moved my hand to rub a thumb across his cheek. "How did you find me?"

"I had some help."

"When did you get out?"

His smile dropped, "Monday morning…"

The relief that I felt seeing him again was losing to the anger I felt about not hearing from him for days. "You are going to tell me everything."

He nodded and relaxed his arms around me. When I took a step back, he bent down to pick up a bouquet of flowers off the ground. "These are for you." I took the small bouquet of different flowers tied together with a bow from him. He nervously ran his fingers through his hair. "Sorry I dropped them."

"No, they're perfect." I grabbed his hand and we started up the stairs to my room.

He quickly asked, "Are you parents home?"

Pulling him down the hallway, I beamed at him. "Nope!"

"Is it cool if we're in your room while they're not-"

My hand was on the doorknob to my room. "Are you always such a rule follower?"

Alex smirked, "If you don't care, then I don't."

I opened the door then pulled Alex into my room. We both sat down on my bed in the same positions we would sit in on the laundry room couch. He leaned against the wall as I turned to face him.

He took both of my hands in his. That's when I noticed the friendship bracelet that I made him had been cut and a safety pin was holding it together.

I carefully ran a finger over the string. "What happened?"

"They cut it off while I was getting booked down at the station."

"I'll make you another one."

He squeezed my hands, "What's wrong with this one?"

"It's ruined."

"Nah, it's what my mom calls a conversation piece now."

A laugh bubbled out of me. "I'll still make you another."

"If you insist."

I swallowed before daring to ask, "So you were actually in jail?"

He took a deep breath. "Yeah, the cops held me in the car for a bit while they talked to the Hamiltons. I'm not sure what was said, but we went to the station and I was processed, finger printed, and then put in a cell. Since I" He held up his fingers to do air quotes, "'attacked' Jake and Lucas, I was facing some pretty serious charges."

"But this was all Jake's fault."

"It was. Everyone realized that but the cops couldn't do anything about that until Jake and Aly gave their statements. All they had to go off was what Lucas said, and that didn't make me look good. So I had to wait until they woke up and were able to talk and while I waited, I was in a cell." He paused and then said, "It was different being in jail this time."

When he looked up at me, I remembered that I needed to be surprised by what he was telling me. My mouth dropped, "This time?"

"Remember when I told you about what my dad did? I had to spend the night in juvie because of it. But juvie is nothing compared to real jail."

My fingers wound into his. "You made it out, though."

"Thanks to Aly's parents. They handled everything and Aly's uncle is a lawyer so he got all the charges dismissed against me. Everything was considered self defense and vigilantism. So I've still got a clean record." He grinned.

"I knew the charges wouldn't stick." I tried not to sound upset when I asked, "But where have you been since then?"

"Aly's parents took me back to camp to get my car and I obviously saw that no one was there anymore. The Hamiltons were instructed not to talk to me so Mr. and Mrs. Green spoke to them on my behalf and got my last paycheck. I didn't know where else to go so I called Aaron and went to stay at his place."

My mouth dropped, "He was supposed to give you my number and let me know when you got out!"

"It's my fault he didn't tell you. I told him not to."

"Why not?"

"I wanted to surprise you." My cheeks went red and he lifted his hand to cup my face. "And I wanted to tell you this in person."

"Tell me what?"

"I love you, Hadley."

I couldn't resist the smile that erupted over my face.

"I love you too, Alex."

Alex's fingers wound into my hair and pulled me in for a soft kiss. But I was greedy and kissed him hard. Too hard.

He winced, sucking in a breath that separated our kisses.

"Sorry!" My hand covered my mouth as Alex touched his split lip.

"It's all good," His breathy laugh hit my ear as he leaned back in. Instead of kissing my lips, he placed slow kisses along my cheek and jaw. "I still love you."

My heart fluttered. "Say it again."

Another kiss landed where my jaw met my neck. "I love you."

"Again." It was barely louder than a breath.

"I love you." His lips met my pulse. "So fucking much, Hadley." He breathed the words against my skin as he kept kissing down my neck.

He pulled away, looking up at me expectantly.

"I love you too." My hands slid up his shoulder and around his neck. My fingers played with the short hair at the nape of his neck. "I missed you so fucking much."

"I missed you too."

I dared to ask, "You'll stay the night, right?"

He stiffened, "Your parents will be cool with that?"

"They're out of town until Friday."

"But," His dark eyes flicked to the door and back. "Your siblings..."

"I'll handle that. Besides, what's the worst that can happen?" I stood from the bed, quickly maneuvering to lock the door before returning to my spot. "If they ground me, it won't matter next week when I move into my dorm."

"I move in Saturday," He tucked a stray curl around behind my ear. "Then you can come stay the night with me."

My stomach flipped. "So you're not staying now?"

Alex moved forward, forcing my body to lay back against the pillows on my bed. "I'll stay if you want me to stay, and I'll go when you want me to go." A soft peck met my lips. He looked in my eyes, "I'm still yours, Hadley."

His nose nudged my head to the side so his lips could pick back up their path they had traced on my neck. Warm hands slid under my shirt, pausing for a moment, just in case.

But there was no need to hesitate anymore. Alex's touch was familiar and comforting as he removed my clothes. I managed to get his shirt off him before he took over and undressed. He stood there naked at the end of my bed, quickly slipping on a condom.

My legs spread out wider as he climbed on top of me.

He slipped inside me and my back arched off the bed. I bit my lip to stifle the moan that threatened to escape.

Alex pulled out slowly, quietly groaning as he guided

himself back.

I let his name slip out.

"I fucking love the way you say my name." His hips started moving in a rhythm that matched my pounding heartbeats. He lowered himself until our bodies were flush, his arms wrapping underneath me as my hands grabbed his broad shoulders.

I peppered his lips with gentle kisses, careful not to hurt his busted lip.

"You feel so fucking good." Alex adjusted his body so his hand could fit in the small gap between us. His middle finger found that sensitive spot and started working me in slow circles. With each pass, I could feel the tension building up.

Alex's finger moved faster and harder, keeping up with the pace he was thrusting into me.

His name slipped out in a louder moan. I threw my hand over my mouth, eyes going wide worry.

Alex slowed the rhythm of his hand and hips, but didn't stop. We held our breaths for a moment to see if there would be any sign my siblings heard. But nothing happened.

I expected him to return back to how he was moving before but he just maintained his torturous pace.

"Alex…" I was desperate for the release he could give me.

He teased me back, "Hadley…"

"Please…"

His hand slipped away from my core.

Alex's breath tickled my ear as he leaned in to whisper, "I want to make you come."

My core pulsed at his words.

"I want to feel you come on my cock more than anything."

All I could manage to say coherently was, "please…"

"But I can only do that if you promise to be quiet. You can't make any noise."

"I won't."

His breathy laugh vibrated through me. "I don't believe

you."

"I won't make a single sound."

Alex looked down at me, "If you do, I'll have to stop."

When I nodded, he adjusted himself so his mouth was on one nipple. His hand moved to pinch my other nipple between his thumb and pointer finger. While he fingers tweaked and twisted one, his tongue flicked the other in the same way. The movement of his hips started to speed up.

My teeth dug into my lip to keep myself from making noise.

Alex lifted his mouth so it hovered just above the hardened peak. His tongue shot out to lick me, and I had to stifle the moan that threatened to leave my mouth. My hands squeezed his shoulders so hard my knuckles were white.

But I didn't make a sound.

He pushed himself up enough so his lips were brushing mine. "Part of me wants you to break. I want to hear all those fucking amazing noises you make." The tingles from his lips on mine went through my whole body. "The other part of me wants you to keep doing good so I can reward you."

A frustrated groan was bubbling up but I pressed my lips together.

He smirked.

"Well played, Hadley." His finger returned to that wonderful bundle of nerves. Alex skipped the circles this time, working me back and forth so quick I suddenly felt that pleasurable curl moving down my spine.

He adjusted his hips so that each thrust hit that blinding spot inside me. Each roll of him into me made my toes curl tighter and tighter.

I wanted to call out his name. I wanted to let out all the nonsense noises and words that would help with the release, but I didn't.

My whole face scrunched as I forced myself to be quiet.

He whispered, "You're such a good girl."

And that was it.

I let myself go, a quiet moan slipping out as I felt myself crumble all over him.

"Fuck yes." Alex snapped his hips into me, careful not to shake the bed too much. As I felt myself pulsing around him, he moved faster and harder. When he found his release, I heard him softly call out my name.

With a shuddering breath, he laid down so our bodies were flush and I could feel his warmth seeping into me.

While he recovered, I ran my fingers through his hair. "I love you."

"I love you too."

ACKNOWLEDGEMENT

First, thank you for reading this book! It has been a long time coming and wouldn't have been possible without the following people:
Mitchell, for fixing this story so it made sense.
Josh, for making amazing art for the cover.
Danny, for being the inspiration behind this.

Made in the USA
Las Vegas, NV
04 June 2024